Sapphire Sea

The Scottish Stone Series, Book Four

Kelsey McKnight

Sapphire Sea

Limitless Publishing, LLC
Kailua, HI 96734
www.limitlesspublishing.com

Formatting: Limitless Publishing

ISBN-13: 978-1-64034-256-9
ISBN-10: 1-64034-256-7

Dedication

This book is for all the wonderful readers who have followed me through the ballrooms of London and into the Scottish hills. Now it's time to go on our final adventure.

Slàinte.

Come, the wind may never again
Blow as now it blows for us;
And the stars may never again shine as now they
shine;
Long before October returns,
Seas of blood will have parted us;
And you must crush the love in your heart, and I
the love in mine!

Silent is in the House—Emily Brontë

Chapter One

Gwendolyn MacLeod skimmed the cases of wine for the fourth time, noting that they sounded rather quiet when they were thumped into the wagon by some of the burlier of her brother's men. They had been unloading goods since the earliest light of day touched the hills, but Gwen was still marking down each item as it passed from the ship to the rowboats, up the bank from the shore, and into the hands of the men. While they were more than capable of sorting everything, she wanted to ensure all was well for Flora's wedding.

"Miss." A MacGregor lad named Peter spoke up as he dropped his load into one of the wagons. "I do no' mean to cause trouble," he said, lowering his voice to a whisper. "But the boxes seem a tad light, if ye catch my meanin'." His gaze slid toward the gathering of swarthy Portuguese sailors near the surf.

She sighed, not relishing the confrontation that was sure to follow her decision. "Open one."

Peter nodded and called for a chisel and mallet

from one of the cart drivers, who handed it over immediately. With several neat whacks of his hammer, the cask's lid was opened. Gwen rifled through the wood shavings and hay used as packing and frowned when she counted five, instead of the six that should have been there. She counted the cases that were already loaded. There were twelve, as ordered, but this particular one was short a bottle.

"Stop!" Gwen called suddenly, forcing the Scots to a halt. "Open every case, every barrel."

"What's wrong, *Senhorita*?" a Portuguese sailor asked, wiping sweat from his brow. It was a mild day in the Highlands, but the morning sun was strong.

Gwen held up her accounting, neatly listed in her notes. "Your goods are short. Everything needs to be recounted before I'll accept it."

The sailor pursed his lips and looked around, eyeing the large Scotsmen, who were watching him in return, their hands on the hilts of their broadswords. "Yes, yes, of course."

Gwen oversaw the boxes and cases being opened, counting and measuring each item as the Portuguese and Scottish men watched. She was pleased to see that everything else was accounted for, save the cases of fine wine, the most expensive of their imports. Each case was one bottle short. She took a deep breath. It was one thing for there to be a mistake—it happened from time to time—but it was clear the Portuguese had wronged them on purpose.

"You shorted me," she said to the same sailor, rage building within her. But Gwen kept her voice even and her expression as placid as she could

2

manage. "Tell your captain that he will not be paid for his services until I have *everything* that was ordered. And don't try to tell me that you received these from the Italian traders like this. It's clear by looking more closely at the lids that each had been opened during their journey and then resealed."

The sailor looked around nervously while several of his cohorts stood silently behind him. "*Senhorita,* the *capitão* is still aboard *La Sereia.*"

"I'll wait." Gwen hoisted herself onto the back of a wagon and sat, her legs dangling. "Go and tell him that unless he rights this appalling wrong, I will sever our contract, have your ship burned, and someone's hand cut off for stealing, as is my right."

The man glanced down at his own filthy fingers before darting off. She watched him scurry down the rocky slope and yell something in his language to his companions before hopping into a boat and madly rowing over the surf toward the ship. She wondered if she had been too harsh with her threats. They were empty, of course; she had no way of burning their ship, nor cutting off someone's hand. Only Conner had the power to order that kind of retribution, which he hardly ever exercised, especially against outsiders. She knew this, but *they* didn't, and she was glad of it.

She waited, watching the Scots below continue to build the long docks that should have been completed weeks before. She herself had initiated the construction, hoping ships could dock closer to shore, making for a quicker process when the boats arrived to trade. The small cove tucked within the cliffs and the stretch of rocky beach was the perfect place for such an addition and the imports were a godsend.

It was some time later when she saw a rowboat begin its short journey from the anchored ship toward the shore. It carried two figures, and she assumed one must be the captain. She tucked her plaid shawl tighter around her shoulders and hopped down from her perch. When she did so, the Scots who were sitting around the wagons stood, each ribbing one another. Gwen knew they were hoping for a good fight. It had been a quiet winter.

One of the men who peered down at the beach stayed at her shoulder. "Takin' his time about it, I see."

"I don't care how much time he takes, I just want my wine," Gwen muttered. That was a lie, though. What should have only taken an hour or two had become three, and she still needed to dress for the wedding.

Gwen watched the same sailor as before scurry up the slope toward her, followed by a cloaked figure moving at a slightly slower pace. "*Senhorita*, this is our *capitão*, Gaspar Florencio." He motioned toward the cloaked man, who lowered his dark hood, shaking out his mane of wavy black hair.

"Captain, we have a problem," Gwen began, striding closer and trying to portray a more menacing height than her flat five feet could offer.

"*Capitão*, this is *Senhorita* Gwendolyn MacLeod," the sailor said before backing away.

Captain Florencio's gray eyes swept over Gwen from the tips of her soft leather boots to the top of her windswept curls. Then his mouth broke into a smile, his teeth made whiter by his swarthy skin. "*Senhorita* MacLeod, I am honored to make your acquaintance," he crooned in accented English. "If I had known what golden beauty was awaiting upon the shore, I would have delivered the packages myself." Then he grabbed her hand and bestowed the lightest of kisses on her knuckles.

Gwen was slightly dumbstruck. She'd been prepared to yell at a crooked old man and get exactly what she wanted, but she knew the ways of men well enough to know that the bronzed seaman before her was not one to give in easily. She was sure of it.

Noting that a strange silence had descended heavily around them like a shroud, Gwen tried to steady herself. Her hand was still within his warm grasp and she pulled it free, placing both her hands upon her hips. "Captain, I have an issue with the goods you've delivered. Each cask of wine is a bottle short and I can say, with near certainty, that it came to be this way during its time on your ship. We've had a trade agreement with this winery for twenty years and they have never wronged us before."

He scratched his cleft chin, which was covered in a light dusting of stubble. "I cannot imagine how those bottles came to be missing."

Gwen pursed her lips at his futile attempt to sound innocent. "I'll only ask you once to not lie to me and I won't require a prolonged explanation. But I *will* ask you to fix this problem."

"And who is it that found this mistake?"

"*I* did."

Captain Florencio raised his dark brows. "You have been taking charge of the delivery, *Senhorita*?"

"Contrary to popular belief, Scottish women can read and count, Captain."

"No offense meant, *Senhorita*," he assured her earnestly, but with a glint of something in his stormy eyes. "We cannot have our contract spoiled by one little delivery."

"Then what will you do to rebuild my faith in your services?"

The captain turned to his men at the shore and let loose a high whistle before looking back at her. "With gifts, *Senhorita*."

Gwen watched as Portuguese sailors carried lidless boxes up the slope like a line of ants. Several minutes later, they reached the wagons, showing her each container as they passed. She saw bottles of wine, more than the ones she'd originally ordered, and tall rolls of brightly colored silk wrapped in paper. She crossed her arms and looked up at Gaspar, who returned her glare with a smoldering stare.

"How is that, *Senhorita*? Will that right my wrong, or will I need to repay you in some *other* manner?"

The tone of his voice was suggestive, and Gwen knew just enough of the ways of men to know he was trying to embarrass her. A lifetime of listening to the rougher sex call out bawdy jokes to one another while she and Flora looked on had prepared her for situations such as this. "I doubt you have anything else that would impress me."

"I'll ask ye no' to speak to the MacLeod's sister in that manner," Big Angus warned from behind her. She heard the distinct metallic sound a sword made as it was drawn halfway from its sheath.

She held up her hand, motioning for Big Angus to step back. "You must do better if you value your ship. You're making me late for my sister's wedding, which isn't warming me to the idea of maintaining our contract."

"A wedding, yes, I can see why that might make you cross with me." Captain Florencio slipped his hand within his cloak.

"Stay your hand," Big Angus ordered, pulling out his blade.

Gwen gasped and looked between the two men, shocked that the captain would think to do her harm. But to her surprise, he didn't mirror her sentiments. In fact, he just nodded and smiled at them both.

"Please, my friends, I mean no disrespect. In fact, I offer another gift."

Big Angus eyed him shrewdly. "Aye, then, show us. Slowly, now."

The captain nodded and pulled out a blue velvet box. He opened the lid to show her a string of diamonds and a pair of matching earrings. "Will this sweeten your mood, *Senhorita*?"

"Do you always carry ladies' jewels with you?"

"You never know what charming woman you may meet on dry land, or what siren will call to you into the sea."

Gwen couldn't resist rolling her eyes at his dramatics. "Fine. I will consider your retribution

7

paid, but if our next shipment is light, I will sever our contract for good."

"I knew you couldn't resist these French gems."

"They will make a fine wedding present for my sister," she told him firmly, snatching the box from his hand and passing it off to Big Angus for safekeeping.

"If your sister is any bit as beautiful as you are, I'm sure she will have a long and happy marriage."

"I'll be sure to relay the message," she replied dryly.

He drug his fingers through his tousled hair. "*Senhorita*, might I interest you in a tour of *La Sereia*?"

"No."

"But the woodwork is divine."

"No."

"Tis so sturdy, you won't even feel the ocean move beneath your feet, Gwendolyn." His voice was slightly dreamy as he spoke, his accent caressing every word, particularly her name.

"I'm sure your ship is lovely, but I'm not interested in a tour." She turned to leave, but paused and spoke over her shoulder. "And don't you dare *ever* call me Gwendolyn."

"*Sim, Senhorita!*" Captain Florencio called jovially as she mounted her horse. "Pleasure doing business with you."

She didn't dare look back at him, for the mere sight of the smug, handsome face would surely enrage her. Instead, she tried to focus on the ride back to the castle and the steady gallop of the horse's hooves beneath her. But with each step, she found her mind taunted by thoughts of his deep gray eyes and bold grin.

***

Gwen was still feeling rather vexed when she arrived at Flora's bridal chambers an hour later. A quick bath in rose oil and a new, pale pink gown did little to ease her frayed nerves. She couldn't put her finger on why the Portuguese captain irritated her so, but she hated that his smooth voice and tanned skin still assaulted her thoughts. The cad.

She turned to Flora and picked up several small orange blossoms, tucking them into her braided, golden hair. "*Lan dhen cac...*" That man was full of shite.

"You're looking awfully irritated," Flora noted. "You never speak *Gàidhlig* unless you're particularly upset or scared. Did something happen?"

Gwen frowned and adjusted Flora's veil before pinning it onto her looped blonde hair. She felt a pang of guilt at bringing her anger into Flora's bridal chamber. It wasn't fair of her. "I'm sorry. You're the one getting married. If anyone should be acting like a brat, it's you. So tell me, are you frightened that you'll be walking down the aisle in less than an hour?"

"No, no, I want to hear why you're stomping about like a child. It's rare you throw such a fit."

"Well, the Portuguese trader tried to short me," Gwen explained, leaning over the dressing table to dab a bit of rogue on her cheeks and lips. She felt she had to do something with her hands. "He arrived late last night to deliver cases of Italian wine for your wedding, among some other frivolities. When they began bringing things up at daybreak, he tried to short me."

"How so?"

She felt the anger bubble within her at the mere memory. "Well, each lot was to be bought for seventy-two pounds each, as each bottle was twelve pounds and sent as cases of six. As our men were loading them into the carts this morning, one remarked that Italian wine was much lighter than the French. Well, I marched right up—"

"You were there?" Flora's lips were turned up into an amused smile. "I thought you would at least stop your work on my wedding day."

"Of course I was! I needed to ensure everything would be perfect. And so I ordered one be opened. The Portuguese weren't too thrilled, but one of our men did and I saw a bottle was missing. They had repacked the cases in sets of five while still charging the seventy-two pounds." Gwen suppressed the volley of curses she wanted to unleash. "The gall of those Portuguese to skim some wine from our cases. Well, I told their captain—"

"Their captain? Is he wildly fierce with a big beard like in the novels?" Flora asked eagerly.

She shook her head and felt her cheeks grow warm as she thought of the devilishly alluring man. "No, his name is Gaspar Florencio and he's terribly young. Perhaps Conner's age."

"And tell me, what did you tell Captain Gaspar

Florencio?"

"I told him that he had best right the wrong done to our house or I'd have his hand cut off for stealing and his ship burned."

"Dear Lord, that's rather extreme."

"No one spoils your wedding day, Flora," Gwen replied flippantly, hoping to lighten the mood of the room.

"I believe you." Flora giggled. "So, did he right his wrong, or is there a burning boat in the sea?"

"We now have eighty bottles of wine, several rolls of silk, and he even gifted some select pieces of jewelry as a wedding gift for you," she announced, feeling a bit pleased with her retribution. "Now, we must get ready to have you wed. You've made Andrew wait nearly four months."

"I needed to have orange blossoms and it was the fastest I could have them readied in London for Charlie to fetch."

"You delayed your wedding for a flower?" Gwen laughed. It was just like her sister to push back her own party for the fine details.

Flora stood and began to shake out her skirts, sending the tulle and lace flying about her legs. "It's considered good luck in England to have orange blossoms. We're already being wed in the highlands in our family's chapel, but I wanted to be a British bride for Andrew."

"He makes you happy, doesn't he?"

"Of course he does, you little nitwit," Flora shot back with a grin.

"There are my two favorite wee lasses!" Conner

11

bellowed as he opened the door to the small room attached to the chapel.

Gwen glowered up at him. "Conner, Flora could have been getting dressed!"

"Do no' fret, she's already in her gown! There's naught to fuss over. Besides, shouldn't ye go find a husband in the crowd? Lord knows one o' my lasses, or my men if ye count Drum, gets partnered off at each weddin'." Conner leaned over and kissed Flora on the cheek. "Ye look lovely, Flora."

Gwen was about to respond with something impudent, but then she thought that it was true. Everyone in the past two years had met their future spouses at weddings. Call it superstition, but Gwen peered back at her reflection and stuck a few orange blossoms into her loose curls for luck. She wasn't one to swoon at romance like the other women and assumed she'd arrange a fair match with an even-keeled man. But if love were to strike her, she wouldn't fight it.

Her mother had seen heartbreak after her father's untimely passing and Gwen would hate to become the ghost she had after his death. Of course her brother and sisters all had love marriages, but Gwen didn't feel the stirring need for companionship that they had. No young men caught her eye in the hall, no one she danced with showered her in sparks. She couldn't imagine how it would feel to accept that kind of heart-racing passion into her orderly life.

"Thank you, Conner," Flora took one last look in the dressing mirror, adjusting the sheer sleeves that covered her arms.

"Stop fussin', lass. Ye look like a right English

rose in that dress," Conner said, holding out his arm for her to take.

Gwen thought to say something to Flora, for she looked like an absolute angel, but worried she might cry when she opened her mouth. With Flora gone, she would be the last girl left at MacLeod castle. Of course Charlotte would be there, and Gwen loved her dearly, but she and Flora had always been so close. It was going to pain her when Flora moved to London for good. So she fought to bottle up those negative emotions, deciding instead to do a final examination of the wedding venue to ensure perfection.

She walked along the edge of the full church, looking at the pews and inspecting the ribbons of ivy and white flowers that had been strung between them. Her seat at the front, closest to the altar, already had Charlie sitting in it. He was making faces at Andrew, who watched the doors with rapt attention.

"Charlie, you're in my place," she told him, tapping him upon the shoulder.

He looked up at her, doe-eyed. "Darling Gwendolyn, I simply must have a good seat. I brought this pair together! If I hadn't told Flora she should shag that Jasper, then she and Andrew would have never fallen in love. I'm practically Cupid!"

"Remind me to not allow you to give a wedding speech." Gwen sighed. "Move over, then."

Charlie slid to the left, his hip bumping against a MacLeod great aunt, who peered at him in elderly confusion. Gwen sat down, and just in time, because the church doors opened and the organist struck up a jaunty bridal march. She couldn't decide who radiated more affection, her stunning sister or the awestruck groom.

The priest cleared his throat as Flora held her future husband's hands. Gwen's heart started racing. While she wasn't the traditional romantic, she loved a family wedding, particularly ones born of true affection. Once the guests had stopped all whispers of good wishes and compliments, the ceremony began.

"Ladies and gentlemen," the priest began in heavily accented English. "We come here this day to join together Andrew Thomas Philips and Flora Fiona MacLeod in the bonds of holy matrimony. At the bequest of the couple, I have been asked to make the vows as short as their courtship, but as meaningful as their love."

Gwen shifted in her seat, curious as to what vows they chose to take.

The priest turned to Andrew. "Andrew, do you take this woman, Flora, to be your lawful wedded wife in sickness and in health, for richer and for poorer? Do you swear to be true to her every day of her life, to pray for her, to worship your marriage, and to hold true these vows which you take today?"

"Always," replied Andrew.

"It's *I do*, lad," the priest informed him in a loud whisper.

Andrew grinned. "I do."

"Better." The priest nodded and turned his attention to Flora. "Flora, do you take this man, Andrew, to be your lawful wedded husband in sickness and in health, for richer and for poorer? Do you swear to be true to him every day of his life, to pray for him, to worship your marriage, and to hold true these vows which you take today?"

"Always," Flora stated with a smile.

"The rings?" The priest motioned and Gwen half-rose from her seat and passed Flora a ring of gold while Andrew took the delicate counterpart from his own pocket. "Now, repeat after me: With this ring, I thee wed."

"With this ring, I thee wed," they mimicked, each ignoring the new additions upon their hands in order to gaze at one another adoringly.

The priest then closed his bible. "Then by the power invested in me by our Lord, I now pronounce you man and wife. You may kiss the bride."

Gwen stifled a sniff of emotion as Flora and Andrew shared a brisk kiss, then whispered in each other's ears. She was happy that her sister had found such a kind and gentle man. Andrew was a perfect fit for Flora. He was the cool winter breeze to her endless flame of passion. He kept her from burning out of control while she kept him ablaze.

When the newlyweds fled the chapel, she took Charlie's hand and squeezed it, savoring his closeness.

"All choked up, are we?" he asked quietly as they stood to leave the church for the reception.

She released his hand and took his arm instead, clutching her white fox fur tighter around her as they stepped outside. A light flurry of snow had begun to fall, adding some of Flora's favorite Scottish treasure to her wedding day. Gwen was glad of it. It was as if the land was saying goodbye to its wild daughter.

Gwen and Charlie half ran into the castle, shaking the snow from their clothes. When a footman had taken his jacket and her fur, Charlie pulled her into the feasting hall, sidestepping several guests. The space had been decorated with bushels of orange flowers and leafy ferns and bunches of candles in silver holders. She was pleased with the work all the maids had accomplished.

"Finally, a drink!" Charlie exclaimed, beckoning a waiter. He plucked two glasses off the tray and passed one to Flora before taking a long swallow of his. "Champagne! Well, aren't we fancy?"

Gwen peered into her crystal goblet, feeling quite confused. "Champagne? We don't have any champagne."

"Well, it's good quality stuff. Quite tasty." He took her cup and drained it.

"Pardon me, I need to go see what's happened," she muttered, crossing the rapidly filling hall and going down to the kitchens, where the clambering of pots and pans assailed her.

"Evenin'," the red faced cook greeted as she shooed away a maid with a fresh tray of sweetmeats.

"Cook, there's champagne being sent about upstairs and I was wondering where it came from. I don't recall ordering any in the past few months, nor did I see any in the wine cellar yesterday when I was there."

She frowned and tapped her round chin. "Some Portuguese fellows brought them in not too long ago. I assumed they were a part of your order for the weddin' and sent them up. Did I misstep?"

Gwen shook her head and picked up one of the bottles on the worn, wooden counter. The label was French. "There was a slight complication with their delivery. I assume it's their way of apologizing."

"Ye can ask them yourself." The cook pointed toward the back of the kitchen with her wooden spoon. "I took them in for a bite. I hope ye don't mind?"

She looked through the crowded space to where Captain Florencio was sitting in the corner with a brawny man. They were talking, their heads together, over a plate of wedding food. She thought she had seen the last of the captain and his ship. She gritted her teeth and stormed over to them, ready to give them a piece of her mind.

"*Senhorita*," Captain Florencio crooned warmly as she stopped before them. "Did you like my gift? A wedding is not so without drink!"

"It was lovely," she replied shortly, annoyed by the mere sight of his chipper face. "What are you doing here?"

"Enjoying all the charms of the MacLeod kitchens. It has been some time since we've had the pleasure of eating such fine foods. I might need to offer your cook new employment on my ship."

"Well, if you need help finding your boat once you're finished eating, please take advantage of my staff to escort you."

"Your hospitality overwhelms me," he told her softly, placing his hand over his heart. The shirt was unbuttoned, showing a sliver of tanned skin and a gold chain that disappeared into the fabric. "As do you in that magnificent gown. The shade suits you, *Senhorita*." He motioned toward the fine pale pink velvet of her dress.

Gwen felt her cheeks flash hotly at his compliment and hoped the shade didn't mirror her dress. "Thank you. I hope you find the seas agreeable to your travels. Goodbye."

He laughed, a deep sound. "Oh, no, *Senhorita*. We cannot leave yet. I need to wait for the rest of my fleet. They are coming from the north and it will be some time until they arrive."

"Does my brother know of your plans?"

"*Sim*. I asked his permission when we arrived. He sent back a note agreeing to us mooring in the inlet among the cliffs."

"Lovely."

"Very. His generosity overwhelms me and my crew. We look forward to immersing ourselves in *everything* Scotland has to offer."

Gwen attempted a smile. She could already tell that he was going to be more trouble than he was worth. Of course he was all talk, just as men usually were, but most would be silenced upon being ordered to do so by the MacLeod's sister. She made a mental note to discuss everything with Conner.

"Well, I must get back upstairs."

"*Senhorita*," he sang with a devious grin.

Gwen turned on her heel and stalked back through the kitchens and upstairs. She had met many merchants and interacted with people from many lands, but none were as only cheeky as the captain. His gaze burned her skin and his smart mouth both infuriated and intrigued her in a most distasteful way. She hoped he would be on his way sooner rather than later.

Shaking her head to clear her mind, she reentered the party. She greeted several people as she passed, finally bumping into Charlie, who had obviously been partaking in his fair share of champagne while she had been gone.

"Darling Gwendolyn, can you believe our babes are wed?" he simpered, looking over at Flora and Andrew, who were seated at the head table.

"I can't believe that bloody man made me miss their grand entrance," Gwen growled.

"Who?"

"Gaspar Florencio," she spat, watching Flora pat at her mussed hair. "He's the captain of the Portuguese ship and the one who sent the champagne."

"Well, tell that foreign bastard he has wonderful taste in drink." He looked around at the guests. "I must say, the gentlemen guests are lacking today. Most are very much older or are towing a wife around. Useless, the lot of them."

"Not every event is held just to hook you up with a new…man-friend."

"It should be." Charlie tipped his glass over with a sigh. "All out."

Gwen laughed a bit to herself as he sauntered away in search of more champagne. She took the opportunity of him being occupied to find another familiar face. She scanned the hall, her gaze settling on Big Angus, who was sitting near to his own future bride, a young, red-haired woman named

Grace who lived down in the village. Grace was pouring Big Angus wine and Gwen thought it almost comical their difference in size. Where Big Angus was brawny and, well, *big*, Grace was delicate and thin-boned like a dove.

Not wanting to intrude on the new lovers, she set her sights on one of her more favorite castle visitors. Penelope sat near the front of the hall, Drum trying to ply her with bits of food. She was pale faced with dark bags beneath her eyes. The usually impeccable lady was looking rather worse for wear.

"Not feeling well?" Gwen asked as she sat beside her.

Penelope shook her head, her cheeks tinted green. "This child doesn't let me eat much of anything." She patted her rounded stomach with a thin hand.

"She's wastin' away," Drum murmured, kissing his wife's shoulder.

"Don't be dramatic," Penelope chastised. "It's all for a good cause and I only have a few months left."

"Are ye sure you will no' eat somethin'?" Drum prompted quietly.

"What about some soup?" Flora suggested. "Something light?"

"Perhaps," Penelope replied, leaning back in her seat.

"I'll go tell the kitchens." Drum squeezed her arm and disappeared into the crowd.

Penelope sighed and smiled lightly. "Finally, a moment of peace."

"Drum tiring you out?"

"Almost as much as the child. He's always following me about, treating me like I could be broken."

"I think it's sweet."

"It is…but it's also exhausting."

Gwen could see where Penelope's thoughts lied, but still felt her cousin was doing the best he knew how. "And you're sure you will have to leave in the morning? Stay on for a week or two."

"If there wasn't a snowstorm beginning, I might have. I want to have the baby at home and soon I won't be able to travel without harming it."

"I wish I could be there."

Penelope reached down and took her hand. "I'll send for you when it's time. You can be there in less than a day."

Drum hurried back over to them and crouched down beside Penelope, adjusting his kilt. "Are ye tired?"

"A bit," Penelope told him. "But I'm all right."

"I've already told them to send ye some soup in our chambers."

"We'll retire now," Penelope said, planting a kiss on Gwen's cheek. "I'll see you in a few weeks when the baby comes."

Drum smiled warmly at her, and then turned to his wife. He held out a hand and they rose up together, as they had been since the beginning, perfectly in sync.

After Gwen watched them leave, she wondered if Conner was right…if her future husband was one of the guests…and whether or not she would find her perfect match one day.

Chapter Two

Gwen moped about the castle the next day, the silent halls assaulting her with their stillness. Most of the wedding guests—it was a small affair—had left early that morning at first light. The quick bustle of carriages and horses departed as quickly as they had arrived, leaving the keep quiet. She hated the quiet. She needed the loud activities that came with castle life. Now that she was the last unmarried MacLeod, the noise had left along with the brides.

She sat in Conner's study in the library; it had become *her* study, in a way, as she had taken over the bulk of his work. She flipped through the papers, ledgers, and contracts, all haphazardly placed there by Conner's steward. Several unopened letters were stacked at the bottom. It was quite the array and she found it quite obvious that Conner had been neglecting his mail. Again. She had taken over most of the correspondence, but until recently he had at least been reading his personal messages.

"Men are so useless sometimes," she muttered,

sifting through one of the desk drawers to find a letter opener.

Then she sat back in the seat and picked up an envelope at random. She inspected it then slid open the wax seal from the Duke of Wellvard with the blade of the opener. Dated two weeks before, it began asking about Conner's health, the state of his lands, the—her name popped out at her. She kept reading and was surprised to find that Wellvard was very interested in Gwen's marital state.

On a hunch, she began opening some of the other letters. They were from grand and moneyed men—a Spanish prince, the Duke of Teller, a trade ambassador to France, an English Baronet. The list went on. Each one offered an alliance with their sons or brothers in exchange for Gwen's hand, and her more than sizable dowry.

After the Scottish finally fell against the English in the early days of her grandfather's time and the clans broke in the highlands, the MacLeods stood strong. While many lairds sold off their lands and allowed the diaspora of their people, her grandfather had kept the farms together and now the family had the means to sell off and give the rich lands when they married. It was no secret that she would come into two manor homes and fifty thousand pounds per year, as well as a nice swatch of farmland in the south.

But the thought of these men, who had never laid eyes upon her, clambering for her hand seemed quite ridiculous. Gwen let out a little laugh. Yes, she was the last unmarried MacLeod girl, but she could be a complete brat with a great, big hump, that never bathed! Besides being amused and a tad flattered, she was almost curious how someone could offer marriage without ever having seen her. After all, no one bought a finely bred horse without at least looking at the state of its teeth.

More laughter fell from her lips. Her shoulders shook with mirth and she felt tears accumulate in the corners of her eyes at the gall of those men. It took her several moments to compose herself, and when she did, she looked to the door to see Charlotte standing there, a strange smile on her face. She set aside the last few unopened letters.

"Care to share the joke?" Charlotte asked, stepping into the study and taking a seat opposite Gwen.

Gwen pushed the letters toward her and wiped away a stray tear. "Just read them and you'll see."

Charlotte scanned the pages, her lips moving. When she finished, she looked back up at Flora, her lips twisted into a scowl. "This is ridiculous. Conner would never entertain such nonsense of selling you off to the highest bidder!"

"Oh, no, I wasn't insinuating he would. I was only showing you what a hot commodity I am." Gwen paused, counting the eleven letters. "Charlotte, do you know any of these men?"

She flipped through the notes again. "Um, let's see…the Baronet Harrison Dudley…well, his son is about your age and is rather handsome. I don't know these two…" She put those letters down. "Ugh, the Duke of Wellvard is a disgusting old man that looks like a goat. Never consider him."

"I wouldn't! Especially just off a quick note. He

24

didn't even say what *I* would receive in the deal."

"Of course, of course. This one I believe I know through Penelope's brothers. The Duke of Teller has a lovely unmarried nephew he's taken on as a ward. I don't think he's particularly handsome, but he's rather kind and the family is an old one. Goodness, here is a Spanish prince!"

"I know!" Gwen giggled. "It says his name is Eduardo. I wonder how old he is." Her mind flashed, albeit childishly, to the book of fairytales she read over and over as a child. Now, the book was with wee Ian and baby Alec in the nursery, but she could still recall the stories of handsome princes and the fair young maidens who captured their hearts. While she had always thought of those tales as nothing more than things to amuse children, a dashing prince with the manners to match might be just the thing to ignite her heart.

"We should ask Conner. He would know." Charlotte looked more relaxed. "How funny would it be for you to be a princess?"

"A princess..." she muttered. "That would be rich, wouldn't it?"

"It would be the best match of all your sisters, that's for certain."

Gwen piled up the letters, leaving the Duke of Wellvard's out to be burned. She tied the stack with the ribbon from the desk drawer. While she wasn't really looking for a husband, it never hurt to keep her options open.

"Are you planning on keeping them?" Charlotte asked, watching her set the stack aside and begin on the accounts.

She shrugged. "I might give some thought to them."

"Are you thinking about marriage?"

"No, not really. I'm only nineteen, so it's not as if I'm an old maid. Still, I'd like to keep score of who desires to take me to wife."

"I completely understand."

Gwen began tallying up the number of sheep still left after the fall culling and the winter storms. But then she stopped and slowly put her pen down. "Charlotte, do you regret marrying? Not Conner, of course, but just...being a wife?"

"Well, I didn't expect that." She laughed.

Gwen bit her lip, wishing she had more of a filter. "Heavens, that was so rude of me."

Charlotte waved a hand. "Oh, posh, it's a valid question. You see, it wasn't marriage I was against initially, but the act of being owned."

"But aren't you now?"

"Owned?" She smirked. "What do *you* think?"

"I think you own Conner more than he owns you, that's for certain." Gwen tried reading the next paper, but couldn't focus on the words. "But Conner's not like other men. He would let you do anything you wished and help you to do it, like with the orphanage."

"Which is why I married him. He made me more a partner than a wife, and that's the difference. Partners are equal, respected. Not that there's anything wrong with being just a wife, but it gives a certain connotation of being owned by your husband, and in many parts of the world, that's true."

Gwen slid her work away and sighed. "That's what I'm afraid of. I know I have more right here in Scotland than you did in England, but the thought of being someone's property...or just being tied to another person jars me."

"You're a strong woman," Charlotte asserted, reaching over the desk to take Gwen's hand. "There are many men out there who have progressive ideas about love and marriage and I hope you won't settle for less."

"I'm not worried, if that's what you're thinking. Thanks to my dowry, I'll have no shortage of men to think of, if I so choose."

"Ach, my two favorite lasses, havin' a moment!" Conner's voice boomed as he came into the library. "Warms my heart, it does."

Charlotte released her hands and allowed her husband to place a kiss upon her cheek. "Hello, Conner, how were the horses?"

"Verra well." His gaze dropped to all the papers and letters on the desk. "What's this, then?"

"Papers for the estate and many marriage proposals," Gwen told him.

Conner nodded. "Oh, aye, I figured as much. A few men came to me with their suits at Flora's weddin'."

"And what did you say?" she asked suspiciously.

"Like I'd give ye away without askin'." He scoffed. "Ye'd stab me in my sleep."

"I never said you would. I was just curious," Gwen assured him, holding up her letters. "A prince has asked for a portrait of me."

Conner raised his brows, looking impressed. "A

prince?"

"From Spain," Charlotte added.

"Ye'd go all the way there to marry him?" Conner asked. "Spain's a long way away, lass."

Gwen smiled and stood, tucking the letters under her arm. "I think I'd like to send my portrait," she announced on a whim. It felt rather nice to be fancied.

"Would ye?" Her brother frowned and looked to his wife, who only shrugged. "Well, aye, I suppose I could call for one to be sent, if you're sure?"

"Goodness, Conner, I'm asking for a picture to be sent, not signing a marriage contract this very moment." Gwen snorted, leaving the room.

She strolled through the corridors and narrow passageways to the front of the castle. She grabbed her cloak from a maid and tied it round her shoulders, squinting in the harsh afternoon light of late winter. The thin layer of snow that had fallen the day before had all but gone, but the frost in the air still remained.

Thankfully, the wind was still and not the biting gusts of the last few weeks. So she was able to walk down to the cliffs, where she often sat when she needed to get out of the castle. Others were frightened to sit among the rocks so high above the sea, but not Gwen. She feared the ocean below and its dark depths, but knew she would be safe atop the stones above.

Gwen sat between two tall, black rocks and leg her legs dangle over the edge, her skirts whipping around her legs. She felt her stomach turn as she peered into the crashing waves, meters below her feet. The feeling sent a short burst of adrenaline through her that made her heart race. Facing the danger of the waters below was the closest she would ever come to true peril.

Once she was comfortable, she set the stack upon her lap and picked up the first unopened one. Sliding the note free with her finger, she scanned it quickly, seeing what lord or trade master was asking for her favor. She frowned when she saw it was a man who had already been married thrice. While one dead wife was a tragedy, three made it a habit. Gwen crumpled it up and tossed it down to the sea. The next two were also uninspired and she wondered if she would find another who sounded as thrilling as the Spanish prince did with his offer of a castle surrounded by a large city. Of course she didn't know much about him, but being the princess to a young prince was certainly a more attractive prospect than being the fourth wife to an old man.

She sifted through the letters for the next envelope when a gust of wind lifted the skirts of her dress and flung the papers around her. Gwen stumbled up, snatching the pages before they could be blown away entirely. She at least wanted to salvage the letter from the prince.

"In need of assistance, *Senhorita*?" a voice asked from behind an outcropping of rocks. She turned around just as Captain Florencio strolled up to her, a paper clutched in his fist.

Gwen groaned inwardly. She had come to the cliffs for some privacy and then he came to spoil it. "No, thank you, I'm fine."

"It does not look so." His gray eyes skimmed her

body in an open way that made her feel as if she were on display. "What are you doing out here alone?"

She swallowed as her heart began pounding anew. She was alone on the cliffs with a Portuguese man twice her size without anyone to protect her. The tales of violent seamen ravishing women on land reached even the most remote of villages and Gwen hadn't even thought to bring a guard—she never felt the need to before. The hills around her were empty and the gate to the keep was some distance away now. No one would hear her call out for help. With the rocks surrounding her, it would be near impossible to reach safety before he grabbed her. There was only one option; she would need to fight for her survival.

Gwen reached slowly into her cloak to grab the handle of the small, bejeweled dirk that was hidden within the folds of her gown. She kept her gaze trained on Captain Florencio, who was watching her with unveiled interest.

"I—I really must be going," she told him, trying to sidestep him in order to get closer to the castle without drawing too near.

"No, do no leave on my account." He held out her letter, which she quickly snatched.

"I really must. It's going to be dark soon."

He looked out at the sun and shook his head. "There's still a fistful of sun left in the sky."

"Lovely, well, I need to get to work..." She had her back pressed against a tall rock and was inching around him, or trying to at least.

Captain Florencio chuckled and crossed his arms

over his chest. "I am not going to attack you, if that is what you fear."

She blanched, feeling her knees go weak. "What? No, I wasn't suggesting anything of the sort."

He took a step closed, a smile on his lips. "You are nervous, *Senhorita*, but you needn't be." Captain Florencio drew closer until he was so near to Gwen, their bodies almost touched. "I would never take a woman against her will. If I planned on seducing you, I would and I could."

Gwen felt her cheeks flush, but she loosened her grip on her dagger. "This is highly inappropriate!"

"I know."

"My brother could have you flogged for your...your..."

"My what, *Senhorita*?" Captain Florencio reached out and twisted a lock of Gwen's golden hair around his finger. "My effect on you?"

Bristling, she reached out and sharply slapped his hand away. Then, with some force, she placed both hands on his chest and tried to shove him back, but he was as hard and immovable as the stones around them. Suppressing the urge to shriek in flustered frustration, she pushed past him and began the brisk walk back to the castle.

But Captain Florencio was incorrigible. "*Senhorita*, you needn't leave on my account," he said again when he caught up with her.

"I need to go back to the keep. I have important work that must be attended to."

"Work? But you're the sister of the master of these lands, *sim*?"

She glared at him out of the corner of her eyes. "Contrary to popular belief, women are capable of more than just bearing children and darning your stockings."

"Ah, you have a fire, *Senhorita*, like the sea herself."

"That doesn't even make sense."

"Oh, does it not?" he challenged. "Does the sea not carry a rage and an energy within her that rivals the flame of the sun?"

Gwen heaved an annoyed sigh. "Still, I wouldn't connect the ocean and fire in such a manner. There are other ways to describe a woman in regards to the sea, such as tumultuous, unfathomable, profound, ever-changing, unpredictable—"

"Beautiful?" he offered, his eyes clearly trained on her face. "Mysterious, breathtaking."

Gwen stopped walking and balled her hands upon her hips. "Captain Florencio—"

"*Por favor, Senhorita*, call me Gaspar."

"*Gaspar*, you're acting ridiculously inappropriate and I won't stand for it."

"Ah, is that why you glow that charming shade of red?" He grinned, flashing his white teeth. "Your words say you wish me to leave you be, but your face tells a different story."

Gwen wished she had the nerve to stab him. She thought it might be the only way to make him stop. But that would mean getting blood upon her sleeve and she was far too practical for that. "If you don't halt this nonsense immediately, I'll tell my brother and cancel our trade contract."

He clutched his heart over his black cloak.

"*Senhorita*, you wound me."

"If only," she muttered, turning to leave, but he grabbed her hand.

"*Senhorita*, don't be angry with me. I cannot bear the look of fury upon your prettily rosy face."

She pulled her fingers free. "You're absurd, has anyone ever told you so?"

"No one so golden and fair."

Gwen made a little noise, akin to a gag. "Do you ever *stop*?"

"I'll stop if you agree to join me for a walk upon my ship."

"Never."

His dark brows lowered. "What if I ask nicely?"

"The answer is still going to be no."

"And if I request it upon my knees?"

"No."

Gaspar pursed his full lips and thought a moment before saying, "And if I offer you French jewels and Spanish gold?"

Gwen gasped at his insolence. "How dare you make such insinuations? I am deeply offended. Besides, when I wed the Spanish prince, I'll have all the gold in the country at my disposal, so I have no need of *yours*!" She stomped her foot and began striding toward the castle, eager to leave him behind. She wasn't sure why she decided to tell him of the engagement that hadn't even become a reality and almost felt as if she told him of someone else's betrothal instead of her own. But if anything would stop his offensive ramblings, it might as well be a royal.

Gaspar followed and jogged before her, his

expression much more serious than before. "The Spanish prince?"

"Yes."

"Which one?"

She paused, her mind blanking to his name. She cursed herself for not remembering such an important detail, but she couldn't let Gaspar realize that she knew so little of him. "Why does it matter to you?"

"I might know a thing or two about the princes."

His words piqued her interest, but she wouldn't give him the satisfaction of knowing that. "I don't care to listen to what you have to say."

"Just know that they all have their vices and sins."

"As do you, I assume."

When they got to the castle, he took her hand again and stopped her right before the gate. "*Senhorita*, I meant no offense earlier. You have just captivated me so and I would hate to let such a golden jewel slip through my grasp."

Gwen looked down at their clasped hands, finding that the warmth of his coarse palm shot through her body. When her gaze found his again, she glowered up at him. "Release me now and never speak to me in this outrageous manner again."

He dropped her hand and dipped a short bow. "*Senhorita*, one day you will beg these hands to touch you." Gaspar then turned his back on her and leisurely strolled back the way they came, leaving Gwen feeling irritated and rather ruffled.

She brushed the confusing feelings aside and hurried through the castle and up to her room.

Maids had been in and piled her white stone fireplace high with wood and built a small fire. But Gwen didn't need the extra heat the low flames brought her. She still felt her body blush from the tips of her toes to the roots of her hair at Gaspar's last words.

"That bloody man," she grumbled, tossing her cloak onto her bed and crossing the room to her small desk. She preferred the large one in the library for her true work, but the delicate one in her chambers was well enough for her personal affairs. Besides, it was nice to have true privacy, which was impossible at times in the library.

Gwen had just shut the crumpled letters in one of the many drawers when something caught her eye out the window. She hadn't noticed before, but the Portuguese ship was directly in her line of sight, the masts standing bare like leafless branches in winter. It was too far away for her to see anything, of anyone upon the decks, but the mere sight of the boat made her heart beat unpleasantly.

Drawing the curtains of her window shut, Gwen stomped the length of her room, her mind muddled with feelings of uncertainty and doubt about her future, something she hadn't been worried about before. But one thing she needed to be absolutely firm on was her match with the prince. He was an attractive prospect that would no doubt be respectful, well-mannered, gallant, and offer her freedoms that other men may not, due to his royal standing that wasn't so high that she would be caged like those closer to the throne.

Out of all the men who had asked for her hand,

or hinted that they would like to, none had sparked any interest. They all seemed flat and often tiresome, and she didn't care to be bored to tears every day for the rest of her life. At least with the mysterious Prince Eduardo, there was a chance of something more.

Feeling better about her future nuptials, she left her letters behind and went down to the library to collect every book they had on Spain.

Chapter Three

Gwen awoke early the next morning to Charlotte shaking her shoulder. Her face was so close that—for a moment—she had no idea what she was looking at and sat up with a start.

"Charlotte, what's happened? Is something wrong?"

"No, not in the least bit."

"Then why bounce about as if there is a fire? I'm exhausted."

"Wake up and you'll see," she sang, sharply drawing open the curtains and letting in the early morning light.

She rubbed her eyes and stretched, noticing a blue box upon the foot of her bed. It was not unlike the one Gaspar had given for Flora's wedding gift. "What's this?"

"I don't know. Open it."

"Who is it from?" Gwen asked, although she thought she had an idea about the identity of the mysterious gift giver.

Charlotte's lips curled into a cat-like grin. "The

Portuguese captain. Now, open it. I want to see what's inside! Why did he send you something that looks suspiciously like it contains jewelry?"

Gwen held up the box and shoved it into Charlotte's hands. "Send it back unopened, please." Then she lay back down among her pillows, pulling the blankets back up over her shoulders. She was fully awake now, but had no interest in drawing herself out from her warm, sleepy cocoon.

"But why? Aren't you curious?"

"No, and you shouldn't open it either."

Charlotte pouted, her fingertips tapping on the gold clasp of the box. "But I want to see."

"Don't," she chastised, her voice more harshly toned than she meant. "I don't want him to get the wrong idea that what he's doing is welcomed. It's not right."

"Fine," Charlotte replied in a stiff tone. "I'll do as you ask and pass it off to be returned. Would you like a note sent as well?"

"No."

Charlotte tapped her chin with her finger, as she always did before suggesting something absurd. "You know…this is awfully reminiscent of when Conner sent me my emeralds when we first met."

"I don't like what you're implying."

"I'm not implying anything, merely pointing out the similarities," she replied, her voice a mask of innocence.

Gwen rolled over so her back was to Charlotte. "Well, stop pointing things out. I fear that the captain is merely trying to provoke me."

"And why would he do such a thing?"

38

"Because he's an obnoxious cad who thrives off making other people uncomfortable."

Charlotte hummed something, but Gwen didn't wish to ask what it was.

She tried going back to sleep once Charlotte left, but she was too irritated to rest. She had been awakened at the crack of dawn because Gaspar wanted to annoy her. Well, it had worked, that was for certain. She begrudgingly slid from the warm cocoon of her blankets and hurried to wash her face and dress simply in a warm plum gown. She pinned back the front curls of her hair and was just about to step out the door when a maid stopped her.

"These were sent for ye, miss." The maid held out two blue, velvet boxes and a book of poetry with fine, gold lettering.

Gwen eyed the packages suspiciously. "Who sent them?"

"The Portuguese captain," she responded meekly. "I took the first gift down to shore but I was given these to bring back."

"Any note?"

"No, miss. A man just gave them to me and said I was to tell you the captain sent them."

Gwen groaned. "Take them back, if you please, or give them to one of the kitchen boys to return."

The maid looked down at the boxes and back up at Gwen. "Ye do no' wish to open them?"

"No, just go."

Gwen pushed past her and stalked down the hallways until she was safely in the privacy of the spacious library. A large pile of accounts and bills of sale awaited her, but she looked forward to the monotony of numbers. They were stable, predictable, fixable, and she didn't need to fear them pestering her unbidden. Unlike men.

She worked through several ledgers, noting the annual income of each tenant's farm into her book with a delicate hand. But after several hours, she was beginning to regret skipping breakfast and rung the bell for a servant. She thought she deserved a break from her work, as did her poor, cramped fingers.

Once she had ordered tea and sandwiches be brought up, Gwen began tidying up the desk. She stacked the old receipts, put away the pens and ink, and got up to burn the soiled and unusable papers she'd used for scratch. She had just begun to feed the small fire when she heard the door open behind her.

"Just place my tray on the desk, if you would be so kind," she instructed, still carefully slipping papers into the flame.

"As you wish, *Senhorita.*"

Gwen felt her blood run cold in her veins, but the hot heat of annoyed anger quickly replaced the sensation. She stuffed the rest of the pages roughly into the fireplace and stood, wiping her hands on her gown more roughly than they deserved. Then she took a deep, steadying breath to calm her nerves before turning around.

Gaspar leaned against the desk, smirking as he observed her. His signature white linen shirt hung open almost to the waist, which was cut by a black belt. A gold chain looped around his neck and lay against his smooth chest, from which a cross and small medal hung.

"Do I leave you speechless?" Gaspar asked.

"Only because all the words I wish to say are not fit for a lady's lips," she answered briskly, going to the desk to pour herself some tea. She was frustrated to see there were two cups on the tray instead of one. Still, she filled a cup only for herself, ignoring the cream and sugar like always. She couldn't serve him.

"I can think of many things a lady's lips are fit for," he murmured, leaning close as she sat down. "And none of them require speech."

"You're sickening."

"Sickeningly handsome." He winked and sat on the other side of the desk from her in a wingback chair. "So, *Senhorita*, why did you send back my gifts?"

"Because I didn't care very much for them."

"Oh, but I know you're lying to me! These boxes were unopened and the book wasn't even cracked."

She took a sip of tea. It was an exotic, Chinese blend she usually enjoyed, but the flavor was tainted by his company. "I know what I like and I didn't like your gifts."

"If you only saw, I am sure you would have felt differently."

Gwen sighed and placed her cup silently back on its saucer. "Gasper, your attentions would be better spent elsewhere. I'm sure your gift would be very welcome at the rather unsavory establishment in the village by the standing stones. They don't often come into contact with the finer goods we enjoy here at the castle."

"I told you before, I never touch a woman who doesn't beg me first. Now, *Senhorita*—"

She gritted her teeth, the word *Senhorita* grating on her already frayed nerves. "Goodness, I cannot take you calling me that a moment more!"

He grinned widely and poured himself some tea. He took it black, just like her. "And what should I call you?

"I am Lady Gwendolyn MacLeod of Clan MacLeod."

"Gwendolyn," he copied slowly, his foreign tongue caressing each letter as it left his mouth. It made her almost uncomfortable...as if she'd been sitting naked before him.

"*Gwen* will be fine."

"No, no, no, I think I will use *Gwendolyn*."

"As you like," she told him, picking up a sandwich, although her appetite was gone.

"Now that we are on a first name basis, will you accept my gifts?"

"Why are you so obsessed with giving me things I don't want?"

"Because you won't accept them."

"That makes no sense."

He leaned back in his seat and propped his booted feet on the desk, regarding her under his dark brows. "Because you pull away from me like my touch burns you, but when I look at you, you don't look away. You gaze right back, like the rogue waves that crash in the sea. Fearless. Challenging me."

She stared at him blankly before telling him, "You're ridiculous. I'm not challenging anyone."

"Then accept my gifts!"

"I don't want to!" she shouted in return.

"But every time you send something back, it will be multiplied until my ship is empty and she is all I have left to give."

"I doubt your crew would be pleased to hear that," she pointed out, thinking of the brawny men who crowded the beach.

"Then you must accept it for the good of my men."

"If it will make you stop and leave me alone, I will take your gifts and leave you your ship."

He clapped his hands together, making her jump. "Good news. Everything has already been delivered to your chambers and I await to hear how you enjoy them."

"Everything? Already delivered?" she mimicked dumbly.

He didn't respond at first, but stood, readying himself to leave her. He snatched a sandwich from the tray and gave her long look. "I await your message."

***

Gwen ate her lunch in silence, trying to buy time before she clambered up to her rooms to see what Gaspar had brought her. She wouldn't put it past him to be hiding in the hall just outside the library, waiting for her to pass in order to harass her some more. She wouldn't give him the satisfaction, so she took eat bite slowly until her tea was cold and she was almost certain he would have tired of waiting for her.

As she walked through the corridors back to her chambers, she wished again that Flora was there to tell her what to do, or even Charlie, even though he was a bad role model. Or better yet, Penelope, who always knew just what to say and how to say it, without compromising her manners. Conner would merely have Gaspar flogged. Charlotte would say his insistence reminded her of her own romance. It was ridiculous.

She was almost afraid to open the door, and cracked it just a sliver to peer inside before entering. Luckily, there was no one within, so she entered the room and locked up behind her. Upon her bed was a pile of packages, boxes, and of rolls of fabrics.

It almost felt like Christmas or her birthday and she couldn't help but smile to herself. She sifted through the pile, wishing she could send it back to save her own pride, but she also knew Gaspar would make good on his promise and bury her in gifted finery until she kept something.

Within the presents were four bolts of silk in rich colors, perfect for the summer season. She found a set of diamond bracelets and a gold locket featuring several black stones. Among the parcels were also four books in French as well as a box containing an entire silver toilette set—a brush, mirror, and a small comb.

The gifts were fine, and of wonderful quality, but she still felt guilty as she placed the silver and the jewelry upon her vanity and tucked the books in her nightstand to be read later. She put the bolts of fabric on the trunk on the end of her bed and wished the other Portuguese ships closer, so Gaspar could finally leave.

She was trying to make a good match of Prince Eduardo. From what she knew, he had never been married, was only a few months older than she, and wasn't in direct line for the throne, as he was the fifth prince. Some might have found his distance from the crown to be an unattractive quality, but it was the opposite for Gwen. He still had titles and land and was looking for an equally moneyed noblewoman to wed, but she wouldn't be trapped within the regulations the elder princesses and princes had to adhere to.

Gwen flopped into bed and lay back among her pillows. She wasn't looking for a great love, as Conner, Drum, and Flora had found. She was much too practical for that and, dare she say, adventurous? She desired a great adventure—which a minor Spanish noble had to allow by the terms of her dowry, expendable riches—of which Spain had plenty of, and to see things she never would have outside a standard honeymoon tour of Europe.

Sure, she could travel from Scotland to Germany and Russia and the Indies, but that would require numerous trips on ships, which she wasn't sure she was brave enough to bear. Spain, however, had direct train lines that were beginning to spider off all through Europe. A train she could handle—the unknown of the sea, she could not. The thought of the necessary sail across the English Channel to the mainland for the hypothetical wedding was enough to make her green about the gills.

If only she could obtain a response from the

Spanish courts sooner. Conner had sent out a small portrait and letters the day before, asking for a portrait, emissary, and even a royal visit, if prince Eduardo's schedule would allow. And, by Gwen's calculations, it would take about two weeks for her messenger to reach Spain and another two for him to return, maybe longer if the prince decided to return with him. This meant she could be a Spanish princess by the end of spring. How novel.

Gwen giggled to herself and picked up her book on Spanish history, excited to learn more of this possible future.

Chapter Four

When Gwen came down to dine that evening, she had dressed plainly in smooth violet velvet that was nipped in at the waist by a black silk ribbon. She forwent jewelry, as she often did. Heavy gems weighed her down and the jeweled cuffs and rings her sisters all favored would get caught in her curled hair, which hung loose. She didn't wish to prick herself with pins that caused headaches.

She meandered down to the feasting hall, in no particular rush. She wasn't one for drink, which everyone else seemed to be. That limited her socialization options and she vaguely thought to the reputation of the Spanish court. It was said to be lively and joyful, and the descriptions of Madrid she had read about was something Gwen found she pined for. They seemed to be a musical and elegant people.

So entrenched in her thoughts of Spain, Gwen barely realized that she had already sat down at her usual seat to Conner's left. She turned to her left, where little Ian sometimes sat, but found herself not looking at the miniature Scotsman she adored, but a swarthy captain, who was eyeing her with one brow raised.

"How did you find my tribute, Gwendolyn?" Gaspar crooned, pouring her some wine.

Gwen gritted her teeth. "Why are you here?" she hissed.

"Conner invited me." He glanced toward her brother. "Isn't that right, Conner?"

Conner tipped his goblet in response. "Aye, it's too quiet around here."

"Perfect," Gwen grumbled as a bowl of soup was placed before her. Once again, Gaspar had ruined her appetite.

He leaned toward her, his elbow almost grazing hers. "Gwendolyn, how do you find life in Scotland?"

"The same as life anywhere else, I suppose."

"Do you not crave the cities of the south?" His voice lingered on the word *crave*.

"I've been to London, went to finishing school in England…I'm quite content where I am now."

"Then why go to Spain?"

Gwen fiddled with her spoon, her gaze still focused on the hall, watching the light crowd eat and talk amongst themselves. "That's none of your business."

"But it is…if I am the one who will take you there."

Her head whipped around to him. "Pardon me?"

"Yes, when my ships come to meet me, we will go do some business. If the match between you and the prince is agreed upon, I will take you to Spain."

Gwen felt her mouth go dry at the thought of sailing over open ocean and took a long drink of wine. "That won't be necessary. I plan on taking the train."

He grinned over the rim of his cup. "Over the sea to France?"

"Obviously not. I can handle the short trip to France well enough, but then I will be taking the train through to Spain."

"There are no direct trains to Spain from France."

"Then I can switch trains on my way," she retorted, her stomach churning.

"You would have to travel by ship anyway, once you reach southern England. You might as well stay upon the vessel and go directly to your new home."

"I'd much rather keep my time on a boat short, thank you," she said primly, trying to keep the blush of embarrassment off her face. "People do it all the time—travel by ship and rail. I believe that is how most people travel, in fact."

"But it would be thrice the cost and your luggage will be minimized upon the train." He gestured with his fork.

"I don't need much, anyway."

"What do ye need?" Conner asked, turning to her.

Gwen was about to speak, but Gaspar cut in. "Gwendolyn was just telling me her plans to travel to Spain by train."

"And I was just telling *him* that the train lines are growing each day and there's no need for me to travel all the way there by ship," said Gwen tightly.

"Aye." Conner talked through his full mouth. "But I've already made a deal with the good captain, if the match goes through. In writin', I might add."

Gwen stared at him, trying to convey her true feelings through her hard stare. "Conner, you know I can't do that."

Her brother frowned. "Do what?"

"Go on a ship," Gwen muttered lowly, so that Gaspar wouldn't hear.

"Ach, ye still go on about that?" Conner waved a hand and sat back in his chair.

Gaspar leaned forward, obviously eager to be included in the whisperings. "Go on about what?"

Gwen felt her cheeks flame. "Nothing."

Conner opened his mouth but Charlotte, always one to look out for Gwen, elbowed him sharply in the side. Gwen made a mental note to thank her later.

"I see the topic distresses you," Gaspar noted. "I will not ask again."

She let out a deep breath. "Thank you."

"But it seems we shall be in close quarters, Gwendolyn."

"Not necessarily. I spend much of my day in the library and you upon your ship."

"But I heard that you are in need of a tutor?"

Gwen closed her eyes for a moment, dreading what he was about to say next, for she could guess what it was. "Yes, this is true. I never studied Spanish. But I did write to my old French tutor to see if she could find a suitable lady for the position."

"Well, you see, Portuguese and Spanish are sister languages."

"So I've heard," she murmured dryly, pushing about a carrot with her spoon.

"I could be your *professor*, Gwendolyn. You needn't wait for a tutor from England when you have me among the cliffs, a short walk away."

While logically she could see merit in his offer, she could also see many distinct issues with his proposition. The man was, apparently, incapable of being serious and seemed to adore goading Gwen into a confrontation. He would make a terrible teacher and she felt quite sure that she would learn nothing of value from him, except for how to possibly kill a man with a textbook.

As if he could read her thoughts, he began, "Gwendolyn, I know what you must think of me. You must think I am a flirt and a lay-about."

"Among other things," Gwen admitted.

"But I am fluent in many languages, as is obvious by my English."

"Your English *is* very good," she conceded, noting that he had never once used words incorrectly while harassing her. "But there's still the matter of your conduct."

"A man cannot help who he is."

She rolled her eyes. "Well, you must learn if you propose to be my tutor. I wish to study the Spanish language, not get trifled with by a cad. If our arrangement is to work, you must uphold yourself to a standard that leaves no room for inappropriate behavior."

"You drive a hard bargain."

"But a necessary one."

"I swear to you that I will attempt to be an honorable teacher." Gaspar's voice sounded sincere, but she noted a gleam of mischief in his gray eyes.

"Conspirin', are we?" Conner asked, leaning toward them.

"Hardly," Gwen responded, tearing herself away from Gaspar's gaze. "The good captain was just offering to be my Spanish tutor."

"Is that right?" Conner grinned. "That's verra good news. Ye needed to begin your study right away."

"Just as I said before," Gaspar chimed in. "The Spanish courts can be a cruel place for a lady not of that land."

Conner put down his goblet of wine and raised an eyebrow. "Oh?"

Gaspar shrugged noncommittally. "Yes, yes. Many of the royal courts can be harsh to newcomers, especially those as fair as your sister. Among the dark haired *senhoritas*, Gwendolyn will be a golden beacon in the darkness."

"And you believe they might be cruel to her?" Conner sounded worried and glanced toward Gwen, who stared at Gaspar with as much hate as she could manage.

Gaspar dared a look in her direction. Although he attempted to appear serious, the corners of his lips twitched. "Well...someone as gentle and temperate as your charming sister could be taken advantage of."

"All right, that's enough," Charlotte cut in sharply. "Conner, don't you have some correspondence to take care of in the library?"

He began to shake his head, but when his wife glared at him, he nodded and said, "Aye, I do."

Gwen watched his brother get up and stride from the room, his wife tittering at his side. She rolled her eyes and pushed her soup away, aware of Gaspar's stormy gaze still upon her. He watched her in a fascinated way, studying, probing. Each skim of his gaze felt like the cold wash of the surf.

She shivered and moved back from the table, eager to leave. "Do excuse me, I'm suddenly very tired."

Gaspar followed suit. "I should go back to the ship. I'll escort you to your rooms before I go."

"Oh, that won't be necessary," she told him firmly, leaving the small platform upon which the family's table sat.

But he followed, quickening his stride to match hers, which wasn't a difficult feat with his long legs. "When should we begin your studies?"

"Whenever suits you."

He held the door open for her to the main hall. "Tomorrow, then?"

"All right, when?"

"Noon? You could come to my ship—"

"No," she said, much harsher than was probably necessary. But then added in a softer voice, "No ships."

Gaspar nodded, taking his cloak from a footman and throwing it over his shoulders. "Then I will come here, to the library, *sim*?"

"To the library," she repeated.

"Until tomorrow, *Senhorita*." And then he left

53

with a sharp flap of a black cape, into the night.

Gwen stood in the main hall for a moment, listing to the quiet castle, waiting for something—anything to happen. She hoped for music, for laughter, for the boisterous sounds of life that used to make the castle come alive. But she knew the welcomed noise wouldn't come. Perhaps the tenants would appear in a few weeks for a festival, or later on for a feast to celebrate something, but then they would leave and Gwen would, again, be alone.

Sighing, Gwen turned and went slowly up to her chambers, careful to keep her gaze away from Flora's closed door. She knew the room within would be bare, save for the furniture, and she couldn't bear it. All their lives, they had been separated by little more than a wall, if they had not been sharing a room, when her older sisters had still lived at home. Now, there was nothing. In fact, she was the only one who still dwelled in that hall and the only sounds she heard were the soft tapping of her slippers on the stone and the crackling of the fireplace, which had been recently fed.

Once her door was closed behind her, she kicked off her slippers and began unbuttoning her gown. She let it fall to floor, leaving her in her silk shift. Her room was too hot, the fire making it far too warm for her liking. She crossed the room to the window, hoping to let in the night breeze to cool her, when she saw a pinprick of light out in the cliffs. She opened the iron frame and leaned into the cold, salty night air, squinting to see into the distance. But then she remembered what was anchored among the rocks…Gaspar's ship.

Gwen drew back and closed the window, locking it with a swift snap, and then drew the heavy brocade curtains shut. She'd much rather bake in the heat than think about the Portuguese ship, or its captain.

Chapter Five

Gwen paced in the library, her nose buried in a short history of Spanish royalty she found buried on a high shelf. While she spoke four languages, she didn't have the knack for them that Conner did. Besides, the French and German had been ingrained in her from a young age, becoming second and third nature. But anything else had been deemed unnecessary, and thus untaught.

"Beginning early?" a voice said.

Startled, she looked up to see Gaspar standing beside a large globe. He prodded it, sending it spinning on its axis.

"Yes, I wanted to be prepared for our lesson." Gwen snapped the book shut and crossed to the desk, taking a seat. "Please, sit down."

He nodded and dropped onto a chair on the other side, leaning far back in the velvet cushion. "So, *Senhorita*, where shall we begin?"

She motioned to the books that had been carefully selected and stacked between them in order of importance. "I thought we would start with some general geography, and then turn to basic conversation. Afterward, I'd like to—"

Gaspar held up a hand. "Please, Gwendolyn. You are learning a language, not planning an invasion."

"I enjoy being precise and methodical in all my doings so I've mapped out a series of lesson plans for you to follow."

"That does not sound like a enjoyable way to live."

"It *is* an enjoyable and rather necessary for things to run smoothly. Now, if you're done picking apart my personal life, let us get to business." She nodded pointedly at the stack of books.

Gaspar regarded her for a moment before nodding. "Yes, we will begin with the basics, but we will not use your plans. I am the teacher and I will conduct your studies. Have you any knowledge of the Spanish language?"

"Not really. I don't have much in the way of educational Spanish volumes. I ordered a few, but there's no telling when they'll come from Edinburgh—that is if they have them in store."

He grinned, flashing his bright white teeth. "All the better. So, repeat after me...*Olá*."

"*Olá*," she repeated slowly. "That means *hello*, correct?"

"*Sim*."

"Which I know means *yes*, based on context clues. But I thought the Spanish for *hello* was *hola*?"

"You wanted to learn to converse with your future husband, *Não*?"

"Yes—I mean, *sim*."

"Then trust me when I say you shall soon be able to speak the true language of love."

***

The lesson passed quickly, with Gwen parroting Gaspar's every word until he deemed the class at an end. She had only learned several words and a few choice phrases: *hello, goodbye, my name is Gwendolyn, yes, no, horse, carriage, castle, how do you do*, and *very well, thank you*.

Gwen stood and began tidying up her sheets of carefully penned notes. But as she placed each paper in a neat pile, she felt Gaspar's gaze, penetrating the side of her head. She turned to look at him. "May I help you with something?"

"*Não*." He was looking about the library curiously, then stood and began to mill about the large room, picking up odds and ends and running his tan fingers down the spines of several books. But he paused before a display of short daggers called *sgian-dubh*, lined up on an elevated rack between two lines of French novels.

Gwen watched out of the corner of her eye as he picked up three of the blades, testing the weight and sharpness of each in turn. "Do take care. Conner keeps all the castle's weapons in perfectly working order, even if they look decorative."

"Do not fear, Gwendolyn. I've handled bigger and sharper knives than these." He then glanced over his shoulder at her, as if ensuring she was watching, before tossing each knife in the air and catching them deftly. His nimble hands caught each one before launching them in the air again. All the while, he kept his gaze trained on Gwen.

"Please do look at the daggers you're juggling. You'll lose an eye playing about like that and then I'll be expected to nurse you back to health," she chastised, nervously watching the blades as they flipped about in the world's most dangerous juggling act.

"Do not fret, Gwendolyn. This is but child's play."

As if the daggers knew he wasn't taking them seriously, one slipped awkwardly and hit him full on the arm, slicing the skin. Gwen gasped audibly as he caught the last two in his uninjured hand. He set them back in their places—after wiping the bloodied one on his pants—and inspected the wound.

He glanced down and shrugged. "Well, that didn't go as I planned."

"Serves you right," Gwen huffed, seeing he wasn't truly hurt. "Careful to not get any blood on the oriental carpet and follow me."

Feeling annoyed to have Gaspar trail in her wake, she led the bleeding man through the corridors and up to her chambers, where she kept several medicinal items out of habit. When she was younger, she was always tending to Conner and some of the lads he played with, as she was the only girl who could stand the sight of nasty gashes and ill-healing cuts. So, tucked on a shelf in her washroom was a slim box filled with odds and ends that still came in handy more often than not.

"Are these your chambers?" Gaspar asked as she opened the door and ushered him inside, careful to leave it open behind them.

"Yes. I keep some necessities tucked away in here."

He followed her through the room, gaping around at her private space. "Rather dull in here."

"Dull? I have some of the finer bedding and furniture in the Highlands, not to mention these tapestries," Gwen said from the door of the washroom, feeling rather offended.

"I see little of you in here."

"There's not much to see."

"But I do see some rather familiar items…such as a book I know for certain I gave to you."

She felt her cheeks heat at being caught actually using his presents. The volume in question was still open upon her bed. "I couldn't let a perfectly good book go to waste."

Although he looked as if he wanted to, he didn't respond. Rather, he came in to join her and sat down at the low stool beside the claw foot tub, his bleeding arm slightly raised.

"It'll be faster to tend to you myself, rather than send you down to find someone else to do it in the kitchens."

"You tend wounds?"

"When I must," she replied, sifting through the cabinet before finding the box. She placed it upon the dresser that held her washbasin and held out her hand. "Let me see it."

"You won't faint?" he asked suspiciously.

Gwen rolled her eyes and heaved a sigh. "For

goodness sake, I'm telling you to let me see it, now comply before you sully the floor."

He raised his brows, but obeyed, showing her the injury. After dabbing at the skin with a clean cloth, she looked it over, bending and flexing his fingers and testing the depth of the cut. Then she filled her basin with clean water and let the arm soak a moment.

"It's not bleeding much, but it's rather deep. I think you'll need stitches."

She pulled out a needle wrap, a spool of silk, scissors, and a small bottle of vinegar and then washed her hands. "It's better to be safe than sorry." She carefully pulled a thin needle from the wrap and cut a length of silk to use. Then she poured some vinegar over the needle and silk until she was content that they were clean enough for her use.

Kneeling down, she carefully withdrew Gaspar's arm from the basin and dabbed it dry. With the basin set aside for washing, she instructed him to keep still before again inspecting the depth of the wound. Then she quickly drew the needle through the skin, noting how still and silent he was while other men might at least tense.

After laying several tiny stitches, the wound was sealed and she cut off the loose ends, then drew out a strip of clean linen with which to wrap his arm. She looped it over quickly, tying it tightly so it didn't slip off, but not so tightly it would hurt.

When she was done, he looked down at it and nodded. "You did very well, Gwendolyn. Better than most ship surgeons. *Obrigado*."

"*Obrigado*?" she questioned, packing up her

supplies, setting some aside to be cleaned.

"Thank you," he explained, peering at her from under lowered lashes. "Your future husband...he is lucky to have you."

Gwen thought his tone odd, but brushed it off. "It's kind of you to say so."

"Is he a good man?"

"I suppose so."

"You *suppose* so?"

She took her time putting away her medicinal box, thankful to not have to face him. "Well...I've never met the prince."

"Yet you will be his bride?"

"It's the way nobles have done it for thousands of years," she retorted, feeling her cheeks flush. "Nothing at all strange about it. In fact, if you look at the timeline of the world, it's very much the norm."

"Surely you have been writing letters? Learning of one another?"

"It's a new engagement."

"And you have no ring? Is there no ring in the culture of the Spanish now?"

Gwen rounded on him, crossing her arms over her chest. "I hope it's acute blood loss that's making your tongue wag thus. It's entirely inappropriate for you to be asking me these kinds of questions."

"Can a *professor* not take an interest in his pupil?" he asked, his gray eyes glinting.

"Not *that* kind of interest."

Gaspar sighed heavily, as if heaving off a great load. "You are correct, Gwendolyn, and I apologize. I merely wish to have an honest *amizade*...an honest *friendship* with you."

"Then let me be honest and perfectly clear. You are my tutor, and I don't appreciate your line of questioning."

"But why? What do you have to lose by being honest with me? I am leaving soon. I have no ties to Scotland, save some shipping contracts, and none at all with the Spanish. Can we not be friends…confide in one another?"

Gwen blanched. "Confide in *you*? Why ever would I do such a thing?"

"Were you not listening? I have no reason to care what you tell me, nor do I have any interest in betraying your secrets. You seem as if you have a lot on your mind and I have an interest in easing it."

She paused, thinking over his words. In a way, he made a lot of sense. There was a lot on her mind at present, where her potential future husband was concerned, and she thought that it might be prudent to speak it over with someone who knew about the country and its royals—or at least claimed to. Besides, she could use a bit of a friend, particularly when the castle was so empty of those she loved.

"But why have an interest in my thoughts on my marriage?" she wondered aloud to him.

He shrugged, bending his fingers in turn, as if to test the flexibility. "It may be some weeks before I can leave for home. What better diversion is there than the company of a beautiful woman who needs my assistance? Much better than my men, and more pleasing to look upon."

"Stop with the constant flirtations, *please*."

"I cannot help it." He held his hand to his heart.

"The blood of a flirtatious people flows through my veins."

"Well…*try* and perhaps we might be friends."

"I can try, but I make no promises, for when I am your company, I cannot control my mouth as it longs only to sing your praises."

Feeling completely exasperated, Gwen grabbed his good arm and pulled him up to stand. "I must say you're off to a terrible start."

"I have always been a slow learner."

"Then I hope you're a better teacher than a student," she said dryly, looking at the bandage. "If you're lucky, there won't be a scar. But try to keep it clean and tell me if you require anything for it."

"I wouldn't care if it did scar. Years on a ship have given me tough skin. What's another mark upon a sea of them?"

For a fleeting moment, Gwen felt an unexplainable urge to touch his hand—to feel the coarse palm and the long, strong fingers entwined with hers. The uninvited thought made her feel flushed and she quickly looked away.

"Really, do as I say and keep it wrapped tightly in *clean* cloth while out or working."

"I take it you will not come to the ship and change the dressings for me?" he asked, a teasing smile on his lips.

Gwen took him by the shoulder and steered him out of the washroom, through her chambers, and into the corridor. "Remember, friends don't flirt, nor do they act like fools."

"Some do."

"Mine don't."

"Then, *senhorita*, you have very boring friends."

***

When the chamber door was closed behind him, Gwen glanced at the window. The sun was slowly falling, signaling the end of day, and probably the start of dinner soon. But there was still some light and she wished to make use of it as much as she could.

She sat in an armchair by the open window, listening to the waves crash upon the rocks. She opened the small book of poetry Gaspar had given her days before. But as she skimmed the words, her gaze kept drifting out to the cliffs. In the sunset shades of red, purple, and orange, the water around the Portuguese ship below was alight with color.

Just as she was about to close the unread book and begin to dress for dinner, movement caught her eye. She stood, leaning slightly out the window for a better look at the small figure. It was too far to tell for certain, but she thought the person she spied was Gaspar. He was striding toward his ship in that confident manner he possessed. But suddenly, he stopped and turned, looking up toward the keep. Gwen almost drew back into her chambers, but thought he surely wasn't peering at her. She was too far and too quiet for him to have heard or seen her.

But still, he looked, standing unmoving against the grass and rocks as the sunlight dimmed. And then he raised one hand—the uninjured one—as if in parting. As if saying goodbye to her. She lifted her hand slowly in return and only then did he turn

65

back toward his journey to the sea.

Chapter Six

Gwen was riding slowly away from the MacLeod keep, balancing a basket of medicinal items in the crook of her arm. She was trotting toward the village below the castle—some several miles—for the wedding of Big Angus and his bride Grace. She had left ahead of the rest of the MacLeods in order to stop by the local healer before the nuptials. The healer, an elderly woman named Sorcha, often traded with Gwen, swapping her herbal remedies for the more modern tonics that often came into the keep.

She had just stopped to check one of her mare's hooves for stones on the path nearest the docks when she heard her name called out amidst the crashing of the waves. Confused, she whipped her head about, looking for the source of the voice. But it didn't take long to locate it, as Gaspar was heading toward her.

Gwen instinctively frowned, dropping the horse's leg and picking up her basket. "Good afternoon, Gaspar."

67

"Gwendolyn." He dipped a short bow, rising with a grin. "On your way to the wedding of Big Angus and his red bride?"

"Peculiar way of saying that, but yes, I was going down before the ceremony to do some trading."

"What a coincidence! I, too, am invited to the blessed event. I was on my way to the castle to borrow a horse, but now there is no need...that is if you do not object?"

"Object to what?"

"Why, me riding with you, *Senhorita*."

Gwen bit her lip. While his company wouldn't be all that intolerable had he his own mount, she wasn't too keen on sharing the back of her horse with him. "Well...my business will be very boring."

"Then I will liven it."

"And my pony is but a small mare."

"She is a fine, strong *corcel* and I am a trim man. Lighter than air."

She looked over his tall, broad shouldered frame and almost laughed at his words. While he was smaller than her giant cousin Drummond, it wasn't by much. "You are persistent."

"A persistent *professor*," he countered. "We can make a lesson of it, and you may learn all the words for the things as we pass."

"Well, that does sound rather educational," Gwen conceded.

"*Maravilhoso!*" He deftly leaped upon the saddle, much to her surprise, and then held out a hand. "Come, we will ride."

"Have you ridden often?" she asked tentatively.

While he had mounted easily enough, she wondered how much practice a ship's captain had on land with such a beast.

"Often enough to get us to the village in one piece."

"What about your arm?"

He held it down for her inspection. The wrappings were fresh and the cut was healing without issue. "You are a fine *médico*, Gwendolyn."

Not wishing to be late, nor argue, she took his proffered hand and allowed him to pull her before him, so she was pressed between his chest and Faodial's strong neck. Her basket stuck out awkwardly between them, but Gaspar remedied the situation with one reach inside his cloak. He produced a short length of thin rope, which he used to tie the basket to one of the flat saddle's straps, so it lay off to one side of Faodial's shoulder and out of the way.

As they began their journey down toward the village—naught but lines of smoke against the sky—Gaspar held both reins tightly. Gwen found herself enclosed between his tanned and muscular arms, which were firmly visible past the rolled up cuffs of his shirt. She tried to make herself small, so she would not touch him overly much, but found it impossible. Her back was pressed against his breast and she imagined she could feel his heart beat as they trotted down the path. And his legs cupped behind hers on the horse, powerful and sturdy. She felt secure in the notion she would not fall off if Faodial spooked, but still felt ill at ease at being in such close proximity to a relative stranger.

And most unsettling was how much she enjoyed the closeness of his body. She longed to lean into him, to touch the bared tan skin and savor the human closeness he could offer. Before she could control her thoughts, the vision of Gaspar dipping down to kiss her upon the neck filled her mind. It flustered her and filled her cheeks with a searing heat. She had never had such a thought in her mind before. While she knew the thought was sinful, it was also thrilling.

"Do you often carry rope with you?" Gwen asked, hoping to break the silence and take her mind off his healthy warmth and solid arms, which all but embraced her.

"When I am traveling any distance, *sim*. I do not like to be ill prepared."

"Do you carry anything else?"

"A small knife, some flint...no more than other men, I expect."

Gwen, unable to think of anything else to say, cursed her suddenly blank mind, which was still whirring madly, the vacant cogs not producing anything of substance for her to work with. So she stayed silent, trying desperately to ignore Gaspar's presence and thinking how grateful she was that he could not see her face, which she was certain must have been beet red.

"Does she have a name, your horse?"

"Oh, yes," Gwen answered, thankful to have a safe topic to speak about at last. "Faodial."

"Faodial...Fao...dial..." he murmured, as if testing out the unfamiliar language.

"It means *lucky find*. My father gave her to me

just before—" She broke off, not wishing to bring up her father so soon. "My father had been at an auction in the Lowlands, looking for some good Clydesdale breeding stock to bring home. He told me that once he caught sight of this little Eriskay foal, he had instantly been reminded of me."

"Reminded of you? This horse is gray and stocky. Not like you at all."

Gwen smiled a bit, hearing the bewilderment in his voice. "I think it's because she was so small, much smaller than the others, as I was with Conner and my sisters. I had been begging him for a horse of my own for months, but he was certain I'd break my neck if I took one from the stables. So he got me Faodial so that we could grow together."

"I see…much like when a boy in my village first builds a small raft to take out to sea and fish—well, I suppose my old home is now much larger than it once was."

"Have you not been back in some time?"

He paused, staying silent for a moment, the sound of hooves against pressed ground the only sound that surrounded them. Then he said slowly, carefully, "I have been to Portugal, but not my old village in many years. The sea is my true home."

***

Gaspar waited outside Sorcha's hut while Gwen traded several small vials of new medicines from London for bushels of dried bog myrtle to bring down fever and tormentil to stop the bleeding of cuts. She could have gathered such plants herself

71

over the course of a few hours' search, but Sorcha wouldn't take the modern English medicine for free. An honest trade was the only way to get the traditional healer to accept Gwen's help.

"Finished with your business?" he asked as she stepped back out into the early afternoon sun.

"Yes, I am."

"But where is your basket?"

"Sorcha's grandson will bring everything owed me up to the keep tomorrow."

"Then where is your next appointment?"

"That was all I needed to do before the wedding. It's at the chapel, just down this road."

Gaspar held out his elbow for her to take, which she did with some trepidation, as being in close proximity to him seemed to ignite strange thoughts and emotions within her. But to refuse the arm would be rude, so she gently took it, as she would that of any other man. With his free hand, he led Faodial by the reins toward the far edge of the village, where the local chapel stood.

As they strode in companionable silence through the dirt lanes and walkways, dodging stray chamber pots and small children running about, Gwen couldn't help but notice how the villagers responded to them. They were always kind to Gwen, having known her all her life, but they peered curiously at Gaspar, almost as if he were some sort of traveling exhibition. She knew why. He was as brown as a berry, compared to the ruddy complexions of most of the Scots. One might think him a Moorish mercenary or a mysterious cutthroat from a distant land. But based on the appreciative glances at him—and the jealous glares at her—from some of the young women, she knew a good deal would think him handsome.

She herself couldn't deny that Gaspar was a striking man, as well as very educated. If he were only a bit more polite and less of a ridiculous flirt, she might wish for his company more. However, his constant dallying made it difficult for her to take him seriously. Although she noticed his gray eyes didn't wander as they walked and he looked past the village girls as if they were empty barrels or trees.

Gwen would be lying if she said that didn't please her, in some small hidden space within.

"This is it?" Gaspar asked, jarring Gwen out of her musings.

"Oh, yes. I'll just take the horse to the public stables to be looked after."

"No, I will do it. Where should I take the beast?"

"It's there, beside the blacksmith's shop. Have you not been here before?" She knew the Portuguese sailors had often gone to the village to dine, and probably to sample some of the girls who dwelled in the local brothel. She assumed Gaspar would be no different.

As if reading her mind, he said lowly, "I have told you, I will never touch a woman who does not wish me to touch her, and that includes those one could pay. So I have never been to this village. Wait for me, I shall return presently." With a small smile, he turned and led Faodial past the slowly congregating crowd.

Gwen's face heated so rapidly, she could almost hear it boiling like a kettle over an open flame. She couldn't imagine how he was able to know her thoughts so easily, but she could curse herself for making them obvious. She didn't mean to imply he was one to visit the house of ill repute...or at least, make it known that's what she was implying.

When Gaspar rejoined her, they entered the small church together, sitting side by side on a worn wood pew near the door. She looked around for Conner and Charlotte with the children, but they were initially nowhere to be found among the crowd. When she finally did spy them, she found that they sat close to the front. Normally, she might have moved to be near them, but the chapel was almost full and she didn't wish to give any fodder to Charlotte's claims that Gaspar was attempting to spark a grand romance.

When the ceremony began, and Big Angus took his place beside the priest, Gwen allowed herself to relax and watch the proceedings. The gentle giant Big Angus had been a staple in her life since she was very young and it warmed her heart to see that he finally found a woman. And that day he was scrubbed clean in a new shirt and a kilt in the woven colors of their shared clan.

From outside, a band of bagpipes, flutes, and drums suddenly assaulted her ears, the mishmash, joyous music announcing the arrival of the bride. Grace entered, her red hair filled with early spring foliage and wearing a new green dress. There were tears in her eyes, and Gwen thought she spied Big Angus wipe one of his own away as she stopped beside him before the altar.

As the priest spoke in Gaelic, she closed her

eyes, drinking in the words. She was allowing it to lull her peacefully into a place of pure contentment when she realized that this might be the last Gaelic wedding she ever saw. From what she read about the Spanish court, there was no way her old traditions would be kept while marrying the prince. There would be no pipers, no penny tucked in her shoe, no heather in her hair. She felt a sharp pang at the thought and opened her eyes to watch the ceremony with renewed attention.

But as she looked around her at the rapt faces, all turned toward the altar in interest, she found that one person wasn't looking at the newlyweds. It was Gaspar…and he was looking at her.

***

Gwen watched the makeshift band setting up near the town square, bringing out fiddles, flutes, bagpipes, and drums. As for her and the rest of the guests, they were seated in the collection of chairs and tables that had been dragged outside from the various homes. Woman laid dishes of food and plates of bread while two men were turning a pig over an open fire off to one side.

Charlotte and Conner, along with the boys, had greeted Gwen quickly after the ceremony, but then left to tend to some village matters, leaving her alone with Gaspar. It seemed to be a pattern, ending up alone with him unintentionally. She found she didn't really mind all that much. It surprised her to discover she felt that way, but one may never have too many friends, even if the friend in question was a terrible flirt, and she thought it was high time for her to embrace his ever-present company, in the most proper of senses.

"I thought all fine ladies had chaperones," Gaspar said, leaning back in his seat. "Why do you not?"

"Conner says that I was born a grown woman with more than enough sense to stay out of trouble."

"Is that so?"

"Oh, yes. Now, Flora…she needed a chaperone. All she thought of was getting married and going to balls."

"And you do not?"

"Me? Hardly!" She laughed a bit, her gaze following a group of boys who hungrily eyed the simple wedding cake. "Have you ever been to a Scottish wedding? I mean, besides Flora's, of course."

He shook his head, grabbing two mugs of ale from a passing platter. "I have not had the pleasure. This is different than that of your sister, *sim*?"

"*Sim*. This is a traditional wedding. Much less formal than the ones we've had at the MacLeod keep. In truth, I find this much more enjoyable than the rigid ways of the castle."

"That surprises me."

"How so?"

"You are a very…structured lady, yet you enjoy this more than a wedding planned to include every detail."

It was then that the band struck up a lively tune and Big Angus pulled his bride to the empty cobblestone square that had been transformed into a makeshift dance floor. They whirled around in a spin of plaid and green, looking at each other with such devotion that Gwen could barely keep the smile off her lips.

"Thinking of your own wedding?" Gaspar asked.

"What?"

"You looked happy yet sad," he informed her, pushing her cup of ale closer to her fingers upon the table. "Happy to be married, sad to leave your home? Or happy to leave your home, sad to be married?"

She was surprised to find truth behind his simple question. She *was* sad and couldn't quite place her finger on the reason her rapidly approaching engagement had made her feel that way. But she hid her rush of unease with a swig of strong ale. It settled in her stomach, quelling the discomfort that filled her. She didn't care much for the taste, but it gave her something to do with her hands.

"Did I overstep again?" One brow was raised and there was a cocky tilt to his lips that Gwen almost wished she could smack off. Smug cad.

She opened her mouth to answer, but was saved when many of the guests and townspeople joined in on the dancing and the noise in the village rose to a roar. Their hoots and yells overpowered her hearing as people left their seats and the band grew more animated in their playing.

"Dance, Gwendolyn?" Gaspar stood and extended a hand.

She looked up. "Truth be told, I'm not a great dancer."

"Neither am I. But it is a wedding and we came

to celebrate, *sim*? Or we could sit and talk?"

A dance would be the only way out of his probing questions, so she rose from her seat, leaving her cloak upon the chair with Gaspar's. Luckily, the dances the villagers favored weren't like those in the keep. The men danged jigs while the women swung with hooked arms, swapping partners. Gaspar and Gwen joined that round, linking elbows and skipping around through the crowd. And every time their circling brought them back together, the moment their hands would touch—for those fleeting seconds—she swore she felt her fingers tingle.

Despite her initial reservations, she found the beat of the drums and laughs of the other dancers infectious and couldn't recall when she'd acted so carefree. It had been a long time, perhaps even before Flora was wed, or longer still. And even when they spun with other partners, circling the cobblestones, Gwen always felt Gaspar's gaze boring into her, watching her as if she was the most beautiful and graceful dancer of them all. And with that knowledge, she threw her head back and danced with even more vigor, somehow hoping to keep his attention.

When she was finally winded, and the sun had set with candles and lanterns lit all around, Gwen left the dancers and slogged back to her chair to rest her tired feet. When she was seated, she scanned the crowd, catching sight of Gaspar. He was no longer passing through partners like the rest, but had one girl by his side. Gwen didn't recognize her, but immediately felt a hot pang of irrational dislike. But the girl was pretty—she had to admit—with long dark hair and cream-colored skin that glowed in the candlelight as she spoke.

It was unreasonable, how terrible seeing Gaspar with this other woman made her feel, but she couldn't help how the sight churned her stomach. Although she kept looking away, her eyes would almost immediately swivel in his direction. She watched as the girl giggled at something Gaspar had whispered into her hair. It was too much for her to handle—her irrational jealousies—so she rose abruptly and stepped away from the party, blending into the darkness of the surrounding houses, far from the fire and lanterns that lit the square.

The air was cooler away from the crush of bodies and energetic dancers, and Gwen gratefully took in deep breaths. But they did little to ease the angry heat building in her chest. She felt so foolish, taking in all Gaspar's flirting, when that was all he was really good for. Well, besides his knowledge of the Spanish language.

She meandered through the darkened streets with no true destination in mind, ignoring the faint ache in her feet. While she had no claim on the man, nor did she want to, being rejected by Gaspar still hurt her pride. The thought of it almost made her laugh, but the sound stuck in her throat when a hand clamped over her arm.

Gwen let out a high-pitched shriek of alarm and kicked her leg backward. Her free hand dove into her pocket to pull out her small lady's dagger. Her foot then made contact with something solid.

"*Droga!*" the mystery man spat. "Gwendolyn, it is Gaspar!"

She whirled, her heart beating violently against her breast and adrenaline coursing through her veins. The dagger was still clutched in her fist, ready to strike. "Gaspar? You startled me, you great lout!"

"In all honesty, I was attempting to *not* frighten you." He released her arm. "Still wish to stab me?"

Gwen shook her head and gently slid the blade back into the hidden scabbard. "No, not at this particular moment."

"You left and I wanted to ensure you were safe."

"Well, as you can see, I'm quite safe in the village loyal to my family, so you are free to return to your...*dance partner*."

Only the waning moon lit his features, but she could see his brows were furrowed. "Who?"

"The girl you were chatting with, obviously."

Gaspar grinned and leaned casually against a building. "Do I sense jealousy, Gwendolyn?"

"Hardly. It's just rude to disappear without a word."

"Like you did?"

She jarred. She *had* left suddenly and without a word. "I needed fresh air."

"Well Big Angus and Grace have...retired for the night. Some others are leaving as well. Shall we? Or will we stay longer?"

"Return to the castle, I think." She had no more desire to stay. The later the hour, the drunker the guests would be. She wasn't a fan of overly drunken people.

"Come, then." He held out his arm for her to take. "We will ride back at once."

***

The night had gone cold and Gwen was thankful for his sturdy warmth behind her. It made for a comfortable journey back and her misplaced anger had vanished as soon as they left the village. In a strange way, she felt as if she won against the dark haired girl, as he had left with Gwen and not the strange beauty.

"Beautiful night," Gaspar murmured softly.

"It is. I've always loved the night in the hills. The sky is so clear, you can see every star."

"You should see them in the open ocean. It is *muito lindo*…very beautiful. In a calm sea, the stars reflect off the waters, making it seem as if you're sailing though the sky itself."

"That sounds like an amazing sight."

"It is. When we take you to Spain, you might see for yourself."

Gwen's stomach lurched. "I hope the journey isn't so long as to allow me to see much."

"Eager to meet your groom?"

"Among other things," she replied, her mind wandering to churning seas and thrashing waves.

He laughed, the sound reverberating in her back. "If you let me, I will rid you of your fear."

"I'm not afraid."

"You lie. I know you fear the ocean, but you should not. The sea is what gives us life. It brings us to exotic lands, allows us to trade, provides us with fish…yes, it deserves respect and fear, but also our gratitude."

"Then I suppose you can thank it for the both of

us," she huffed as a gust of wind swept through the valley, cutting through her cloak and light dress. She shivered involuntarily.

Without a word, Gaspar took one hand off the rein, using it to settle the sides of his own cloak around her, helping to shelter her from the breeze. Then he wrapped an arm around her waist, holding her more tightly against his chest. As indecent and intimate as it may have appeared, Gwen found she didn't mind the closeness. She was much warmer and terribly comfortable. She knew she should have fought the feeling of ease, but she was too tired and too content to worry overmuch.

They rode in the quiet until the keep came into view, torches lighting the tops of the wall surrounding it. The night was still quiet though, the only sounds being the hooves of the horse upon the hard packed dirt and the distant waves of the ocean. When they reached the gates, a man waved them in with a nod and Gaspar brought Faodial to a halt beside the darkened front door of the castle.

He leaped to the ground, leaving Gwen feeling his absence behind her. But then he raised his arms and swung her down, his hands lingering on her waist. Gwen felt her breath hitch in her throat at their closeness and almost wished he would lean down and kiss her.

But as he seemed to do often, he read her mind and whispered, "I never touch a lady unless she asks it of me." He leaned down a bit, their foreheads almost touching. "Do you ask it of me, Gwendolyn?"

She bit her lip, unsure of how to proceed. Then

the sound of a group of men approaching made them pull apart. The sentry was changing, and neither Gwen, nor Gaspar apparently, wanted to be found in a compromising position.

He nodded at her, a short bow, and asked, "Then I will see you tomorrow? For our lessons, of course."

"Of course," she agreed, a little breathlessly. Despite herself, she silently cursed the guards, but felt underlying guilt as she did so. She had no claim on the man, especially as she was a semi-engaged woman. But she also found that that it didn't stop her from missing his company already.

"Goodnight," he said, but still didn't move.

"Goodnight," she replied, just as still.

He regarded her for a moment and then grinned and shook his head slightly, as if brushing off an unbidden thought. "I will take your horse to the stables. Go inside now. The night grows cold."

"Thank you for riding with me," Gwen said politely, trying to prolong the moment.

"Then I bid you *boa noite*." He turned, leading Faodail to the stables.

Gwen watched him disappear into the darkness—murmuring Portuguese into the horse's ear—before going inside the castle. When she came to her room and whipped off her cloak, she found she was incapable of sleep. Her heart still raced from their evening together and the closeness in which they had spent it.

So she sat by the window, watching the black waves by the cliffs and the single lantern that lit the ship below.

Chapter Seven

Gwen sat among the rocks, tucked in her usual corner between two stones. Her knees were drawn up to her chest and she relished the lull in the wind that left the air mild. The sounds of the waves below roared in her ears. She closed her eyes, thinking of how it would feel to be out in the middle of the sea, hearing nothing but that distinct murmur of rushing water, having it surround her for miles. It was horrifying.

"Am I interrupting?" Gaspar's voice inquired from behind her.

She looked over her shoulder, secretly pleased to see him. "No, I was just out here thinking."

"About your husband-to-be?" he asked, sitting down in the new spring grass beside her. His long legs dangled over the edge of the cliff and Gwen forced down an admonishment for him to be careful, lest he fell to his death.

"No, not exactly." She tore her gaze downward, but caught sight of a large ruby signet ring on his hand glinting in the sunlight. She had never thought to ask if he had been married, but he wore it on his ring finger. Gwen wondered how a woman would feel about having her husband gone for months at a time with no word. She watched Charlotte worry by the window every time Conner's business took him away for more than a day.

"Gaspar, do you…do you have a wife?"

He laughed a bit and lay back, crossing his arms behind his head. "A wife? No, of course not! What made you think that?"

She turned a bit to look at him. His eyes were closed and his breathing even. "Your ring…my brother didn't always wear one, but shortly before my nephew Alec was born, he took to wearing his signet ring, as you do, as a sign of his marital fidelity to Charlotte."

"This was my father's. I've never taken a wife." He opened one eye to look at her and grinned. "But if a golden haired woman who can use a dagger and dress a wound walks into my life and begs me to marry her…" He shrugged and lowered his lids.

"Stop teasing," Gwen chastised. She followed a lone gull with her eyes as it dipped into the waves and flew higher up, past the top walls of the castle.

"You will need to rid yourself of this fear of boats."

"I'm not afraid of boats."

"Then what are you afraid of?"

"The sea," she admitted quietly. "I told you that. If Eduardo does call me to be his wife, then I don't know what I will do."

"Then we should remedy that. Come." Gaspar stood and stretched his hand out to her.

"Where are we going?" she asked as he lifted her to her feet.

"To my ship."

She felt the blood rush from her face. "No, I can't."

"It is docked. No harm will come to you as long as I am beside you. I swear it."

Gwen shook her head violently, feeling her knees grow weak. "No, Gaspar, I can't do it."

"Why not?"

"What if something happens? What if the mast crashes into the boat and sinks and we all drown?"

The corners of his full lips twitched, but to his merit, he didn't laugh aloud at her fear. "You will not drown. I am an excellent swimmer."

She shook her head again.

"Here, wear this." Gaspar reached for his crucifix and medallion, pulling it from his shirt and placing it around Gwen's neck. "Saint Nicholas is the patron saint of sailors and merchants. He will not let you sink and neither will I."

Reluctantly, Gwen allowed Gaspar to take her hand begin pulling her down toward the low shoreline. If she was really going to go to Spain and marry the prince, she would have to overcome her fear, and soon. She wouldn't like to enter her new country as a weak and fearful ghost of herself. Still, she kept her mouth clamped shut in fear she'd be sick from fright. Seeing the water from afar—safe in her little alcove—was vastly different than being on top of it with nothing more than some fancy pieces of wood to keep her from being dragged under.

"Do not be frightened, Gwendolyn," Gaspar whispered, squeezing her fingers. "I swear to you that you will be safe by my side. Always."

She looked up at the massive ship at the end of the hastily built mooring. It seemed bigger up close and she wondered if Gaspar would allow her to merely watch it from afar, but he was already trying to move them slowly forward to the dock. Gwen dug the heels of her shoes into the wet sand at the base of the beach. Gentle surf lapped at the pebbled shore and the boat swayed slightly with each motion.

"I feel as if I'm going to faint," she said. Gwen was never one to faint, but she assumed there was a first time for everything and whipped her head about, trying to find somewhere soft to land as her vision began to darken.

Gaspar suddenly stood before her, cupping her cheeks in both of his palms, forcing her to look into his eyes. "Breathe deeply," he ordered, holding her gaze.

She mimicked his exaggerated breaths, feeling less like she might drop to the ground, but still scared out of her wits. "Can we go?"

"You have come this far, *meu único ouro*, don't stop now."

Gwen was so frozen and sick with terror, she didn't even care to ask what he had just said to her. He was right; she was too close to turn back and may never allow him to bring her this close to the ship again. If she left now, her fear may follow her forever.

"Are you ready?" Gaspar asked, releasing her

face and taking her hand again.

"Yes." Her voice was barely audible over the waves.

Gaspar pulled her gently toward the docks and Gwen wished she could close her eyes. But she knew she needed to be able to see to tell whether she was still on the wood or crashing into the water. Still, she chose to keep her gaze fixed on their tightly joined hands. They were firm, real, and something she could hold on to—literally—as she walked toward the unstable boat.

"*Capitão!*" a voice called out from the deck of the ship as they reached the gangplank.

Gwen stopped moving as she looked up to the boat. It was massive, enormous, a dark wooden vessel with tall masts and a bustle of activity within like a busy beehive. She took several tight breaths and cursed herself for wearing a corset that day. She could pretend the dock was more secure and sound than it really was, but she couldn't ignore the light rocking of the ship, moving with the waves.

Gaspar bent his face down toward her. "Hold tight to me. And step onto the plank with your right foot."

"Why?" she asked, her eyes fixed on the boat.

"Just do it." He drew her tighter to him and willed her forward, up the gangplank.

She stepped with her right, as instructed, and moved onward. Her legs felt like lead and she allowed Gaspar to half carry her up. Her heart thumped against her breastbone, almost painfully, and she dared not look to the side of the fenceless walkway. The ocean below called her and she was thankful when her feet were planted firmly on the deck of Gaspar's ship.

None of the sailors, who were each preforming some kind of task, gave her more than a polite nod as she joined the fray. Some were painting rails, others carried ropes or boxes. One was even polishing a large brass bell. For something that had been docked for more than a week, there was obviously much to be done to keep up appearances.

"My ship is so large, you can barely feel the sea below," he told her, releasing her hand and allowing her to get her bearings without his support.

Gwen had to admit that she felt no different on the deck of the ship than on dry land. But she had the sensation she would feel differently if they were out on the open ocean and she could no longer see the cliffs around them. Still, she nodded in agreement as she followed him around the boat to the bow, which was pointed at the mouth of the cove, toward the sea.

"Look down," Gaspar directed, walking to the end of the bow and leaning over, pointing at something.

"No, thank you," she croaked, happy to not fall over the side and into the frigid water.

"You must," he said with a grin. "Trust me."

Gwen shook her head. "I'm quite content to not look down, thank you."

He held out his hand. "I cannot move until you come look."

"No."

"Please, *senhorita*," he said seriously. "One look and then we can pretend the sea does not exist."

She bit her lip. On one hand, she had no interest in seeing the distance she would drop to her death if she fell. On the other, she knew that Gaspar wouldn't stop pestering her if she didn't, and she needed his help to get back to land. The gangplank was too frightening to even consider approaching alone.

He grinned as she approached and sat down on the deck. She took his hand and gripped it tightly. "Look." He nodded down toward the front of the ship.

She lowered herself beside him, tucking her legs beneath her, her eyes wrenched closed. "I'm fine here."

"Open your eyes."

Gwen did as she was bidden and peered over the edge of the deck. Her vision began closing in as she saw how far below the water was. It was a dizzying sight. "Hold me," she breathed. "I don't want to fall."

"You would never," he murmured into her hair. His arm was already hooked around her waist. "I have you, and I will not let you fall."

She inhaled sharply as she tried to focus downward. But all she could see was dark water and white tipped waves. She felt the cross and Saint Nicholas medallion hanging heavy on her neck. She grabbed it and tucked the gold against her breast. "What…what is it that I mean to be looking at?"

"*Meu único ouro,*" he told her, gesturing to a carved figure below his hand, off to her left.

Gwen saw where he pointed. There was a cut wooden woman on the bow of the ship. In fact, she saw it was an intricately carved mermaid, her scaled tail wrapping around the bow. The mermaid must have been freshly painted, as her scales gleamed a bright sea foam green and her hair shined a deep yellow. For a moment, Gwen wished she could see the figure's face.

"She is lovely, *não*?" Gaspar asked. "*Meu único ouro* always guides *La Sereia* safely to port."

Gwen pushed back, away from the bow and planted her hands on the deck, facing the inner parts of the ship. While the mermaid was lovely, she couldn't ignore the crashing waves below.

"What do they mean—those words in Portuguese?" Gwen asked, looking down at his hand, which rested on the curve of her hip. Although it was improper, it made her feel safer, knowing he was holding onto her.

"*Le Sereia* is the name of this ship. It means *The Mermaid* in your tongue," he explained, his fingers tracing one of the small pink lines on her cream silk dress. "*Meu único ouro* means 'my golden one.'"

"Oh, you called me that earlier, did you not?"

His fingers went the length of her skirt to her knee and ran back up to her hip, leaving a hot streak below the fabric. "I did. My mermaid once had dark hair and olive skin, but when I met you, I knew that she must be changed—must be painted to reflect the good fortune I have."

"You repainted the mermaid because of me?" She felt her face flush and she was both flattered and confused. It seemed a good deal of work just to flirt.

He didn't answer, but she heard him laugh a little

behind her.

She watched his fingertips slide farther up to her waistline, skimming one of the bodice bones that ended right below the curve of her breast. Then his hand trailed back to her hip, where it stayed. She found it hard to focus on much more than the lazy way he caressed her. The feeling of his palm on her hip almost made her forget where she was.

"Are you well, *meu único ouro*?" Gaspar interrupted her thoughts.

"Yes. But may we move, now? The mermaid is beautiful, but I can't sit here any longer." Her fear of below was only one part of why she wished to move. His touch was stirring something within her that hardly had a name.

"Of course." He stood, pulling her up with him, careful to support her. "I'll show you some of the rest of the ship."

She hooked her arm through his offered one, drawing nearer than she normally would. The inappropriate way he often teased her was gone. Gaspar was in his element upon the ship. He strolled down the edge of the stern, letting her walk on the inside. He seemed calmer, less…obnoxious. He was lord of his vessel, and acted accordingly.

"This is the helm," he said, helping her up a small set of stairs. "Do you know much about ships?"

"Only what I've read." She placed a hand on the wooden wheel, worn smooth from use.

He released her and stood at her back, taking both hands and putting them upon the spokes. His fingers rested over her own. "From here, you have total and complete command."

She looked out over the open water, imagining the frightening thrill of being the captain of such a massive ship. "And you say you have more boats under your charge?"

"Four more. They should be here in a week, perhaps longer, depending on the sea." He stepped back. "Care to see where you will be staying, if you choose to go to Spain?"

"I suppose I must," she murmured, letting go of the wheel and following him down to the main deck. There were two doors on either side of the brass bell.

Gaspar opened the one to the left. "The other leads to the deck below, where the crew sleeps and eats."

Gwen shadowed him into the cabin, her eyes taking a moment to adjust to the dim light within. It was a small space, with two more doors, one beside her and another ahead. He opened the one by her arm and pushed her inside. It was a quaint, but cozy room. It held a wardrobe, a bare bed, a dressing table that also functioned as a desk, and a side table. A single, thin window let in enough light to brighten the cabin comfortably.

"Of course it will be better furnished, if you do come," Gaspar assured her.

"I hope I'm not taking your accommodations?" she asked, wondering if he would sleep in the hold among the men, as she had read in books.

He shook his head and nodded toward the other door. "I will show you." He swung the silent door open to reveal a much larger room.

She stepped inside the elegantly decorated chamber. It was all dark wood from the carved beams above to the massive desk covered in maps and ledgers. Several fine paintings hung on the walls and six tall windows trimmed in stained glass lay behind the desk, letting in colorful beams of light. In the corner was a great four-poster bed, the red brocade hangings showing only a glimpse of the bedding within.

"This is my cabin." He strode over to the desk and leaned against it. "Has been since I was sixteen."

"Sixteen? How old are you?"

"Twenty-four."

Gwen was puzzled. She hadn't thought he was that young. It was odd for someone of his age to command so many ships. But then again, her brother took charge of the clan when he was but twenty.

A crashing sound came from above and Gwen ran straight to Gaspar, grabbing onto his arm tightly, her fingers digging into his bare skin. "What was that?"

He chuckled and stroked her back as she drew nearer still. "Just the crew, *meu único ouro*. They must maintain the ship."

There was another loud bang and Gwen buried her face into his chest, on the verge of tears. She waited for a wave to crash down upon them, or for the boat to split in half, letting her drop into the ocean. She clung to Gaspar, barely noticing that he had his arms wrapped tightly around her, his fingers in her curls.

"Hush, Gwendolyn," he murmured, his accent thicker than usual. "*La Sereia* is a fine ship. It's only the crew you hear. You are safe, I swear to you."

Gwen allowed herself to be comforted, breathing in his scent of leather, wood, and salt. She counted each intake of breath as Gaspar purred Portuguese into her ear. Slowly, her heart began to steady and she opened her eyes, feeling embarrassed and ashamed. She pulled out of his embrace and turned her back to him.

"I'm so sorry I reacted in such an inappropriate manner," she whispered. Gwen hated showing weakness, and that's exactly what she was doing.

"It's all right. It takes time to become accustomed to the sounds of the ship."

"And I'm sorry I clung to you like that. It would have been horrible if we had been thrown into the water. I just...panicked."

"I'm not sorry. I know I told you I would never touch you without your permission...but sometimes I feel as if I cannot help myself."

She heard the sound of his thick boots approaching before he laid a heavy hand on her shoulder. Gwen relished his touch; her fear of being drowned at sea was quickly replaced by the sensation of his fingers trailing down the length of her arm. They swept away her unease, replacing it with an elated gush of heat.

"Do you want me to stop?" he asked, brushing her hair away from her neck.

"No," she replied in a hoarse whisper.

He placed his lips on the curve of her throat, one

hand drifting to her stomach, flattening her back against him. He nipped at the sensitive skin, sending jolts of energy coursing through her body. Gwen reached one arm back, brushing the side of his rugged jaw, savoring the feeling of his mouth on her neck. For a brief second, she thought it strange that her first kiss wasn't on the lips, but on her neck.

As if he read her thoughts, he stopped kissing, but allowed his hands to lightly roam over her bodice. When his palm ran over the swell of her breast, she gasped, but pushed her chest outward, allowing him greater access. But then he spun her rapidly in his arms to face him.

"Do you want me to stop?" His voice was throaty, deep, and Gwen saw something flash in his gray eyes. She didn't know much about the ways of men, but she knew what lust looked like.

"No."

He fell upon her then, pressing his full lips to hers, clutching the back of her neck. His tongue probed her mouth, and she allowed him entry as he crushed her to him. She moaned as he bit her bottom lip and she tangled her fist in his dark hair. The feelings he was arousing in her were dangerously primal and addictive. Gwen wanted nothing more than for him to rip open her gown and take her where they stood.

She slipped her hand to the front of her dress, popping off the top button. The moment the silk-covered fastener came free, Gaspar pulled back, panting. He looked down and his eyes widened.

"What are you doing?"

Gwen challenged his gaze and unhooked the next

button. "Are you blind? I know you know what a button is."

He shook his head, his mouth slightly open. "But…but Spain…the prince?"

Another fastener came undone. "Merely a contract to benefit us both. There can be no lost love where there was nothing there to begin with." She didn't know the words were true until she said them aloud. She didn't give a fig about the prince, Spain, or her possible future vows—only the feelings she was experiencing in that moment, in Gaspar's embrace.

Gaspar took her hand away from the buttons and pressed the knuckles to his smiling mouth. "There is no rush then."

Gwen wished he *would* rush; otherwise she might lose her nerve. She had spent her life being perfectly in control and wished to let go of her inhibitions and give in to her desires. A few hours to live as if she had no rules or plans was as intoxicating as Gaspar's touch.

She let him be her captain as he took her by the hand and steered her toward the four-poster bed. He kissed her again, slower then, his hands skimming her face, caressing her neck and shoulders, and then settling on her buttons, undoing each one without sight, his movements swift and expert.

He slowly let her silk gown crumple around her ankles, leaving her in her corset and lace shift. Gwen had a passing flash of clarity where she was thankful for her recent accumulation of fine French undergarments suitable for an adult woman. Gaspar was clearly in appreciation, as he brushed against the tiny embroidered roses along the top, his breaths becoming shallow.

She brought her hand to his belt and pulled his shift free, yanking it over his head and tossing it to the floor. The moment his face was clear, he took to her lips again. She felt a pang of disappointment that she didn't get a chance to see his bare chest, but the feeling was short-lived. Gasper pushed aside the brocade hangings and grabbed her round the middle, sitting her on the edge of his soft bed. He knelt to the floor and gently slipped her shoes off and brushed up the hem of her shift. She watched him, her breath hitched in her throat.

"*Meu único ouro*, I will worship you," he whispered, slipping his hand beneath her skirt and taking the top of each stocking. He slowly revealed each leg, placing his lips on her knees in turn. "You are so beautiful."

Gwen felt her cheeks flood with heat at the feelings of his skin upon her bare thigh. But then he stood and looped a finger round the chain she still wore. He pulled it off her and hung over the lamp beside his bed. Then he brushed his lips over her bared collarbone, his fingers working the strings of her corset.

She grabbed hold of his wide shoulders, her nails digging in as he freed her from her stays. Then he pulled off his boots, standing over her in naught but a pair of black, low-slung pants. She pored over the sharp lines of his hipbones, the hills and valleys that made up his muscular stomach, and the flat planes of his chest. She bit her lip and looked up at him, almost unsure of what to do—or if they should discontinue. But she knew they had reached the point of no return.

"Do you want me to stop?" he asked again.

She didn't answer. Instead, her fingers flew to the wide silver buckle of his pants and then the small tie that held them closed. She couldn't bring herself to look at his newly bared manhood when she finally loosened his pants enough to allow them to slide from his trim hips.

Gaspar climbed on the bed beside her and moved her so that she lay over the blankets. She watched as he settled between her legs and ran his palms from her knees, over the curves of her thighs and helped pull her shift over her head, tousling her curls. He stared for a moment, his gray eyes grazing over her body, leaving strips of burning heat in their wake.

"Do you want me to stop?"

Gwen felt the tips of her lips curve up. "Ask me that one more time and I'll put my gown back on and leave this ship for good."

Gaspar grinned and hovered over her, cupping a breast in one hand, his thumb teasing her nipple, making her gasp. She knew she should feel ashamed of her actions, but the overwhelming tingling that filled her arms and settled in her chest was too delicious to pass up. But then he brought his mouth to her breast, circling the sensitive peak with his tongue. When she thought the heightening sensations could go no further, he gently touched the juncture of her thighs, slowly swirling his finger around her most sensitive place.

When she let out a loud gasp, his head rose up. His light eyes were wide in alarm. "Are you all right? Do you want me to—"

"*Don't* stop," she panted, her back arching.

Gaspar let out a sound akin to a growl and pressed his lips to hers. She let herself melt into his arms as he slipped a finger into her sex. But it wasn't enough. She needed more before she lost her nerve completely.

"Gaspar," she sighed into his mouth, gripping his shoulders.

"I love the way you say my name," he moaned, his stubble scratching her face.

She lightly pushed him away before he could continue his exploration. "I'm ready, Gaspar."

"Are you certain?"

Gwen paused and skimmed her hands down his hard sides. If men could do as they pleased—and her marriage would be nothing more than a contract—there was nothing for her to lose and every pleasure to be gained. No one need know what she and Gaspar did in the captain's quarters of his ship. It would be their secret.

"Yes," she whispered, biting her lip. She could feel his member pressing lightly against her opening and she spread her legs wider as he steadied himself.

"You can tell me to stop at any time," he murmured, hitching one leg up, settling it in the crook of his arm.

Gwen nodded, wrapping her arms around his neck. With a final caress of his lips against hers, he pushed inside her, making her cry out. It wasn't that it hurt—she had expected blood and tears by the way the older women spoke—but it was still a new and unfamiliar feeling.

As soon as Gaspar was fully sheathed within her, he stopped and looked down at her, brushed the loose hair away from her face. "Are you certain you are all right?"

She took in his concerned expression, almost wondering if he knew she had been a maid. "Yes."

He pressed his lips to her forehead, then her cheek, then her mouth again. Then he began moving slowly, tenderly, his strokes filling her to the brim with a carnal longing she didn't anticipate but welcomed. She buried her face the crook of his shoulder, her nails raking his back as she tried to get closer, though it wasn't possible.

As his thrusts quickened, she wrapped her legs around his waist and moaned in ecstasy. He returned her expressions with deep groans of desire and soft croons of gentle Portuguese and he reached his climax. Gwen sucked in a sharp intake of breath as the feelings of pleasure reached a peak and crashed over her, carrying her to shore.

***

Gwen lay on Gaspar's chest, listing to the gentle ebbing thump of his heart. He lazily drew circles on her bare shoulder as their collective breaths slowed. Her eyes were closed and it was easy to ignore the fact that she was in a ship on the ocean—well, the cove was still part of the ocean. What's more is that she couldn't ignore the reality of the act which had just taken place. She was in bed with a Portuguese captain and had just willingly given her maidenhead

101

to him without a single regret.

The more she thought about their tangled legs, her breast pressed against Gaspar's side, and the plush Persian pillows they lay upon, the more ridiculous the situation felt. She had bedded a man out of wedlock, a handsome man, but not one she loved nor planned a life with. She felt like some manner of...well, she felt like *a man*. Unable to control herself, a small giggle burst from her lips.

Gaspar turned to her, a smile on his lips. "I hope you are not laughing at me?"

"No, never," she replied lightly.

"Then what is it, *meu único ouro*?"

She rolled onto her back and stretched, looking up at the dark canopy overhead. It was inlaid with gold strands that made up a most peculiar pattern. "Might I be frank?"

He lay on his side, propped up by his elbow. "I would prefer it."

"I'm just thinking how darkly humorous this is. I'm in bed with a foreigner to whom I am not wed while my brother prepares to collect my dowry to give to another man."

His face fell. "And you regret it?"

"Certainly not! I rather enjoyed myself."

Gaspar smirked and ran his fingers through his mussed hair. "Oh, did you?"

"No complaints," she replied, watching as he raked over her body. "Rather surprising, considering it was my first time."

His dark brows rose slowly, disappearing into the shock of wavy hair above. "*O Que*?"

"What?"

"You were…you were a maid?" he choked out gruffly.

"Emphasis on *were*." She sighed, extending her arms above her head to touch the headboard.

"Are you all right? I didn't hurt you?"

"No, not at all. I found the entire situation entirely gratifying."

Gaspar fell onto his back and ran his hands through his hair again, but that time it was a gesture of aggravation. He muttered something in Portuguese. "I had no idea. I would have been gentle, perhaps not done it at all! I would have—"

"You *were* gentle. You kept asking me if I wanted to continue." Gwen frowned. She hadn't meant to make him feel guilty. "I wanted this. *All* of this."

His mouth curled into a smile. "You little minx. I had no idea, by how deliciously wet and writhing you were."

She was about to say something when she saw, upon the slope of his broad shoulder, a love bite, clear as day. She tapped it with a finger and laughed. "Oops."

"You've marked me!" he exclaimed, faking shock. "Now I must do the same to you."

Gwen covered her chest with her hands and shrieked playfully. "No!"

"Yes, my fair Gwendolyn," he growled, pouncing upon her. He nipped at her ear and twisted his long fingers in her hair. "Mmm, you smell of lavender."

"So much for the monstrous revenge," she tittered, running her hands over the smooth expanse of his back. She felt him harden against her thigh and she became excited at the promise of another round.

He began moving his mouth lower, sweeping over the swell of her chest and dipping over each tip. As his light kisses swept past her bellybutton, Gwen arched her beck, turning her head to the side. She could see the diming light streaming into the cabin, the orange glow of sunset filling the room. Gwen sat up quickly, surprising Gaspar, who drew back at once.

"What is it?" he asked, lightly touching her shoulder. "Did I hurt you?"

"No, no, not at all. Just look how late it is!"

He glanced around her at the wall of windows before pulling her back down into bed. "No, no, *meu único ouro,*" he rumbled, snaking his hand down her stomach. "There is still a fistful of light in the sky. No need to rush."

"But I must," she stated firmly, even though she regretted saying it. "As much as I would love to stay abed with you, I need to be back in the castle for supper. I don't even know how long I've been gone!"

"Only a few moments," he assured her, placing a feather-light kiss upon her wrist. "So if you stay a few moments more, no one shall notice."

"Stop trying to seduce me."

Gaspar groaned playfully and nipped at the tips of her fingers. "Well, *meu único ouro,* if I must take you back to the castle, at least let me fix your hair."

She brought her hand to her head, feeling how her curls were tangled and mussed from their romp.

"Oh, goodness, now everyone will know what has happened." She began to feel ill. She couldn't imagine her being bedded by Gaspar was something that would go over well if her brother heard.

"Do not fear, Gwendolyn, we will fix your hair and your cheeks."

"My cheeks?"

He brushed his stubbly jaw with his hand and then touched the curve of her chin. "Nothing. You look lovely. Come, I'll help you dress."

Gaspar slipped from bed and grabbed his pants from the floor. Gwen took a moment to appreciate the generous slope of his behind, and couldn't contain the frown as it disappeared behind thick, black fabric. After he buckled his belt, he collected Gwen's clothes off the floor.

"Enjoying the view?" he asked with a mischievous grin.

"Perhaps," she admitted, sitting on the edge of the bed, feeling a dull soreness between her legs. "Will you be playing my lady's maid?"

Gaspar knelt down beside the four-poster and pressed his lips to her inner thigh. "It's like cream." Then he put on each stocking and raised her to stand. But he didn't immediately help her put on her shift. Instead he ran his hands down her sides, resting them upon her hips. "You are perfect, *meu único ouro.*"

She felt her cheeks burn. "Oh, do stop your flattery and help me dress, it's bloody cold in here with nothing on."

When she was decently outfitted and her knotted hair had been tamed with a borrowed comb of

Gaspar's, she was ready to return to the castle. At that point, the sun had truly set and the cabin's windows showed nothing but black sky.

"Still a fistful of light, is there?" she asked him as he dropped his cross back around his neck.

"It was a very small fist." Gaspar tucked his shirt into his pants. "The night chill may have come. Here, take this." He reached into a wardrobe and pulled out a dark cloak.

She fastened it about her neck. "Thank you. Aren't you taking one?"

"You'll be leaving me with a fire in my belly. I need the cold to quench it," he told her as he took her hand to lead her to the main deck. "Hell, I might even jump in the ocean!"

Gwen's throat tightened at being reminded of how close they were to drowning. She strengthened her grip on his hand. "Don't say things like that."

He looked down at her when they were out in the night air. The deck was deserted, but the sound of the crew below could be heard. "I'm sorry, *meu único ouro.*" He kissed the back of her hand and looped an arm around her waist. "Now, remember to stay close to me."

There was no moon, only the sprinkle of stars in the sky as they began their descent down the gangplank. She could hardly see anything, but Gaspar strolled down the narrow walkway with ease, apparently able to see in the dark like some manner of cat. She clung to his chest, eager to get back to the rocky shore and away from the sea, which was only made more frightening by its new inky darkness.

106

Once she was standing on dry land, Gaspar released her, instead choosing to take her hand, entwining his fingers with hers. When they began the walk back to the castle, she was grateful for his cloak. He was right by saying that the night winds had come. He, on the other hand, seemed totally fine, oblivious to the spring chill.

As they strolled in silence, Gwen had time to think. The addition of clothes did much to enhance her thoughts. If she and Gaspar had still been lounging in his bed, there was no possible way she would have the strength of mind to be able to speak. But then, with the only sound being the waves and the wind, she pondered her next move. Her afternoon in Gaspar's arms had been carnally perfect and she knew she would always look back upon her first time with relish. But would there be a second? A third? She had to know.

"Gasper..." she began, trying to find the words to convey her tumbling thoughts. It was easier to speak with him in the darkness, but still a difficult subject. How was a highborn lady meant to ask a roaming captain to continue pleasing her in bed? None of her lessons in finishing school had taught her *that*.

"You want to know if you can see me again?" he asked quietly, as if reading her mind. "Do you want to see me again?"

"Well, I'll see you every day for my Spanish lesson," Gwen pointed out, avoiding directly answering his question.

He squeezed her fingers. "Then you will see me every day in whatever capacity you wish."

"That's rather vague."

"Then you want to know if I will bed you again?"

Gwen didn't answer. For the first time that evening, she felt embarrassed. It should have been simple to tell him exactly what she wanted. But as they walked hand in hand to the castle, the words evaded her. She waited for him to say something until they reached the gate, but he was equally silent.

"I suppose this is where I leave you, unless you wish to dine with us?" she asked him as the sentry on duty began his walk away from the gate around the wall.

He regarded her for a split second, and then pulled her between the two sections of wall, hidden from all sides. They were enclosed in darkness, their chests touching.

"Gaspar, what are you doing?" Her voice was low, but held a hint of excitement.

Without speaking, he pressed his lips roughly to hers. His hands slid in the fabric of her borrowed cloak to caress her breasts through the silk of her gown. Gwen moaned into his mouth and held tight to his shoulders, wishing she had done as he commanded and stayed in the bloody boat.

When he pulled away, Gwen was left speechless and she leaned back against the cold wall, trying to catch her breath.

"I will see you for our next lesson tomorrow," he told her as he backed away. But just as he was turning to go, Conner came out the door, his figure lit from behind by the lanterns in the hall.

"Ach, where have ye been, lass?" Conner asked when he spied her. "It's dark as sin out."

Gwen debated lying, as she knew she had the face for it. It was a skill that always made Flora jealous. But she decided to go for a half-truth, to save what was left of her clean conscious. "Captain Gaspar was teaching me a few things," she said smoothly, stepping forward toward the door.

"Is that right?" he asked.

"*Sim*," said Gaspar, stepping into the light.

Conner ushered them both inside. "Gaspar, ye'll stay for supper, aye?"

"If it is no imposition," he replied politely.

"No' at all." Conner took Gwen's borrowed cloak and passed it to a maid.

When they entered the family dining room, Charlotte was already seated with little Ian and baby Alec. As soon at the manservant spied Gaspar, he busied himself with making another place setting. Gwen sat on the left side of Conner, who was at the head of the table, and across from Charlotte. Gaspar sat to *her* left and she repressed the urge to glance his way. It felt almost sacrilegious to sit at the MacLeod table beside him, the evidence of their encounter still slick between her thighs.

"Are you well?" Charlotte asked Gwen, a light frown on her lips.

"I have been working her quite hard," Gaspar explained seriously.

Conner began filling Charlotte's goblet with wine. "Did ye learn anythin' useful?"

Gwen regretted this course of action, but there was no way out. "Oh, very, but I'm not an expert by any means."

Charlotte nodded. "It takes time. Just be a good student and work as diligently as you can, as frequently as you can."

"Do not fear," Gaspar assured her. "I will be giving her many lessons and seeing how *malleable* she can be."

Gwen bit the inside of her mouth to keep from bursting out in inappropriate giggles. Gaspar's hand snaking under the table and squeezing her knee playfully did nothing to quell the sensation.

"Wait," Conner cut in. "Ye were no' in the library today. I just met ye outside."

"Because I was on the ship," she admitted slowly, her focus on her dinner. She wondered if that would be the thing that undid her lies.

Conner and Charlotte exchanged looks of pure shock. But it was Conner who broke the silence. "You were on a boat...a *real* boat in the...the *water*?"

Gwen speared a potato with her fork. "Yes. I was on his ship for a large part of the afternoon. It's why I was so dreadfully late."

"I'm so proud o' ye, lass," Conner said in disbelief. "I never thought ye'd get over your fear o' the water." He looked over at Gaspar. "I can no' believe ye got her to do it. You teach her Spanish *and* have her get over her fear? Unbelievable."

"You must be a very good teacher in order to get Gwen to go on your ship," Charlotte mused, dabbing some droplets of soup off Ian's face. "I wish I studied more languages. But I guess Gaspar has a very talented tongue."

Conner nodded. "Aye. Tell us, Gwen, does he treat ye well? Or does he have a hard hand?"

Gwen nearly choked on a potato and it took several moments for her to regain her breath. She had no idea how Gaspar was sitting there so silently, calming eating. "He's a fair teacher."

As the conversation moved to other things, Gwen found it hard to follow. She couldn't focus on the current conversation of land sales and trade agreements when she had just lost her maidenhead on a Portuguese merchant ship! The mere thought of it sent her skin aflame, and not due to embarrassment. Of course, she knew she should be ashamed for her wanton behavior, but she didn't have it in her to give a damn. It wasn't as if she would marry the Spanish prince for love; it was quite possible they wouldn't even meet until she got to Spain. And until the time came for her to step into the church to say her vows, she didn't see the harm in having some fun.

As Gaspar gently stroked her thigh out of sight of her family, she knew he saw no problem with their relationship either.

Chapter Eight

Gwen was in the library when Gaspar came for her. She hadn't seen him for two days and she had begun to wonder if he was over their dalliance. But the playful flash in his eye as he pored over her body told her a different story. Gwen thought about speaking to him directly, but decided it would be better for him to wait, as he made her do. And after taking her virginity no less! It was shameful. So she kept her eyes on her work, leisurely flipping through her pages.

"Good morning, Gwendolyn," Gaspar said, his hands in his pockets.

She glanced up at him briefly, then back to the desk. "Good morning, Gaspar."

"Are you well, this fine day?"

"Exceedingly. And yourself?"

"Fine, Fine…" He meandered through the room a bit, poking at some of Conner's odder collectables. "Are you very busy?"

"Just going over the spring seeding plans for the farmland."

"And you do all that yourself?" he asked, coming closer.

She shuffled a few pages aside, looking for the notes on the previous year's barley crop. "Of course I do. I have for several months. I rather enjoy numbers."

"Is that right?"

Gwen looked up at him. "They are very predictable, stable, *dependable*." There was a pregnant pause in which Gaspard regarded her closely. She knew that didn't need to be said, but if their casual arrangement was going to work, he needed to know that she waited for no man.

"I admire that," he told her, coming to stand on the other side of the desk. "Many women would be content to sit and sew."

"Everything well with the ship?" Gwen asked mildly, changing the subject. She didn't like being reminded she wasn't like other women. If she were, then she certainly wouldn't have been in bed with him. She jotted down a few numbers in her receipt book.

He placed his hands flat against the desktop and leaned forward. "Perfectly. I needed to survey the supplies for our journey back to Portugal." He lowered his voice. "I would have sent a note…but I could not trust myself to not write all the things I wish to do to you."

Gwen closed her pen and looked up at him, feigning innocence. "You mean how you wish to teach me to become fluent in conversational Spanish?"

"Yes. I was thinking we might go over parts of

113

the body? Anatomy, their functions…if you would be agreeable to such a lesson?"

She felt the stirring in her loins, something she had tried to ignore for the two long days she had waited for him to contact her. "Quite," she responded evenly, rising from her chair. "Where shall these studies take place?"

"I was thinking we could go to the ship. We need quiet for our lesson."

"But the crew?"

"Mostly gone to the village," he explained, straightening his back and raising his brow at her. "So, *meu único ouro,* will you join me?"

"I suppose I could fit you into my schedule."

"Clear it, Gwendolyn," he growled as she passed him to leave the library. "What I have planned for you might take all day."

***

Gwen thought she should feel nervous when the door to the captain's cabin was locked tightly behind them, but it was quite the opposite. She trusted Gaspar implicitly, although she hardly knew him. Besides, she felt oddly at home in the lavish quarters and immediately kicked off her shoes and began unrolling her stockings before Gaspar stopped her, his shirt already gone. Her fingers itched to touch his chest.

"No, Gwendolyn," he said lowly, kneeling before her as he did the first time they came to the cabin. He reached up her skirts, skimming her leg. He pinched the tops of her stockings and pulled both off. "*Meias*—stockings."

"*Meias*," she repeated, watching him with interest.

"*Vestir*." His rose and his fingers made quick work of the fastenings to her gown. "It means 'dress.'"

"*Vestir*." Gwen tried to put her arms around his neck, eager for him to continue disrobing her.

But Gaspar dropped the gown to the floor with a satisfied smirk. "No, no, this is all part of the lesson. Now, this is *espartilho*." Gaspar began unlacing her corset. "And this is your *pescoço*." He brushed his lips against her throat.

"My neck? *Mmm*…what else?" She was beginning to thoroughly enjoy his lesson.

He kissed her shoulder. "*Ombro*." His fingers hooked over the straps of her shift and let it puddle on the floor. "*A bainha*."

"And this?" Gwen asked, grabbing him by the belt.

"*Cinto*." Gaspar helped her to unbuckle it and it fell with a clatter upon the wood. "*E calças*." He gestured to his pants, which she hurriedly lowered.

They fell into the bed together, and Gwen reached for his member, but Gaspar grabbed both her hands, holding them above her head. Her breathing quickened in anticipation, but it seemed that Gaspar had other plans than taking her as she hoped he would.

He nipped at her lower lip. "*Boca*." And his knee thrust her legs apart, making her gasp. His mouth caressed her breast. "*Peito*."

"*Pieto*…" Gwen hummed when he found her

115

nipple. "Gaspar, can we—"

His head darted up. "Hush, I have not gotten to the best part."

"I think I'm fine. We can continue to the next step, if you don't mind."

Gaspar shook his head and released her wrists, sliding his hands down her arms, over her breasts and down her waist to cup her thighs. His lips followed, halting at the gentle peak of her hipbone. Gwen's voice hitched in her throat as he continued his journey south and dipped his tongue at the juncture of her thighs.

And try as she might to pay attention, Gwen couldn't recall a single word.

***

"I swear, I'll never be able to say a single thing in Spanish," Gwen murmured into her pillow. She was watching Gaspar pull on his pants, leaving his belt on the floor. "You're a terrible teacher."

"You mean to say you didn't learn anything today?"

"Oh, I learned plenty." She laughed, brushing her hair away from her face. "Just nothing useful in conversation."

"Then I suppose our next lesson should be at a desk, in your brother's study? There I can instruct you on all the grammar and uses of this glorious language."

Gwen groaned. "Never mind. I'd rather continue my study in biology." She reached out to him with a lazy hand. "Will you come back to bed?"

He walked over to her and brushed his knuckles on her cheek. "I am just going to get us something to eat from the galley. I will be back in a moment."

Gaspar turned and left the room, giving Gwen a good look at the dimples on his lower back. She also spied a series of thin scratches above she knew were from her nails. She peered at her hands and stifled a small laugh, then sat up, holding the brocade cover to her chest. All around her were tokens of his travels—wondrously strange things she had only ever read about in books.

There were Russian nesting dolls, an African mask, tusks of gilded ivory as tall as she, and fine paintings that simply covered every available space on the walls. It was a cluttered cabin, but not a dirty one. Every exotic piece was clear of dust and even his bed smelled of soap and fresh linin. She rather liked his chambers. It suited him, and if she were honest, it suited her as well.

"Preparing to leave?" Gaspar asked from the doorway, a bottle of wine tucked under one arm and a plate of bread and cheese on the other. He shut the door behind him and came to sit on the edge of the bed beside her.

"No, why would you say that?"

"You look it." He nodded toward his wardrobe. "If you ever feel the need to go on a jaunt, I have put a dressing gown there for you. It is meant for a French countess, but it would suit you better."

She felt the gesture oddly intimate, but decided not to question it. "That won't be necessary. I was just hoping to get a look at some of your things."

He put the cork of the bottle between his teeth

and pulled, letting it fall to the ground. "So you wish to snoop, do you?"

Gwen flushed, taking the bottle. "Goodness, no. I've just never seen any of these wonderful treasures and paintings. Some I don't recognize the artist, although I do spy some classics."

"Because I painted a few of them."

"*You* are an artist?"

"I enjoy painting at times, but I would not call myself an artist."

"Which are yours?"

He stood and made a quick round of the cabin, pointing at three small canvases. "This, this one with the ship, and that one beside the wardrobe."

She pulled on his discarded shirt, which fell to her thighs and covered her up enough so she wasn't too scandalized, and went to join him to get a better look at the works. The first was simple, a landscape featuring the coast in the distance. The second was, as he said, of a ship, crashing against a harsh wave, lightning lighting up the sails. The last was of a dark haired woman, bathed in moonlight, wearing a flowing blue gown that brushed the cobblestone beneath her feet.

"She's beautiful," Gwen whispered, brushing a finger across the filigree frame. A strange twinge of jealousy filled her at the sight of that lovely woman, so carefully painted.

"My mother."

"Your mother?"

"Yes. She died when I was very young, so I do not remember her face."

She placed a hand upon his arm, feeling ashamed

of immediately thinking the worst. "I'm sorry."

"There is no need." He cleared his throat and smiled at her. "What else here caught your eye?"

"What didn't? Everything is so exotic."

"Then travel and you will see many more amazing things."

"I can't," she whispered before taking a liberal gulp of wine and crossing back to the bed.

"Why not?" he asked at he followed her and settled himself next to her.

"I can be on this ship when it's docked like this, but never...*out there*."

"You will have to at some point, when it comes time for you to go to Spain."

The wine soured in her mouth at the mention of Spain and she passed him the bottle. "Yes, but I will have no choice in the matter," she explained, watching him take a drink. "I must go on a boat to the mainland or forfeit the wedding. I would never set sail willingly and never just for sport."

"Can I ask you, Gwendolyn, why do you fear the sea?"

She felt her throat tighten and the heat of fresh tears pooled in her eyes.

Gaspar noticed and cupped her cheek with his hand, setting the bottle aside. "Forgive me. I should not have asked."

Gwen shook her head and swallowed. "It's a fair question."

"One that need not be answered."

"Yet, I shall." She took a deep breath. "My father was fascinated by the sea. Granted, his duties as chief kept him on land, even before the restoration of the clans. But he loved to sail for pleasure, fish, and bring my mother shells—she gave me one, a delicate, spiraled thing of pure white and purple intertwined. I still keep it in my writing desk."

"A man after my own heart."

"But a man not as lucky as you. He drowned several years ago, just before I turned thirteen. We don't know exactly what happened, and we never will. My father took his small sailboat out with another man. He wished to see the cliffs from all angles, as he was plotting the ways in and out of the castle, and wanted to see the wall during low tide. He was looking for any more hidden passages and sea caves. But something happened...something bad. Their boat flipped and crashed against the rocks. When he didn't return, some men went to find them. They found...they found my father, at least. It was some comfort to my mother, being able to give him a funeral. Shortly after, she left to go live with my eldest sister and her husband, and Flora and I were sent to school in England."

"I am sorry," Gaspar said in a hushed tone. "If I had known...I should not have pushed you to rid yourself of the fears you rightly hold, *meu único ouro*."

"I needed to. I needed to overcome them somehow."

He brushed his thumb over her cheeks and his fingers came away damp.

"Goodness, I'm a sight!" She forced a laugh and swiped at her face, ridding herself of the evidence of her grief.

"The most beautiful sight I have ever seen," he assured her, pressing his lips to her shoulder. "And I have seen a great many sights."

Gwen lay beside him and burrowed into the crook of his arm, looking up at the side of his handsome face as he spoke. The mere sight of him calmed her wounded heart and offered a very welcome distraction. "What kind of things? Tell me. I need to think of something good."

A smile played on his lips and he closed his eyes as he spoke after a final, short kiss. "The markets of the middle east, for one. There are dozens of tables with spices, jewels, fruits you have never tasted and mysterious jars you dare not open. To get to the markets from the sea, you travel by camel, a great animal with humps upon its back."

"How novel," she whispered.

"And there are the ruins of Greece. Some monuments and temples to their old gods are naught but piles of stone now. But the mystery is still there and great cities hide beneath the earth."

"Beneath the earth?"

"*Sim*. Several cities were buried by dirt and volcanic ash long ago. Now people sometimes find what's left of homes and farms, deep beneath the ground."

"Amazing. What else?"

"There are northern lights in Greenland—"

"We have the lights in Scotland, too."

"Yes, but the colors are purer and reflect off the sheets of ice and icebergs, filling the water with vibrant greens and strips of violet I could never truly describe."

"That does sound beautiful," Gwen admitted regretfully. "But it's still only accessible by ship."

"If you could go anywhere, ship or not, where would it be?"

She thought back to all the books she had read and maps she had studied. But reading about something and actually experiencing it were so terribly different. "You tell me, where should I go?"

Gaspar paused a moment before speaking. "Well...I could see you on the streets of Paris, walking along the *Champs Elysées* in that cream and pink frock you favor, buying flowers from the shops and taking tea along the River Seine."

"You remember my dresses?" She smiled into his shoulder.

"I'm not colorblind."

"Where else?"

"Maybe on the shores of the island of Hispaniola," he mused, his fingers drawing lazy patterns on her bare skin. "They have white sand beaches and water so light and clear, you can see straight through to the bottom of the sea. You can see the pods of dolphins and the vibrant corals that lay leagues below your ship. And the ocean there is so warm, it is like stepping into a bath."

Gwen thought of the icy waters of the loch near the keep, which was cold no matter the season. "That sounds lovely."

"It is."

"Tell me more."

He opened one eye and looked down at her. "You are very curious for someone who does not wish to leave Scotland."

"I'm allowed to be curious."

"How about you tell me something about your home, here."

"There's nothing to tell." She sighed. "It's green, wet, cold—"

"Is that why your people drink so much? To ward off the cold?"

She frowned, confused by his words. "What do you mean?"

"When your man Angus married, we gifted them all the drink for the celebration. When I returned to the ship, I found the guests had almost completely wiped out our stores!" He laughed a bit. "It was very impressive."

"You gave them all that?"

"Why not? I was a guest at a wedding in which I was welcomed with open arms. It was only polite."

"Are you always so overwhelmingly generous?"

"How can I not be when in a beautiful country such as this? It really is amazing, full of effervescent culture, and savage in a way that makes me think of what man used to be like…almost like you."

Gwen giggled. "That isn't a compliment."

"Is it not?" he asked, turning to face her. "Aren't you beautifully savage but perfectly refined?"

"I…I don't know." She couldn't really understand what he was trying to say.

"You are classically beautiful like a Botticelli painting, round in the right places and golden like the sun's rays." Gaspar ran his fingers lightly over her shoulder and to the swell of her breast. "But natural. You do not color your hair and paint your face like some women do. And you are smart, *meu único ouro*. Smarter than most men."

"Well, I can't argue with that!"

He pressed his lips to hers. "And so humble."

"Says you." She laughed as he hooked his fingers around the back of her neck. "You're the least humble person I know."

"Who could be humble with a face like mine?" Gaspar teased.

"You're ridiculous."

He touched his forehead to hers and closed his eyes, inhaling deeply, as if breathing her in. She thought to lower her lids as well, but found she wanted to look at him—to take in each arch and angle of his handsome face. As she took in his long lashes and the rounded curve of his lips, her heart lurched in a feeling she couldn't quite place. Still, she stared at him, longing to memorize him.

But suddenly the boat lurched and Gwen's heart dropped to her stomach. "What was that?"

"The wind," he replied, opening his eyes.

"Are you sure?"

"Quite."

Gwen tried to keep her voice steady. "Shouldn't you check? What if we're drifting away?"

"We are not."

"But how do you know for certain?"

"I have lived on this ship since I was sixteen," he assured her, running his fingers through her hair. "If we were drifting off to sea, I would know it."

Gwen thought the motion was meant to be calming, but there was no way a mere fondling of her follicles could slow her heart rate. "But you can't be absolutely sure without seeing for yourself, surely?"

He sighed and kissed the top of her head as he moved to leave the bed. "I shall be back in a moment."

She was about to settle back in the wait when she realized that if the ship were to float away from the dock, the waves would probably send it smashing into the cliffs that surrounded the cove. If Gaspar was above deck and she was below, there was no way she could escape when the vessel began to sink.

"Wait for me!" she called as he reached the door. She scrambled out of bed, throwing on just her gown and shoving her feet into her slippers

He tilted his head. "What are you doing?"

"You're not leaving me here to sink," she retorted crossly, hurrying to tie her loose hair back with a ribbon. She wanted to look respectable if her drowned body was to be pulled from an icy grave, and not as if she had just been ravished.

"Leaving you here to sink?" he repeated dumbly.

"Never mind, just hurry. We're running out of time."

"After you." Gaspar stepped aside, allowing her to dash past him.

Gwen thought she heard him laugh as he followed her through the hall and up the stairs to the main deck. While it took her a moment to adjust to the fading daylight, she was extremely relieved to see they were still safely in port. She slumped against the wall beside the brass bell and tried to quell the shaking of her legs.

"Come, you must lie down." Gaspar cupped her cheek. "You are even paler than usual."

"I'm fine," she muttered, her gaze fixed on the steady rocks of the cliffs to her right.

He took her hand and began pulling her to the bow. "Come."

"Where?"

"Just do what I ask without question for once, *meu único ouro.*"

Gwen allowed him to lead her to the front of the boat. He helped her to sit on the edge, and even pushed her legs off the side to dangle. She tried to not look down, although she feared she would lose her slippers. He sat behind her, wrapping his arms tightly around her and making her lean back against his chest. It made her rather nervous for him to be the only thing that kept her from falling to her death, especially as she still hadn't completely relaxed yet.

"You won't let go?"

"Why would I? Then I would have to explain to Conner why his beloved sister is dead. I have a feeling he would burn more than just my ship."

"Also, we shouldn't be sitting like this," she whispered, looking back at the empty ship. "What if someone sees us?"

"Has any Scot but you come to this boat?" He didn't wait for her to answer. "No one will see you and none of my crew will say a word, not that most could, anyway. Many do not have even a basic grasp of the English language. So do not fear, Gwendolyn, you are protected."

Gwen took a deep breath and tried to quell the

battle of emotions within her. She reached up and held his hands, which were locked firmly around her torso. They were warm and steady. They made her feel safe. When she was in his arms, it was almost easy to forget that the ocean was waiting to swallow her up...almost.

Chapter Nine

Later that week, Gwen lay in Gaspar's empty four-poster for a quarter of an hour before growing bored of waiting. He was up with the crew, supervising some provisions they had bought in the nearby village. While he had said he would be but a moment, he obviously had no true concept of time. This was evident in the full four days they had spent in bed, exploring each other's bodies until the sun set. Until it was no longer passable as sunset, Gasper kept telling her there was still light left in the sky.

Rising from the warm bed, she crossed the room to the wardrobe, where he had once said he placed a dressing gown for her use. Curious, she pulled open one heavy door, seeing a straight line of stacked shelves of plain shirts and other clothing. She opened the other and found a row of hooks. There were several overcoats and furs, then on the end, tucked behind something she thought might be bearskin, there was a flash of color among the browns and grays. Gwen took out a long pink robe of the finest silk. Small cream roses ran about the trim and it tied with a strip of silk the same color.

She donned her new addition and milled about the cabin, as she hadn't done before. During her visits they hardly ever left the bed. But without Gaspar to distract her, she had the freedom—and the clear mind needed—to inspect his exotic collection.

There were delicate Chinese vases and containers on a shelf filled with colorful powders and bits of dried herbs and plants. She thought she recognized a few from her trading with Sorcha, but most were foreign to her. Stacked atop the desk were a pile of nautical maps and odd tools she had never seen. Along the walls, covering almost every exposed piece of paneling, were framed pieces of art, the likes of which would belong in almost any fine home in London.

But one particularly large piece caught her eye. It was of a nude woman—perhaps a nymph—and she was lying peacefully upon a pile of cushions in a green wood, gazing dreamily up at the canopy of trees above with a smile on her lips. But it wasn't the canvas that Gwen was drawn to, rather the frame. The gold filigree was thick and shined with careful care and maintenance. But the edge was slightly worn on one side. While the normal visitor might not have seen such an irregularity, Gwen had not found so many hidden passages in the MacLeod keep by being unobservant.

She knew she shouldn't; it wasn't her business. But she couldn't help herself.

The frame pulled away easily from the wall, just

as she suspected it might. The small room within was dark, but as her eyes adjusted to the sight, she was confused. While Gwen didn't know exactly what she was looking at, she knew it was worth a great deal of money and she didn't blame Gaspar for trying to hide it. So she climbed inside, impressed at how well it was secreted, but more impressed at the quantity of hidden objects within.

Floor to ceiling shelves filled all three walls of the concealed chamber, which was no larger than a stairwell. Atop each shelf on the far wall, attached to the wood, were small boxes. Intrigued, she went to the closest one, unhooked it, and peered inside. Dozens of uncut diamonds shone dully in the feeble light that came from the cabin.

Gwen had seen the ship's ledger when it first came to port, and while she saw several gemstones and jeweled pieces in the log, there wasn't any note of the diamonds. One box, such as the one she held, could be easily worth a hundred pounds. It would have been impossible to neglect such a collection in his note taking.

Her feeling of unease grew as she opened each lid, seeing how every box contained more precious gems. While most were diamonds, there were also stones of deep blue, canary yellow, and something akin to an emerald but paler. All in all, there was a substantial fortune hidden away in the ship and Gwen thought she might have been the only person to know—aside from Gaspar, of course.

"I see you have found my little storeroom?" he asked from behind her.

In alarm, Gwen dropped the small chest,

scattering diamonds all over the darkened floor. But she made no move to pick them up. Instead, she found herself staring back at him, wondering if he would yell, fight, banish her from the ship…but as the moments passed, he did nothing. In fact, he didn't look angry at all, merely amused.

"Well, you weren't very much impressed by the silks, jewelry, and books I sent you before. Are these more to your liking?" he asked, holding out his hand to her. "Shall I offer you boxes of gems?"

She took his hand, allowing him to help her back into the main cabin. "I might have accepted, had they been a *legal* import."

He laughed. "You are a sharp one."

"You say that like it's a surprise."

"You always surprise me, *meu único ouro.*" Gaspar closed the portrait hole with a dull *click.* "And I will not lie to you, for I think you would see through me in an instant. No, these gems are not in my books, nor will they ever be."

"But that's terribly illegal. I don't know the laws in Portugal, but I know enough to be fairly sure that you could be incarcerated if they were to find you to be a…a…"

"Smuggler?" he offered helpfully. "Pirate? Man of fortune? Brigand?"

She crossed her arms over her chest, annoyed at his calm attitude toward his illegal activities. "Any one of those apply, I believe. Now, I don't know about your homeland, but I do know that in several countries, you could be tried for some manner of piracy, Gaspar. It's a very serious matter and—"

"You are adorable when you worry," he

muttered, toying with the cream tie that held her robe shut.

She slapped his hand away. "Stop that, this is serious!"

"Do not worry, *meu único ouro.* I have never been caught before."

Gwen rolled her eyes. She couldn't believe he was so stupid as to be taking such chances with his life and those of his crew. He was concealing a sizable fortune on his ship, and if the wrong people found out, he could be killed. "Should that make me feel better?"

"I did not know you felt any sort of way. Tell me, what is it that you feel?" His gray eyes scanned her face as he waited for her response. While his words might have been innocent coming from anyone else's lips, Gwen felt weight behind them.

"I feel that you're an idiot," she snapped, turning away and crossing the room back to the bed. "I feel that you're making very poor choices that could result in the death of your crew and yourself. I also feel that you are far too intelligent to throw away everything you've worked so hard for and you must rectify this immediately, lest you draw attention to yourself at a later date."

He came up behind her and placed his hands upon her shoulders. Then he bowed his head down to speak in her ear. "It is sweet that you fret, but you should not. I know what I must do and how to get my items where they need to go. That is why I waited here for my ships." He pressed his lips to her neck before continuing, "We will split up the gems among us, each going to a new port. The jewels are tucked into orders, when necessary, hidden among larger purchases."

"And this works?" she questioned, feeling her heart race. She knew she had no right to be, but she was angry with him for being so stupid and reckless. "It's a foolproof plan that will *never* fail?"

"No plan is without error," he conceded, sounding weary.

"Let me see," she demanded, rounding on him.

He frowned. "The jewels?"

Gwen took a deep breath and stalked over to his desk, taking a seat in the plush captain's chair. "Let me see your plan. Show me your accounts and I'll tell you what I think."

Gaspar raised a brow, but did as she commanded. He crouched down to open a hidden panel on the base of his four-poster bed and removed several leather bound books. He placed them before her then leaned on the edge of the desk, watching her as she scanned each line.

While she wasn't familiar with hiding goods from officials, she was always quick to find the indiscretions in any logbook. But the ledgers didn't read anything odd, nor did any particular account jump out at her as being untruthful. Gwen was surprised at this, for she had known the moment Gaspar had tried to short her wine shipment on the morning of Flora's wedding.

"See anything?" Gaspar looked down at her with a small smirk. "I told you I was good."

"But what of when you sell the gems?"

He shrugged. "We haven't had such a large shipment before. But I got a good deal from the new mines in South Africa."

"South Africa?" Her mind wandered to the giant elephants and proud lions she had read about. "How exotic."

"Oh, it is."

She shook her head, putting herself back to the task at hand. "Right. So what's your plan to sell them, then?"

He shrugged. "I did not have one. I just purchased another ship almost a year ago, so I cannot put out any more funds. I suppose I will just…keep the money, *sim*?"

Gwen blanched, snapping one of the books shut. "You foolish man. You're just going to trot about the sea carrying thousands of pounds?"

"Thousands?" He sounded surprised.

"Yes. The resale value will be enormous."

"Then what do you suggest?"

She leaned back in the seat, biting her lip in thought. "Well, if I were you…I would sell as much of the gems as I could to a trusted account. I take it you give large gifts often, as you did to me when you first arrived?"

"Oh, no, *meu único ouro.* You are the only one I lavish with finery." He reached out and brushed a curl away from her face.

"Be serious for a moment, Gaspar." She waved a chastising finger at him. "As I was saying, you need to rid yourself of as much of your gem stock to someone you trust, not anyone who may betray you. Do you have such a contact?"

He shook his head.

"Well, then we should—" Gwen slapped her

hand on the desk as a thought came to mind. "Penelope's father!"

"*Quem*...who?"

"Penelope, Drummond's wife!"

"*Who*?"

She smiled. "I forgot, you don't know anyone."

"Apparently not."

"Drummond is my cousin. He married a woman named Penelope whose father owns The Piccadilly Emporium. It's a sort of large shop that deals with imports and you can buy all manner of wondrous good there from books to gowns to furniture."

"And how might he help me?"

"He's always looking to expand, and I know that he made some jewelry there for the ladies to purchase last season. I'm sure that if you brought your gems to him, he would buy a large quantity, and quietly. Truth be told, his business was failing before Drum gifted him the money to pay his debts and having such fresh stock would be a very attractive business prospect."

"But that still does not explain how we would hide the jewels from the accounts," Gaspar pointed out, all mirth gone from his features.

"Easy. Really, I don't understand why you haven't thought of this before. You would make a purchase of, say...Arabic spices. Well, you could seal the spice container, which really had diamonds within, and stow them in your cargo hold, as you would any other good."

"I don't like the idea of such riches being below."

"And I don't think it's very smart to hide them

so. How fast did I find them? It's not safe."

"I see your point," he conceded, toying with the gold crucifix around his neck. "But how would your friend's father account for the jewels?"

"It's not uncommon for ladies and gentlemen of standing to have gems reset from older pieces and family heirlooms they already own. Or sometimes they even buy loose stones from a third party to be later set by a trusted jeweler. They could be hidden thus in the official papers, saving both of you from any legal woes." Gwen took a deep breath when she finished, feeling quite pleased with how well she plotted and planned. It could do with some polishing, but it was overall a fine strategy that she felt very secure in.

But Gaspar was silent. He merely stared at her, his expression unreadable.

After several terse moments, Gwen whispered, "Are you all right?"

"Of course I am," he replied, his mouth splitting into a grin. He knelt beside the chair, turning it so she faced him. "*Meu Dues*, Gwendolyn, you are a marvel."

She felt her cheeks flush. "Do stop, it only takes a bit of thought."

"No, it only takes *you*." He took both of her hands in his and pressed them to his lips. "You have such a mind, Gwendolyn. I am in absolute awe of it."

"Do stop, you're embarrassing yourself," she told him. But really, she enjoyed his lavished attentions on something other than her looks. It was quite a new notion for her talents to be appreciated, instead of overlooked as they often were in the castle. She relished it.

"I cannot help it." He kissed her wrist. "Your mind is so *maravilhoso*…so wonderful."

Gwen giggled and leaned forward to allow him to tend to her lips. "You're too much."

"Just please, tell me what I can do to repay you. Shall I give you some diamonds, perhaps? Some gold combs for you hair that were meant for a duchess?"

She glanced over his shoulder at the four-poster. "Oh, I think I have an idea."

Chapter Ten

"It's here!" Charlotte jostled Gwen roughly awake, shaking her shoulders.

She opened her eyes groggily and batted her away. "What's here?"

"A letter from the prince!"

Gwen shot up, untangling herself from the blankets. Charlotte held a sealed note in her hand. "Is that it?"

"Yes! Conner's opened the rest about your dowry, but this one is addressed solely to you. I haven't read it either, before you ask." She held out the letter and Gwen snatched it from her fingers.

She ran her thumb over the wax seal that preserved the message. Suddenly, Gwen felt nervous. It bubbled in her stomach, making her feel ill. The discomfort wasn't rational, but she thought it might be the unknown that filled her with dread.

"Should I...should I leave you?" Charlotte asked, though Gwen knew she had no desire to leave.

Gwen, still looking at her name written in

spidery script, answered, "Yes, I suppose so."

She waited until the door was shut before slitting the letter open with her finger. She cursed herself for feeling so anxious. After all, it was naught but an arrangement, an agreement that brought on the potential union. Several deep breaths later, Gwen was prepared to actually read the words within. As soon as her gaze met the page, she was pleased to see it was written in perfect English. If the prince was fluent in her own tongue, then her poor Spanish would not be an issue.

Eagerly, she began to read.

Gwendolyn MacLeod,

I have begun several messages, all which have been unsent. Your portrait spoke to me. Your eyes were languid pools of beauty and tales of your gentle nature and amenable personage have reached the court of my father.

Although I am a fifth son, and far from the crown, I do hold titles and lands that will hold you in comfort and jewels befitting my bride. As the youngest daughter of your family, surely you can commiserate.

As my father and your brother finalize the bargaining that will determine our match, please feel secure in knowing that I will make you a good husband and will enter into this contract of my own free will. Hopefully, you feel the same and we can enjoy a pleasant union.

Yours,

Prince Eduardo Ferdinand Juan Pablo de Bourbon

She held the paper tight, unsure of what to think. On one hand, he had sounded like a kind and understanding man, but on the other, she felt nothing more than the kind of admiration one might feel for a nice neighbor or a stranger one might meet in the village. Of course, he *was* a stranger, but she thought that, perhaps while seeing something written in his own hand, she might feel a spark of...*something*. But all Gwen felt was dread.

It was an odd and heavy feeling that pressed down on her chest. It held her tightly, squeezing the breath from her lungs and weighing her down. She read the letter again, hoping it would ignite something positive within her, but it was just words that meant nothing to her, even though she knew they should. After all, he was to be her husband.

Her thoughts should have been directed firmly toward Eduardo, but her mind drifted to Gaspar. Gaspar was devilishly handsome, good-natured, quick to laugh, and even quicker to kiss. He was also a patient lover who lavished her body with passion, while also worshiping her mind. On the other hand, Eduardo was naught but a distant figure—a thought that hadn't quite been finished, but was destined to be.

Gwen shook her head and slipped from her bed, dressing hurriedly in a deep blue gown. She pinned a shawl over her shoulders and tucked the letter within her dress. As soon as she had tamed her curls and slid on her slippers, she crept down the stairs, careful to not draw attention to herself. She knew Charlotte would be curious to see what the prince had written, and she wasn't sure if she wanted to share it.

But as she passed the library, Conner called her in. He sat at the desk, scratching something in a book. "Have ye read the letter, lass?"

"I have," she replied. "How are the dowry arrangements?"

"No' bad. I've already sealed the response and sent it out to be delivered. There's a portrait here for ye as well."

Gwen swallowed. "A portrait?"

"Aye." He nodded to the side. "I did no' tell Charlotte, she'd go mad if she knew and I wished to spare ye her excitement for the time bein'."

"How compassionate," she grumbled, stepping over to where Conner had gestured. Upon a low side table beside an armchair was the painting in question. She took a deep breath before picking up the small, framed canvas.

The man—Eduardo—was nice enough to look at with brown, slicked back hair and dark eyes. A pair of thin lips sat below a mustache. He was pale of skin and wore a black and red military jacket, trimmed in a fine gold braid. Several military metals sat upon his chest, although Gwen had a sneaking suspicion he had never held a weapon, save for ornamental pieces. Overall, he wasn't unattractive. He just wasn't…Gaspar.

Gwen put the canvas face down upon the table and tried to take a deep, sobering breath. She had looked upon her future and saw nothing there. She turned on her heel, feeling uncharacteristically claustrophobic in the spacious library. Conner called out something behind her, but she quickened her step, fleeing the keep with her skirts raised above her knees.

The note she had tucked into her bodice burned the skin of her chest as she ran, almost unconsciously, to the stable where her horse was eating. There were no stable boys to be found, but the horses were all fed and watered, tucked away in their stalls. They pawed at the ground as she passed, probably hoping for a spare apple.

The mare nuzzled her nose into Gwen's shoulder when she let her from her stall. Gwen savored the familiar touch of her animal and murmured low endearments in Gaelic as she quickly saddled and harnessed her for a ride. She had no destination in mind, but knew she needed to leave, to clear her head.

As she began her gallop over the land, going farther than the sight of the castle, and even the small loch Charlotte was fond of visiting, she felt the tightness in her chest begin to loosen. But it did little to lift the numbness that still gripped her heart.

She knew she should feel happy, excited, touched, and the fact that she felt none of those things almost began to deeply worry her. She wondered if she was broken—incapable of feeling these deeper emotions that one should feel toward their intended. Even when looking into his—painted—eyes, she felt absolutely nothing warm toward Eduardo.

Her thoughts still fluttered about in her mind when her final destination came into view. A clearing of ancient stones greeted her. They probably stood tall once, looming over their human visitors in the form of a home or maybe a circle of standing stones, but now some lay tumbled to the side, others broken clean in half, giving in to years that passed.

She leaped from Faodail's back and left the pony to graze, content in the thought the beast would stay near to her, and stepped lightly over the grass to the nearest rock. They were old, there before even the massive keep she called home. Some said they came from the Picts who once roamed the land, but Gwen suspected they were an even earlier installment, one whose age or true purpose could never be rightly guessed. Her father, who stayed true to the old gods, thought the hill and its stones contained magic of some kind that couldn't be put into words. She hoped to drink in some of their magic now as she fought to catch her breath.

The stones were rough against her palm, but warm from the sun. She unpinned her shawl and tossed it aside, letting the cool spring breeze chill her. She strode around them, touching some as she passed and trying to call to mind something to inspire her into action. She pulled the letter from her bodice and read it again. And then again. And yet one more time before sighing and folding it back up and sitting down upon one of the fallen stones with the new spring grass lapping at her ankles in the breeze.

It didn't feel real. It was as if she was reading someone else's missive. By now Conner would have already listed out her dowry for their approval. In fact, knowing her brother, he would have already sent out his reply without speaking to her. And why wouldn't he? After all, it had been Gwen herself who pushed for the match and she was rarely one to change her mind once she decided on something.

Logically she understood that it was a fine match, one that would make her a wealthy woman and help to bolster the admittedly mostly ceremonial Scottish clan system. A pact between two strangers was all it was—all it was meant to be—but Gwen was no longer sure what she wanted. It was as if all her plotting, planning, and leaving her emotions out of the equation finally came back to haunt her.

Before, the thought of marrying the Spanish prince invited dreams of travel, adventure, and a carefully laden plan of two adults meeting for a common goal—marriage. But something had changed within her. Now all she saw was herself adrift in a foreign land with a man she had never even seen, save in portrait form. The once thrilling idea now weighed her down like a stone.

She had felt true passion and what it was like to be cared for and desired by a man. It had only been two weeks, but she wasn't sure she was ready to throw away those feelings for the rest of her life. However, the bonds of matrimony and the strength of contracts was enough to give her pause. The plan to have her wed to the prince was in motion, and it was *she* who made the first move. It was too late to turn back. It was too late to change her fate.

"I thought I saw you here." It was Gaspar. He towered over her a moment before crouching down. "You have been crying?"

Staring at him, she swiped at her cheeks, surprised to find them wet. "I...I suppose so." She turned her head away. She was embarrassed at having been seen crying, even though she had no idea tears had fallen. Was she grieving for her old life? Was the thought of leaving her home and family paining her? Or was it Gaspar?

"What has happened?" he asked, pulling her to his chest and gently rubbing her back.

Gwen caved in to his touch, welcoming the warmth and comfort of his body. She opened her mouth to try to verbalize her feelings, but no sound issued. Perhaps she was in shock? She had read that people in stressful situations sometimes shut down their mind and disassociated from their surroundings. Yes, that sounded right...

"Gwendolyn, speak to me, *por favor*." His dark brow was furrowed and he regarded her with a strange expression akin to fear. She had never seen his face look so torn, so frightened.

Still unable to speak, she unattached herself from him and held out the letter from Eduardo with a shaking hand. Then she watched Gaspar's expression as he scanned the note. His full lips rapidly turned into a thin, hard line as he read and his expressional darkened.

When he had finished, his stormy eyes turned to her. He regarded her for a moment before whispering harshly, "You are to truly marry him? Is it arranged?

"No," she replied in a voice no louder than the wind. "There are many things to be prepared before the match is formally announced, although I believe we are in the final stages. I just…I don't know."

"What do you not know?"

"I thought I…I thought I would be prepared for this," she admitted, taking back the letter and fingering the wax seal, raised with the crest of her future husband. "I thought I knew what was to come and that I could handle all that went with it. But now? Now I'm not sure of anything."

Gaspar reached out to her and brushed back her hair from her face. "You will marry him, though?"

"I suppose I must. It's being finalized." Gwen rose shakily to her feet, her hand against a rock for support. "How did you find me?"

"I saw you riding from the castle. I borrowed a horse from the stable and rode it like hell to follow you."

She began to weave in and out of the labyrinth of broken rocks, keeping a steady pattern as she stepped around and over them. It helped her to stabilize her movements. She didn't need to think in order to walk. But her gaze kept wandering to the center, where Gaspar now stood, watching her intently. His hands were fisted to his side and his shoulders tense.

"Must you do it?" he finally asked, his voice cutting harshly into the silence surrounding the hill.

"Do what?"

"Marry him."

She stopped and caught his gaze. "I suppose I must."

"As you keep saying," Gaspar growled, striding toward her frozen form. "But *will* you marry him?"

"Yes."

"Do not do it." His voice still sounded severe as he came to stop before her. But after a moment, his gaze softened and he repeated, "Do not marry him, *meu único ouro*. I will not deliver you into his arms, into his…bed."

The tone of his words and the use of their secret pet name sparked something within Gwen. The weight in her chest felt heavier than ever, so much so that it forced her to lean back against a stone for support. For the briefest of moments, she felt as if the rocks would fall and crush her, and she almost hoped they would as Gaspar's eyes bored into her. She could no longer handle the pain of knowing what was to come. So many things had changed between them—within her—she didn't know how to fix any of it.

"Do not marry him," he commanded again, stepping closer.

Gwen swallowed, feeling her heart beat madly against her breast. "It's done. The riders will have already left for Spain by now with talk of the dowry."

He reached out and cupped a hand to her cheek, forcing her to look up at him. "Then we shall send a faster rider to call them back. *I* will go myself."

"Why?" Her mind whirled. Gaspar looked pained and pale, which was an odd thing indeed for one with his usual golden complexion.

"You just…you just *cannot* marry him!" He turned away abruptly, leaving Gwen's cheek cold. He ran his fingers through his thick black hair as he paced within the circle.

"But why can't I?" she challenged, feeling the tears fall, unbidden. "I agreed to this bargain with Spain. I asked for it, even! I thought it's what I wanted."

Gaspar rounded on her. His face was now unreadable. "And now? And now what do you want?"

"I…I don't know!" She sobbed, her shoulders beginning to shake and knees weakening. "I made this decision and now I must go through with it."

"You cannot. I *forbid* it!" His voice was a roar, but when his gaze settled upon Gwen, he groaned softly and gathered her up to his chest, burying his face in her hair as she cried into his shirt. As the tears began to ebb, she held Gaspar closer, breathing in his rugged scent of salt water and leather and the fine oiled wood that made up his captain's quarters. She closed her eyes as she took it in and then pressed her lips to the sliver of smooth chest that showed in his open shirt.

"Gwendolyn, what are you doing?"

She silenced him with a kiss, wrapping her arms tightly around his neck. Gaspar tensed for a moment, but followed suit. His fingers tangled into her hair as he parted her lips with his tongue. She melted into his embrace, feeling his body tear away the tension that encased her.

Gone were the tender, playful moments they had shared on his ship. Now there was only the primal need to feel his hands upon her body, to fill the emptiness she felt within her soul. And Gaspar complied fully, matching the pace of her lips and skimming her body with the palms of his hands. If he had any desire to stop her, he didn't show it.

She yanked his shirt over his head as he began to undo the buttons of her gown. He drew the neckline off her shoulders, baring her chest to him. Losing herself in Gaspar was what she craved. But as soon as Gwen touched the silver buckle of his belt, he finally stopped her.

"Don't marr—"

Gwen pressed her fingers to his lips. "Don't say it. Please. I…I need you, Gaspar."

Nodding, he dove back into her mouth and pressed her against what may have once been a stone wall. The rock scratched at her back, but she welcomed the slight pain, a punishment for her own decisions. His hand found her breast as Gwen undid his buckle. Gaspar rifled through her skirts, finding her bare legs beneath the fabric. He hitched both hands beneath her and lifted, holding her against the rock and impaling her on his member.

"*Meu único ouro*…my golden one," he murmured as he thrust into her.

Having him take her there, on the ancient hill of her people, felt terribly blasphemous, but right. The primal act flooded her with a whirlwind of tossed emotions, more volatile than the sea and even more deep. She had never drowned—never even come close—but in that moment, she felt lost in his arms. It was as if all the air had left her lungs and she began to feel lightheaded. She was overwhelmed by the sensations of his hands upon her body and his lips upon hers. But she relished it.

Finally, as the surge of orgasm brought Gwen back above water, she clung to Gaspar, unwilling to let him go as he reached the peak of his own desire within her. But then he placed her feet upon solid ground. Then, wordlessly, he pulled away to buckle his pants, and with tender fingers, buttoned her gown carefully. He even untangled her pressed curls, arranging each one around her face with delicate intent. Finally, he dropped his hands to his sides and peered down at her intently.

"Gwendolyn," he began, his perfect English more accented than usual, the slight tang of Portuguese threatening to bubble to the top of his words. "I will not beg and I will not ask again after this time…but…come with me, *meu único ouro*."

Gwen's breath caught in her throat and the sound of her own heartbeat filled her ears. "Come with you?"

"Yes." He nodded and grabbed her hand, pressing her knuckles to his lips. "My ships have come, I can see them in the distance, and we will soon leave to new ports. But I do not wish to leave without you."

She was stunned by his offer of running away with him. Upon first thought, without thinking of the consequences, she wanted to answer in the affirmative. She couldn't say that she loved Gaspar;

it was something she had never even brought to mind and it was something she wasn't sure she even understood. But having him there, asking her to leave with him for a new life, forced her to consider it.

But as much as Gwen...*cared* for Gaspar, she couldn't bear the thought of life at sea. It was too frightening and too horrid to picture. And yet she couldn't ask him to throw away his fleet, his livelihood, and his passion of the water for her. And then there was the agreement that was made with Spain. Soon, she would be expected and Gwen was never one to throw away a contract.

"Say something." Gaspar's voice was pleading and his eyes searched her face.

"I don't know what to say."

"Say yes. Say you will come with me. We could have a good life together, you and I. I could take you to Greece, Hispaniola, the orient...you would have finer jewels and gowns than any Spanish princess could ever dream of."

She pulled out of his grasp and turned away, unwilling to continue looking up into the penetrating gray stare. "I can't."

"Why can't you?"

"You know why, Gaspar. I've told you a dozen times." Gwen fought back a new wave of emotion. He needed to leave and she needed to return to the righteous path she had strayed from. "I'm not leaving Scotland with you."

"Please." His voice was barely a whisper and it broke Gwen's heart. "I said I would not beg, but if I fell to my knees before you, would you come with me?"

"No."

The word hung in the air, hidden among so many others neither dared to say. The only sound was the low sweep of wind through the hills and the distant snorts and pawing of the horses. But there was something else tucked into the quiet—a heaviness that was settling in between them, building a wall so high, it would soon be impenetrable.

"As you wish." He stepped up behind her, his boots barely making a noise in the grass. "Look at me."

"I can't." Her voice cracked when she answered.

"Look at me," he repeated firmly, grasping her wrist.

Gwen complied, but shut her eyes tightly when she turned.

"*Maldito seja*, Gwendolyn!" he shouted. "Look at me! It is the least you can do!"

"The least I could do for what?" she asked, daring to look at him.

His gray eyes, so much like the sea he loved, were filled with unshed tears. "For breaking my heart."

Gwen felt as if she had been doused with freezing water and whatever words she could have spoken became trapped in her throat. So she said nothing, but pulled him down into a kiss. But it wasn't a primal one like before, when he had taken her against the stones. It was tender and full of longing for the future they would never have.

When they pulled away, neither made a move to speak. But Gaspar reached up and took off his crucifix and medallion necklace. He then pressed his lips against the charms before fastening it around Gwen's neck, careful not to tangle her hair in the chain. It hung heavy against her breast.

She couldn't take his necklace. It wouldn't be right of her. "I—"

"No. You must have it. I cannot give you my love, nor my name, nor any of the riches on my fleet, though I would if you had let me. But I can give you this. I want you to keep it always, even if you never wear it. I hope that it can bring you all the luck it has brought me these past years and you find happiness in your new life in Spain."

Gwen could feel her cheeks dampen with tears. She didn't know what to say. If she had been a stronger woman, a braver one, then maybe things would have been different. Maybe she could have begged him to stay in Scotland, or joined him on his ship for a life of adventure. Maybe she could have found a way for their secret meetings in his cabin to transform into a life they could share together.

But as she watched Gaspar stride quickly from her to his horse, her vision obscured by emotion, Gwen said nothing. There was nothing left to say. Not even goodbye.

Chapter Eleven

Feigning illness, Gwen scurried up to her room, brushing past Charlotte and the bevy of maids preparing for luncheon. She needed to escape to the safety and privacy of her chambers before completely falling apart. As soon as shut the door behind her, she was thoroughly sick in a chamber pot, sobbing and retching, feeling as if her insides had been torn from her body. But, then again, it almost seemed fitting for her to have these pains searing from her broken heart.

Sobbing, she crawled to the window, desperate for a glimpse of Gaspar's ships, but a heavy fog had settled upon the cliffs, almost completely hiding them from view. She could barely make out the shape of a mast. She pushed open the glass, leaning out and squinting, desperate to see some sign of Gaspar—the brilliant white of his shirt, or perhaps even him, holding out a hand in farewell.

She knew he wouldn't stay long in Scotland. His ships had already arrived, according to him. And though she knew there was no point in them ever meeting again, she wished dreadfully that she could have one last lingering moment with him. She longed to kiss his lips and be held in the strong arms she had spent so many long afternoons within. It was selfish of her to wish for something so strongly, but she had never truly allowed herself to be selfish before.

If they did meet again, she wasn't even sure what she would say that hadn't already been said. It would only be cruel to bring him into her shattered world again. It was entirely self-regarding, and she hated herself for it. And, if she were honest, she hated Eduardo. She hated his pale skin and dark eyes. She hated his wiry mustache and how dreadfully pleasant she expected their future to be. There was no feasible way she would ever be able to open herself to him fully. The mere thought of giving her body to Eduardo in the way she had to Gaspar disgusted her, but Gwen knew there was no way out of it.

And as the fog lifted, the sun fell below the horizon, and the ship left the cove for the open sea, Gwen closed the window and drew the drapes firmly shut. She would soon be bound body and soul to the Spanish prince and would never lay eyes upon Gaspar again.

***

After three long days and nights of lying abed, Gwen knew she needed to rise and rejoin life in the castle. Charlotte had been in several times, trying to ply her with soup and tea—even calling Sorcha, the medicine woman from the village, to attend to her. But Gwen brushed both women out, letting in only wee Ian. The lad would bring his pack of dogs to see her and was often content to merely sit beside her, reading aloud from his children's book. He asked no questions, expected nothing, and would leave as quickly as he came.

But there was work to be done and Gwen could stew in her sorrow no longer. So she quickly bathed, dressed, and came down one morning, just in time for breakfast.

Conner and Charlotte exchanged silent glances as she sat, but it was wee Ian who spoke. "Gwen, are ye feelin' better now?"

Her mouth creaked into a forced smile, feeling unnatural upon her lips. "Much, thank you."

"What did ye think ye came down with?" Conner asked.

Gwen shrugged and picked at the plate of food set before her from a servant. "I'm not entirely certain."

"The shock of seein' your betrothed, I expect." Conner laughed. "I did no' think him that ugly, lass. Sure, he's probably got soft hands and manners, but he's well enough to look at."

"Yes, he looks quite kind," Charlotte added, giving Gwen a reassuring smile. But she still peered at her queerly, as if she longed to say something.

Not wishing to be asked any more questions, she willed herself to sit up straight and down her food without gagging. She needed to wash her hands of the past and look toward building a new future—and that meant not wallowing in self-pity for what could have been, no matter how much she wanted it. She was to marry the prince and there wasn't anything more to it.

When she had eaten a good deal and participated in some general niceties with her family, she excused herself to the library. She wanted to ensure that Conner hadn't made a complete mess of her accounting and perhaps peruse one of the few books in Spanish hidden among the shelves. While her grasp of the language was relatively poor, there was nothing more she could do to remedy the situation other than read. It was a small comfort that Eduardo could write and presumably speak in English.

When she saw the pile of disheveled papers upon the desk, she opted to read before tending to the disaster that waited. Her mind wasn't up for the challenge just yet. She picked up a Spanish poetry book she had found weeks before but hadn't actually read, and curled up in a chair beside the window, cloistered in the back of the library. If anyone were to come in, they would never see her behind the shelves.

Taking a deep breath, she opened the first page and began to read. But then stopped. She looked over the written words again and again, flipping through the book to random pages, seeing if she recognized a single thing. Surely her understanding of the Spanish language wasn't so terrible that she didn't recognize even the smallest of words?

Snapping it shut, she strode back to the front of the library and looked through another in Spanish. It was the same: pages upon pages of words written in a language she knew nothing about. She was dumbstruck, tossing the book upon the desk, mind awhirl. It was true, she hadn't exactly been studying during her long hours with Gaspar, but she knew some words and phrases. Unless…

Moving on a hunch, she climbed to the second floor of the library and sifted through the little read and largely ignored volumes, finally finding the one she sought. It was a thick black book with large silver embossed letters. As soon as she opened the cover, she found the truth. Gwen could read the passages—not all, but enough to know the book covered Portuguese history from the time of Julius Ceasar's invasions up until the early Brigantine era.

Collapsing to the floor upon her knees, she let out a wracking laugh that sounded rusty to her own ears. She couldn't believe the truth of it. She couldn't believe that she hadn't known and never expected Gaspar to do what he did—the cheeky lout. But it was done. Gaspar hadn't taught Gwen a lick of Spanish. It was *Portuguese* he had taught her, and Portuguese she knew. It was one final joke from the man who could coax laughter from her lips even in the darkest of times.

"Gaspar, you foolish man," Gwen whispered to the empty library, tears slipping silently over the curves of her cheeks and dampening the pages of the book. "God, I will miss you."

***

Gwen had spent the rest of the afternoon in the library, trying to compose a letter to Eduardo. It had to be done. She needed to begin building some sort of relationship with her future husband, if they were to have a comfortable life together. She ended up with a rather strained and awkward message that she wasn't sure she would even dare to send…

Eduardo,

I hope this letter finds you well. All is well in Scotland, and with me. The castle is busy preparing for my possible departure and I find myself rather active as of late. I've been studying Spanish, but though by your letters, I see you have a great grasp of the English language. It's quite a relief, given my slow learning of your mother tongue.

I have also received your portrait. What a grand uniform you have. I very much look forward to seeing it in person and learning more about your military prowess. Perhaps you might tell me about it in your next letter? I would love to know more of your life and experiences.

Do you care much for horses? I have

a lovely dapple-gray named Faodial that I hope, very dearly, to be able to bring with me if I come to Spain. But I know journeys on a ship can be difficult to great beasts such as horses and I wouldn't wish her harm.

Since we cannot meet for some time, I'll tell you a bit more about myself. I'm rather good with numbers and can take care of a large household very easily. I'm not much of a cook, though, but I expect my prowess in the kitchen isn't really your main concern! I adore the outdoors, but despise spiders. I also don't mind the cold at all, though I've read the temperament of Spain is very agreeable.

What about you? Is there anything I should know?

All the best,

Gwendolyn

After she signed the letter, she rolled her eyes at her effort and pushed the paper away, disgusted.

She sounded like a complete dolt and honestly didn't care much for what Eduardo liked, didn't like, wore, or anything else about him. Still, she felt he needed some sort of personal message from her, even if it was a little odd. If they were to be married, they would at least need to tolerate each other.

"Writin' love letters, are we?" Conner asked with a grin as he entered the library, baby Alec asleep in his arms and a staghound following close behind.

"Hardly. I think I'll toss this one out in favor of one less…terrible."

He looked over the desk at the note and frowned. "That will no' do, lass. The prince has no English."

"No English?" Gwen shook her head. "That is impossible. He's written me a letter in perfect English."

"By the hand o' a scribe, I expect. It was in one of the missives I received on the matter. I thought ye knew, or at least Charlotte told ye."

She groaned, crumpling up the paper and setting it aside to be burned. "That's terrible news."

"Ach, no. Ye've been studyin' Spanish all this time with the good captain. Surely ye can read and speak enough to get ye by?"

"Of course," she lied, her stomach churning. "But I'm still learning and I wish I had a better grasp of the language in order to write him a letter at least."

"A shame the captain had to leave so suddenly."

"Yes, a shame."

"An even worse that I'll have to find a new trade

ship to work with."

Gwen's eyes widened. "Whatever for?"

"The captain said he would no longer be comin' north though our waters." He bounced the baby in his arms as the bundle began to fidget. "He will no' even be able to take ye to Spain when the time comes, as his new trade route keeps him south. I'll have to sort that out as well, but do no' fret, I'll right it soon enough and find ye a new way to Spain."

"I can take care of it," she assured him, trying to keep a pleasant lilt to her voice.

"Eager to get to your new home?"

"This will always be my home," she said quietly, feeling tears prick her eyes.

Conner frowned and drew close, Alec kicking his blanket off and beginning to cry. "O' course, lass. I only meant that you're eager to sort out your married life. Ach, I think there's a great ye need to be told about married life…and your weddin' night for that matter." His ears pinked at the realization. "With our mother livin' with our sister…well, I suppose ye'll need to be told—"

"I know enough, don't bother!" she said hurriedly, not interested in hearing the ins and outs of marital life as explained by her crass elder brother. "I can handle myself."

"Just know, lass, that I will no' tolerate him treatin' ye with a hard hand. I will no' abide if he mistreats ye in any way." His tone was suddenly serious and Gwen almost felt as if she were in trouble by the sound of it. "This is your home as long as I am laird, or wee Alec, or even wee Ian, if it comes to that."

Gwen looked up. "Ian?"

"Aye. There's always a chance…" He drifted off, pausing for a moment before continuing. "Ye never know what the future holds and ye should live in the present, but always be prepared for what may come. When I took Ian in, he had my protection. But when I married Charlotte, I gave him my name as well."

"Yes, I remember."

"If Alec passes with no heir, the title and lands will pass to Ian. Now, I know that may be strange, seein' as it should be one o' our sister's sons, but Ian's my lad now, through and through. He has his place here as my son and ye do as my sister."

Gwen sniffed, fighting back tears. She wasn't ready for Conner to speak in such a manner, as he was usually just a giant tease. "Oh, stop it. I get all red when I cry."

"Aye, ye do. Ye look like a squashed rhubarb pie. Now get up, lass. I think ye've had enough o' the library for one day."

Chapter Twelve

A few days later, Gwen had just sat down at the desk in the library when a harried-looking Charlotte dashed in. Her face was pink with excursion and she grasped a bookshelf for support as she fought to catch her breath.

"Well, spit it out," Gwen commanded, growing nervous at seeing Charlotte so flustered. "Was Ian hurt? Did something happen to Conner? Where is baby Alec?"

"Penelope…Penelope…" She gasped. "Shes—she's having the baby!"

"Now?" Gwen felt her stomach drop. It was too soon for Penelope's child to come. If her timing was correct, she was only several months along. That was may be too early for a healthy babe. "It's too soon."

"I know." Charlotte's hazel eyes were wide with worry. "I'm leaving straight away. Will you come with me?"

Gwen nodded, rising from her seat. "I'll meet you in the hall as soon as I've packed. Have you called for a carriage?"

"No, I thought horses would be faster. Would you mind riding such a distance?"

"Not at all."

Charlotte turned on her heel and ran from the library. Gwen soon followed, her heart pounding against her breastbone so hard it almost pained her. Strange to think the first strong emotion she had felt in the week since Gaspar's departure was fear—fear for Penelope, her unborn child, and even Drummond.

What would the gentle giant do without his dainty English rose? Drum was devoted to his wife and Gwen wasn't sure if he would be able to bear her loss. And Charlotte! Those two had been friends since girlhood, two pieces of the same fine china who had been lured from home by the magic of Scotland.

She hastily redressed in a deep green riding habit and tied her hair up tightly into a bun. Then she shoved some sturdy dresses into a saddlebag and topped it with several packages of medicinal herbs. While she knew there would be medicine at Penelope's home—if not a true midwife—she'd rather be safe than sorry. Finally, almost mechanically, she reached under her pillow to where the cross and medallion necklace had lain hidden.

Gwen pressed her lips to the crucifix before attaching it around her neck and shoving it into her bodice. It was almost a full day's ride to Drummond and Penelope's home in the best of conditions and there wasn't a moment to be spared for hesitation.

They needed to reach their lands by nightfall, and it was already nearly noon.

She had just turned a corner when little Ian stepped out from the stairwell.

"Ye leavin'?" he asked, his dark brows furrowed seriously.

Gwen paused, feeling irrationally vexed at being stopped midstride. "Yes. Penelope is having her baby, so Charlotte and I are going for a visit to help her," she explained patiently, trying to keep her tone calm.

"Can I come? I want to play with them."

"No, Ian. It' messy women's work we'll be doing. When the baby is born and Penelope feels well enough, we'll all go for a visit together and you can see the new baby. Won't that be fun?"

He screwed up his tiny face for a moment, then responded in a mock grown-up voice, "Aye, that'll do."

Gwen's lips twisted into a small smile. "Good lad. Now, keep an eye on Alec for us while we're gone."

"Goodbye!" He wrapped his arms around Gwen's legs.

She patted him fondly on the head. "Run along, now. I mustn't be late."

Once Ian was back on his way, Gwen continued hurriedly down to the main hall where Charlotte stood with Conner, deep in conversation. But as soon as Gwen reached the landing, they both turned to look at her.

"All ready, then?" Conner asked her.

Gwen nodded, taking in Charlotte's unnaturally

pale face. "I believe so."

"Then let's be off." Charlotte kissed Conner swiftly on the lips before leading Gwen from the hall and out into the bright sunlight.

Her usual horse, Faodail, wasn't hearty enough for a hard ride, being more suited to leisurely jaunts. So two large warhorses had been prepared. It was good Gwen was an accomplished rider, for the giant beasts were frightening at worst and formidable at best. They were bred from Conner's finest stock and most men wouldn't dare touch them, but no others would do for the ride ahead of Gwen and Charlotte.

The second she was seated and their bags secure behind them, they were off, the thundering of the horses' hooves filling Gwen's ears. As they reached the bit of pressed dirt road that passed the way to the dock, she instinctively turned her head and felt the cross around her neck burn into her chest. She hadn't been able to look at the sea since Gaspar had cast off, and she doubted she ever would again, save for when she left Scotland for Spain.

For a moment, she allowed herself to picture casting off on *La Sereia,* watching the keep disappear into the far distance, separated by dark ocean waves. She remembered the initial feeling of being onboard her first time, how horrified she was and how tightly she clutched onto Gaspar. It was as though he had been the only thing keeping her afloat in the tumultuous waters. But wasn't that just what he had been to her—a safe harbor in the sea?

She shook her head roughly, trying to scatter the vivid memories of Gaspar's arms around her and the sound of his heartbeat as they lay in the quiet of his four-poster bed. They would watch the light of the sunset slowly sink, casting multicolored gleams upon the ceilings, then the walls, the floor, and finally disappearing, leaving them in darkness. And even when the moon rose and the candles were lit, they would stay there, wrapped in an embrace until the time came for Gwen to reluctantly retire to the castle.

She tried to push the bittersweet remembrances aside, but it was no use. He had branded her. Not with a hot iron, though sometimes she felt the searing heat in her heart, but with his mouth, his hands, his sweet words of longing. She was forever changed, and she thought it might kill her.

"Are you all right?" Charlotte called loudly, steering roughly to the side, cutting Gwen's horse off with her own.

Gwen pulled the reins, forcing her mount to a halt. "What?"

"You're crying."

She put her fingers up to her face, feeling the wetness on her cheeks. Embarrassed at being seen in such a state, Gwen dabbed at her eyes with the edge of her traveling cloak. "I…I'm just worried about Penelope," she lied, steering her horse around Charlotte's to continue on the path in a trot.

"No, you're not." Charlotte came up to her side, matching her horse's stride.

"Yes, I am."

"Stop lying to me, Gwen. I don't think you have it in you to be a proper fraud. You never did."

She glanced at her sister-in-law and then took a

deep breath. Charlotte hadn't always been good at reading people. Perhaps she really was a terrible liar. It would have been so easy to tell Charlotte the truth—to admit that it felt as if her heart had been torn from her breast when Gaspar's ships sailed away. But she hardly felt that she deserved the peace of mind that came with verbally announcing her feelings. It wouldn't do any good to reopen a wound.

"I suppose you needn't tell me," Charlotte said. "But you might feel better if you did."

"How is it that every woman in this family, born into it, or married, has a hard time settling into life?"

Charlotte tapped her chin in the way she often did when she was surprised or faced with an interesting question. "Oh, well, I hadn't given that much thought."

"You don't find it strange that we all have had our heart broken, then mended, or almost married the wrong man?" Gwen knew she probably wasn't making much sense, but it was as if the words left her lips before she could sort through them. "That all four of us haven't traveled the easy path to love? When I look at my older sisters, they all found their husbands easily, married without fuss, and now live perfectly average lives. Why didn't we?"

"Are you thinking about that Spanish prince?"

"I suppose so." Gwen trained her eyes on the empty hills ahead and the distant wisps of smoke rising from a faraway village. "But shouldn't we be galloping just now? We've hardly just left."

"We were for nearly two hours before we

169

stopped. The horses could do with a walk and a rest, and so could I."

Gwen started. She couldn't remember traveling that amount of time. "Has it really been that long?"

"Yes. Now, what about Spain worries you?"

"Are we being honest? And will you keep my secret?" She dared a glance at Charlotte, who was staring at her intently.

"Of course."

"I…Gaspar…." Gwen felt her stomach flip at saying his name aloud. The last time she dared to utter it was when he left her upon the hill. It felt odd and foreign on her lips, but she savored it all the same. "We had a…a liaison."

Charlotte smirked. "Is that what we're calling it these days?"

"You don't sound very surprised," she pointed out, picking up the pace of her horse.

"And you don't need to marry that Spanish prince," Charlotte asserted. "I mean it, Gwendolyn. You can turn around now and ride back to the keep to Conner and call the whole thing off and no one will be angry with you."

For a moment, Gwen half considered it, but knew she couldn't do something so foolish on a girlhood crush. After all, Gaspar was gone and he wasn't coming back. He made that quite clear when he cancelled his contract with the MacLeod lands. Even if she called off her contract with the Spanish prince, there was no way of knowing she would even be able to contact Gaspar again. When she first offered him a shipping contract, it was through other avenues that were now closed to her.

It was clear that she would never see Gaspar again, no matter how much she dearly wished to see his face one last time. Gwen needed to move on and focus on the future, not dwelling on a whirlwind romance that merely lasted a few weeks. Spain was her future and Gaspar, her past—no matter how much it hurt her.

"Come," Gwen began, breaking the silence. "We've dallied too long. We must ride."

Chapter Thirteen

"Thank God ye came," Drummond bellowed as he stomped down the stairs of his large stone house, a young lad following shortly behind. There were deep circles beneath his eyes, visible even in the dim light from the lantern he held.

"How is she?" Charlotte asked as the boy led their horses away into the darkness.

He ran his fingers through his tangled hair and Gwen's heart lurched sickly for him. "No' well. She…" His voice cracked. "She's asked for her mother, but London's so far…."

"We'll sort her out," Gwen promised, squeezing Drummond's arm as he turned to take them into his home.

It was larger than Gwen thought it would be, warm and filled with hints of Penelope in the décor. There were several things she recognized from The Piccadilly Emporium, and the interior felt decidedly British, but it suited the pair, Gwen thought. Even through the small hints of construction that still carried on, she knew that Penelope must have been hard at work to make the house a home before the baby came.

"She's just in here," he told them lowly as they approached a shut door. A sliver of light shone beneath the wood.

When it opened, Drum passed them to go directly to Penelope's bedside. She lay on her back among the fine bedding, almost disappearing into the blankets and pillows that surrounded her. Her fair hair plastered to her white face with sweat. She uttered a series of small moans, but quieted as her husband neared. A woman hovered beside the fireplace, mixing something in a small black cauldron, but made no notice of seeing Gwen and Charlotte enter.

Charlotte whimpered before dashing to Penelope's side. They put their heads together and began to whisper, but Gwen didn't hear what was said. Instead of intruding on their moment, she crossed to the woman beside the fire.

"Are you the midwife?" Gwen asked.

The woman looked up from where she crouched, startled. Her brown eyes were wide and she was much younger than Gwen expected, younger even than her. "Oh...well, aye, I suppose so."

She gaped, not sure if she heard her correctly. "You *suppose* so?"

The woman—*girl*—pinked. "Me *mum* is the midwife, but she's visitin' with me sister down south and I was to look after things for her."

Gwen bent down next to her, feeling her knees weaken. Then she asked the question she already knew the answer to. "Have you...have you ever

173

delivered a baby before?"

She shook her head, her lips pursed.

"Have you ever assisted in a birth?"

She shook her head again.

"Get. Out," Gwen growled, her teeth bared. "Get. Out. *Now*."

"Wh-what?"

Gwen rose to her feet, hot rage building in her core. "Get out! Ye wee pretender!"

"But I…I can try and—"

"Out!" she shrieked, pointing at the door.

The girl scrambled from the room and Gwen found three sets of eyes settle on her.

"She wasn't a midwife and she's never even delivered a baby before," Gwen explained hurriedly, dropping her cloak to the floor and beginning to roll up her sleeves.

"Not a…a midwife?" Penelope hissed as her face contorted into a rough grimace. "Oh, no."

"Bloody hell," Drum cursed, crossing the room to Gwen. Then he lowered his voice. "What was *that*?"

"She's never delivered a baby, Drum. Hadn't even assisted."

"And none o' us have." His green eyes were wild. "That lass was the only one we had!"

"Charlotte's had a baby…and you have me," Gwen responded stoutly, crossing her arms over her chest.

"Have *you* ever delivered a child?"

"Well, no, but I've read about it and assisted in the delivery of many animals."

Drum leaned forward. "My wife is no' an

174

animal, Gwen…Christ!"

She thought back to the pile of medical texts she had pored over several weeks before when she wanted to learn more about the anatomical ways of a man and a woman. She could see the diagrams and structural drawings as clearly as if they were before her. Of course, she had never even seen a woman give birth, as she was the youngest of her siblings and even Charlotte demanded privacy in her chambers when Alec was born, but she was the closest thing to a healer they had.

"I can do this," she asserted firmly. "I know that I can."

"Ye must. I will no' lose my wife." Drum then glanced briefly at his wife before lowering his head to Gwen's. His voice was barely more audible than a faint breeze as he spoke his next words. "If it comes to it, and Lord willin' it will no'…save Penelope. There can always…always be more bairns, but I will never find another woman like her."

"Drum, I—"

Penelope let out an ear-splitting shriek containing language more befitting a barmaid than a wellborn lady.

Gwen snapped in her direction. She had never heard Penelope curse before and that frightened her much more than anything else. "Don't fret, Penelope, it'll all be over soon."

She released an animalistic groan before pointing at them. "Both of you…Stop. Bloody. *Whispering*!"

"Go…go call for a maid to boil water," Gwen ordered Drummond. "And I'll need clean—"

"Linen, aye." He nodded to a neat pile of bone white fabric atop a dressed. "And you'll find water ready in the pot."

"Good, good." Gwen looked around the room and saw a door to her left. "Is that your washroom?"

"Aye," he mumbled before going over to Penelope.

Gwen entered the washroom and shut the door firmly behind her, her eyes taking a moment to adjust to the dimly lit room, where the only source of light was one lone candle on the countertop. Then she stared at her reflection above the sink. Her blue eyes were round as saucers and there were little worry lines between her brows. Even her lips were set in a firm line that didn't bring confidence to mind, but fear. She looked scared and that would be no help to Penelope.

"Pull yourself together," she demanded gruffly to her reflection. "You're the only one Penelope has and you can't fall apart now. You can do this."

She repeated those words to herself as she turned on the water and began washing her hands with some fragrant soap she found beside the basin. The cold water froze her already numb fingers, but she read how important cleanliness was for both mother and child and she would leave nothing to chance.

After one last sobering breath, and a quick dry of her hands, Gwen felt collected enough to return to Penelope. But before she left the stillness of the tiny room, she placed her hand over her heart, feeling the outline of the crucifix beneath her palm. She needed his strength, his steady force that made her feel as if all things were possible. She needed him there with her, at least in spirit, to calm the riotous storm dwelling within the MacGregor home. She needed him.

But Penelope needed her more.

***

"The baby is turned the wrong way round," Gwen whispered to Drum and Charlotte as they huddled together beside the fire, pretending to be boiling cloths. It had been almost an hour since Gwen left the washroom and Penelope was still no closer to having the baby.

"What does that mean?" Drum asked worriedly.

"It should be head first, facing down—that's the right way of things. But I believe the baby is trying to come feet first, which is why she's having such trouble."

Charlotte glanced at Penelope and shot her a smile before turning back to Gwen. "Is there anything we can do? Alec came so easily."

Gwen paused, calling to mind some of the more graphic scenes in the texts she'd read. "Yes, I believe there is…but it won't be very enjoyable for anyone, especially Penelope."

Drum cringed as Penelope's exhausted moans grew quiet. "Ye must do it…do whatever it takes."

"Right. Well…I'm going to need you to hold her very still. She'll be very…uncomfortable, but it's important that I do this right and on the first try." Gwen looked hard at Drum. "Can you hold her down for me?"

His face looked pained, but he nodded. "Aye."

When Gwen reached Penelope's bedside, it was clear she was rapidly losing her strength. Her eyelids fluttered and she groped around the covers, stopping only when she found Drum's hand close around hers.

"Penelope, the baby is coming feet first," Gwen explained gently, pulling down the blankets and lifting up Penelope's damp shift to reveal her swollen stomach. "I'm going to press down hard and turn it. Do you understand?"

Penelope nodded, but said nothing.

"Now." Gwen looked to Drum and slid her gaze fleetingly to Charlotte, who was looking rather green, but still dabbed at Penelope's forehead with a damp cloth.

Drum climbed atop the bed and slid behind Penelope, wrapping his massive arms around her. He began singing something into her ear, an old lullaby by the sound of it, but Gwen couldn't listen closely enough to make out the Gaelic. Her mind was set in English and Latin—the languages of the books she was trying to picture.

When it was clear Penelope wouldn't put up too much of a fight, Gwen took a deep breath and placed both hands on her stomach, trying to ignore the fact that she felt no movement within. Penelope squirmed though the first few presses, but when Gwen began exerting more pressure, she began to cry out. It broke Gwen's heart to hear her in so much pain, but she was determined to save both her *and* the baby.

"Stop!" Penelope wailed. "Stop! You'll hurt the baby!"

"No, she will no'," Drum crooned, looking anguished.

When Gwen could feel the smooth line of buttock, and things that she imagined might be legs, under her fingers, she leaned back. "It's done. The baby should come now."

Drum let out a great sigh and kissed the top of his wife's head. Charlotte looked as if she might faint, but Gwen imagined the Persian rug beneath them was thick enough to soften her fall.

Back to the matter at hand—it was just as Gwen had hoped. Penelope's body began to convulse gently, then with more might. It was just as it should be, and Penelope began breathing more deeply as she bent her legs into her chest.

"I...it's coming," she groaned, digging her nails into Drum's arm. "Bloody *hell*, Drummond. Your child is just...*ahh*...just as bloody...*ow*! Just as bloody big as you, you bloody bastard!"

Gwen dared a peek between Penelope's knees to find something...*there*.

"Lord above, it's the baby!" Gwen practically yelled, a grin splitting her mouth. "Charlotte, ready the cloth! Penelope, I need you to push."

Penelope complied, her face red.

It was several short bursts later when a tiny, slimy, still baby was born into Gwen's hands and into a clean blanket. As Gwen wiped off the little face, its lips tinted blue, she went deaf. She was slightly aware of voices shouting, but she continued her work. Following the instructions she remembered, she used a short length of silk cord to tie off the umbilical cord before picking up the boiled sewing scissors to sever the tie.

Still, the baby did not move.

Gwen flipped the baby onto its stomach over her knees and rubbed its back furiously, patting intermittently and praying silently to God. The baby couldn't be gone. She would never be able to face gentle Drum and sweet Penelope again knowing that their firstborn child had died on her watch. Certainly she knew several women who had lost babies, but she had never been the one to deliver them.

Finally, a small cry emitted from Gwen's lap and a pair of miniature fists began to wave madly.

"It's alive!" Drum shouted.

Gwen flipped the baby over. "*She's* alive."

"She!" he yelled out, holding Penelope tight. "We have a *she*! A dainty, wee lass!"

Gwen wrapped the baby up tightly and passed her to Penelope, who was looking rather pale.

"A girl," Penelope croaked to the cooing babe.

Charlotte held a cup of water to her lips. "A beautiful girl. Look at that marvelous head of dark hair."

"She's perfect," Drum murmured, reaching around Penelope to stroke a finger over the rounded cheek of their daughter.

Charlotte put the cup back on the side table. "Gwen, I can finish the rest. I remember how to rid her of the afterbirth. Go sit down and rest."

Gwen nodded, but went to wash her hands up to the elbows before sinking into the chair beside the fire. She hadn't realized she was so tired, but at that moment, she couldn't remember a time she was more exhausted. But as she watched Penelope and Drum admire their child, Gwen felt as if it was all worth it.

And as Drum murmured something into Penelope's hair and followed it up with a look of pure admiration and love, a searing pain settled in Gwen's chest. She knew that look. It hadn't come to her from Drummond, but she supposed it was the look all lovers exchanged when they felt such a deep bond. Someone had once gazed upon her that way—as if she alone set the favorable tides to suit his ships and blew the wind toward safe harbor. Someone had once looked at her with such adoration that she felt her whole life melt away in an instant of safe and pure love.

Someone had once looked at her like that…and she had sent him away.

Chapter Fourteen

"Nearly home," Charlotte announced wearily, trying to adjust her waterlogged bonnet to keep the worst of the rain off her face.

"Good. I'm soaked to the bone," Gwen replied through chattering teeth.

They had been traveling most of the day, but it was slow work in the mud brought on by a sudden storm. Gwen would have liked to stay with Penelope a bit longer, but Charlotte couldn't stand to be away from Alec for more than two days. Besides, Penelope's mother was bound to be on her way, and neither MacLeod women wanted to crowd the new mother. It was decided that in a month's time, they would return to the MacGregor home with Conner, Alec, and little Ian to visit baby they named Rose.

"Oh, no," Charlotte murmured as the keep's surrounding lands came into sight.

Gwen craned her neck, but saw nothing amiss other than the gray sky around them. "What is it?"

"Ships in the harbor," Charlotte called over a

particularly loud burst of wind. "They fly a Portuguese flag."

Gwen felt her already cold limbs freeze even more and her heart heave. If there had been anything in her stomach, she was sure she would have retched atop the hill. For a fleeting moment, she considered turning round and riding straight back to Drum and Penelope, but knew that wasn't an option. She would have to deal with whatever happened like a grown woman.

"Just ride on to the castle and I'll send them away," Charlotte affirmed briskly, urging her pony forward. "They severed ties with us. Why on earth would four of their boats come to dock if we're no longer doing business?"

"Four?" She was confused. Gaspar had *five* ships to his name. But it was possible that he had stayed behind and sent only four to the MacLeods for some unknown venture. Still, there was no reason for *any* of Gaspar's small fleet to visit.

As they drew nearer, she could see the ships fairly easily. She scanned the waters and her eyes were immediately drawn to the largest boat, a blood red banner flying atop the bare mast. It was *La Sereia*. Gwen would recognize it anywhere.

"He's here."

Charlotte's brown furrowed. "But why?"

Gwen didn't answer. She kicked her heels into her horse's sides and took the beast on a swift gallop the last mile or so to the keep. What she needed to do was lock herself within her chambers for the foreseeable future—perhaps feigning a headache and exhaustion. There was no way she would allow Gaspar to look upon her again, nor was she too keen on seeing him. She couldn't take any more heartbreak.

***

As soon as a boy came to front of the castle to collect the horse, Gwen leaped from her saddle and brushed past the staff that tried to collect her sodden cloak. She even ignored Conner, merely calling out that she was tired.

When she was safely closed away in her chambers, she crossed quickly to the windows and drew them shut. Although the shadowy light outside was slowly dying, the silhouettes of the ships were still clearly visible among the cliffs and she didn't want to take the chance of setting eyes upon them.

Sighing, Gwen went to the washroom and began filling the tub, dropping her soaked cloak and dress to the floor as she did. When her boots and stockings joined the damp pile, she was left only in the gold of the crucifix and medallion. She considered taking it off, but felt that it had brought her such luck in the delivery of Penelope's baby that she wasn't ready to part from it. Besides, the piece was probably missing the sea, and since Gwen had no plans on jumping in the ocean any time soon, a lilac scented bath would have to do.

The steaming water eased her aching joints and she submerged herself to the neck. Gwen hadn't even been aware of how sore she was. But the lack of sleep and the long day's ride had left her legs feeling tight and her shoulders pinched. She was just about to drift off, encased in the warm bath, when she thought better of falling asleep in a tub full of water. It would be a terrible lesson in irony for her to drown in a bath while she had so recently thrown away a chance at true love for her fear of the ocean.

So she quickly washed and dried herself, slipping into a clean nightgown to nap before calling down for supper. Someone had been in to stoke the fire as she had been bathing, but the sheets were cold as she slid between them. Still, sleep beckoned her. But as soon as her head hit the pillow, the bedroom doors burst open, hitting the stone wall with a shocking bang.

Startled, Gwen let out an involuntary shriek and sat up.

"Quite the welcome!" Flora giggled, running over and climbing atop the bed to embrace her.

Gwen grinned. "Flora, goodness, I had no idea you were even coming home! Well, I suppose it's not your home any longer...when did you get in?"

"This morning. We've been sleeping all day since the early morning."

"How was your honeymoon?"

Flora waved a dismissive hand. "We'll discuss that later. We'd heard that you and Charlotte went to assist in the birth of Penelope's baby?" she asked eagerly, leaning forward. "Boy of girl?"

"A girl—Rose Victoria."

She clasped her hands under her chin and sighed. "Is she a perfectly fair little doll?"

"No, hair as dark as Drum's, but her eyes are the same pale blue as Penelope's."

Flora groaned. "I do wish I had come back in time to join you."

"Why *did* you come back? I thought you planned to go straight to London?"

"We had another week before he had to return to his work, so I asked Andrew if he would mind very much coming to visit for a few days instead of going to the English countryside."

"I'm glad to have you here. It's been so quiet without you."

"Poor hen," Flora clucked. "You'll just have to come stay with us in London once we're settled. Wouldn't that be fun? We can get you married off and living in a townhome beside mine. Wouldn't that be lovely?"

Gwen bit her lip. She had so much to tell Flora—some of which she wouldn't dare, but other things her elder sister needed to know. So much had happened, she had no idea where to start.

"Is something a matter?"

"No…not exactly."

Flora frowned and raised a brow. "Don't try to lie to me. What's happened?"

"I…you've missed a lot, I hardly know where to begin."

"At the start, I think."

Gwen took a deep breath and drew her knees up to her chest. "Well, there's an engagement in the works now."

"Really? Who is getting married?"

"Me."

Her deep blue eyes widened. "*You're* getting married?"

"Don't sound so surprised," she chastised, feeling her cheeks burn. "It all came about rather fast and I believe the match will suit us both quite well."

"How romantic," Flora murmured dryly. "Who is the lucky man?"

"Prince Eduardo of Spain."

"A prince!" she shrieked in glee. "You're going to be a princess? My bossy, wee sister will be a *princess*! You lucky duck!"

Gwen laughed, ignoring that it didn't sound right to her. "I suppose so. He's a minor prince, mind you, far removed from the throne. But we'll have land and a nice income."

"I can't believe it. Where on earth did you meet a prince? I've only been gone a little over a month."

"Oh, I haven't met him exactly. Many men inquired on my martial status after your wedding. I assume my dowry lands sound quite attractive. Prince Eduardo merely seemed like the most attractive suitor of the bunch."

"You're going to marry a man you've never even seen?" Flora sounded so…sad. Pitying, even. It embarrassed Gwen, but she wouldn't let it show.

"I have seen him, in the painted sense. There's a portrait in the library if you'd like to see for yourself."

"What does he look like? Is he dreadfully handsome?"

"He…um…" She suddenly couldn't recall more than the basic facts of the prince's appearance. "He has…brown hair and brown eyes."

"And…?"

187

"Ears and a mouth and a nose," she shot back tartly.

Flora peered at her strangely. "All right then. And when is the wedding?"

Gwen shrugged. "As far as I know, Conner is sorting out the details of the dowry and I could be married in the coming months."

"How queer. I never imagined I'd come home to visit and find you an engaged woman. Does that mean you'll be living in Spain soon?"

"As far as I'm aware, yes. But as I said, he's the fifth son, so it's possible that we'll have a bit more flexibility where our housing situation is concerned."

"Does he write you romantic letters?" Flora questioned with a sly smile on her lips. "I heard that distance makes the heart grow fonder."

"He and I haven't exchanged correspondence, actually. I recently learned that he has no English."

"Then however will you communicate? Will you learn Spanish with a tutor?"

Gwen's heart flipped at the remembrance of Gaspar's lessons, but she swallowed it down. "Yes, I plan on employing a lady's maid who's fluent in the language as soon as the engagement is firmly set. She can travel with me and instruct me on the voyage."

"Are those ships down at the docks Spanish? I can't say I know anything of their flags."

"No. They're Portuguese."

"Ah, yes, the traders." Flora slid off the bed then and crossed to the wardrobe. "By the way, I passed a maid as I came up to greet you. She said that you were going to dine in your rooms? Obviously, I told her you would be eating with us downstairs instead."

Gwen fell back against the pillows. "But I'm exhausted!"

"No excuses."

"But I've been riding all day," she moaned.

Flora pulled a cream gown from the wardrobe and threw it down upon the covers. "Up!"

Groaning, Gwen complied. She knew Flora to be quite stubborn. So she let her sister dress her up in the pale gown and affix some heavy diamonds into her ears. Flora had tried to take the cross, citing that the strong chain would clash with her delicate features, but Gwen batted her hands away and tucked it into her dress.

"I feel a tad bridal," Gwen complained as she brushed out her still-damp hair at her dressing table.

"Nonsense, you look exquisite."

When Gwen was deemed fit for public view, and tucked neatly within a tartan shawl, the sisters left for dinner. "We started our trip in France, then took a train to Austria," Flora was telling her. "The architecture is amazing and Andrew was telling me all about the Hapsburg family. Apparently they're so interbred, they're very sickly."

"I think I've read about them. They rarely marry outside their family tree."

"It's more like a family bramble bush." Flora giggled, putting her head close to Gwen's. "They don't branch out enough to be a tree."

Gwen thought it was rather grand having Flora home again, even if it was only for a few days. She didn't know she was in need of a kindred spirit at the castle until she saw the ships docked among the cliffs. Flora would be a lovely distraction.

But when they reached the landing, Gwen knew something was wrong. Andrew and Conner stood together, muttering softly, while Charlotte was waiting by the bottom of the stairs. Her lips were pursed and she balanced Alec on one hip. When she spied Gwen, she passed her baby to a maid and stepped closer.

"Is everything all right?" Flora asked. "Aren't we going in to dinner?"

Charlotte trained her eyes upon Gwen. "No, we're not. There's been an accident."

"What's happened?" Gwen began to feel uneasy and clutched her plaid tighter round her shoulders.

"Conner told me why the Portuguese came back," Charlotte whispered carefully. "A few of the sailors came to speak with him this morning. They don't have much English, but from what he could understand, they were set upon by some manner of pirates. We were the closest friendly port, so they came straight away as soon as they could."

Her blood ran cold and she leaned against the stairway wall for support. "What else has happened?"

"Nothing good. They lost a ship and a dozen or so of their crew," Charlotte told her gently.

"And the captain? He was still aboard his own ship, yes?" She pulled the cross from her dress and clutched it tightly. She couldn't imagine Gaspar ever leaving his boat, which she had seen clearly docked and firmly in one piece.

She put a hand on Gwen's shoulder. "Conner went down to the docks and to the ship where the injured men lay to offer them food and the help of the local healer. He thinks that the captain was on another boat when the pirates lay siege."

"What are you saying?"

"Gwen...Conner believes...he thinks that in the fray, the captain left his ship and boarded the one being attacked. The boat sank, Gwen. There were no survivors."

Chapter Fifteen

When Gwen came to, she was in her own bed. It took her eyes a moment to adjust to the darkness, as the only light came from the dying embers in the fireplace. She saw Flora asleep by her bedside, her arms crossed on the edge of the bed and her head lain atop it.

Gwen was about to wake her up and ask why she was there, but a jarring wash of horrid recollections tore through her mind. She vaguely remembered slumping to the floor. Conner had carried her upstairs—she was slightly sure of that. But the memories were hazy and unclear. However, the only thing she was truly concerned with was Charlotte's terrible news—news that Gaspar was dead, taken by the same sea he loved so much.

She clapped a hand over her mouth as she stifled an anguished wail. She had been able to handle Gaspar sailing off for good, as she was comforted by the idea of him living his life on the ocean, forever the bronzed Adonis who captured her heart—never aging, always looking upon her with laughter in his gray eyes. But now that picture had been torn to shreds. He had been snatched from the world of the living, taken down to a watery grave.

And what of his body? Had they found it like they found her father's—bloated and rotting? Or was it still out in the water, food for hungry schools of fish?

Gwen felt sick. She leaned over the side of the bed, opposite Flora, and retched quietly into a chamber pot. The thought of Gaspar out in the great blue sea alone was one of the most grotesque imaginings that had ever crossed her mind.

Taking several sobering breaths, she slid from the sheets and padded out to the washroom. She rinsed out her mouth and splashed cool water upon her face. When she rose from the basin to pat herself dry, she caught glimpse of her pinched face in the mirror. But it wasn't the dark circles beneath her eyes that chilled her, nor the pink blotches upon her pale cheeks. It was the small crucifix and medallion that made her feel faint.

She had his good luck charm. He had told her, *Saint Nicholas is the patron saint of sailors and merchants. He will not let you sink, and neither will I.* Gaspar had an ornament to ward off the dangers of the ocean and *she* had it instead. She had killed him! The reality of the situation was too cruel for Gwen to handle.

Gaspar deserved to have it back in any way she could return it. She knew it was possible his body was aboard a ship, awaiting a proper burial as befitting a captain, so it was probable she could at least give him back his cross before he was truly gone for good. Or if he was truly lost, and there was no hope of recovering his body, then she would release it into the sea.

***

When Gwen had slipped from the castle, wrapped tightly in a dark cloak, the rain had stopped. She daren't bring a light, so she relied on the crescent moon to keep her from stumbling too much among the uneven rocks of the hill.

Oddly enough, she didn't shed a tear, nor had she since the moment Charlotte told her of Gaspar's untimely demise. It was almost as if she was too torn to cry—too wretched to even put her feelings into productive action. The only thing she could think of was reaching one of the ships and inquiring as to what really happened to Gaspar. While it would be painful, she had to know about his final moments.

As she reached the docks, there was only one great ship tied tightly to the wooden posts. The other three were anchored near the mouth of the cove. But it wasn't the boat she had been on. Gaspar's was out in the distant water. Still, she guessed this was the one that held the injured and possibly dying men.

"Hello?" she called out as she reached the bottom of the gangplank. Then she remembered she knew a bit of Portuguese. "*Olá?*"

A dark figure appeared at the open deck above, holding a lantern. "*Sim?*"

"I am here to see your captain? *Seu capitão?*"

"*Capitão?*" The man motioned for her to climb the strip of wood that would lead her onto the ship.

Gwen paused. She had never been on a boat without Gaspar. And although she would be happy to never be aboard another, she owed it to him to return his gift. She gripped tightly to the worn rope that served as a makeshift railing, and made her way cautiously to the deck.

"MacLeod?" the unfamiliar sailor questioned.

Gwen nodded. "Yes...*sim*. My name is..." She wracked her brain for some more of the Portuguese Gaspar had taught her. "*Meu nome é* Gwendolyn MacLeod."

The sailor's eyes widened. "Gwendolyn? *Ùnico ouro?*"

Gwen gasped at being addressed by Gaspar's pet name for her. "How did you know that?" Then she shook her head. "Never mind that. I need to see....where is...*onde está o capitão?*"

He motioned for her to follow, and she did, passing the somber faces of the men who were standing about the deck. They walked down the small set of stairs, much like the ones of *La Sereia*, but instead of a small landing, it opened up into a wide crew area. Hammocks and pallets were scattered about the dimly lit cabin, and most contained wounded men.

Gwen put her hand instinctively to her nose as the putrid scent of rotted flesh and ill bodies slapped her full in the face. It smelled of blood, sweat, and fear—a rancid stink that made the air seem thick and too corrupt to breathe. She peered around at the men, looking for Gaspar, and many looked back.

Those who were capable of moving leaned upward to see who had entered their sickbay.

Some didn't appear too badly hurt, but it was hard to tell in the faint light. Some had burned arms, scraped torsos, or bandaged heads. She wasn't sure of exactly what had happened, but she knew it was something violent and probably unnecessary. Her heart tore for the young ones who were no older than herself, all of them nursing cuts and gashes.

A particularly bruised young man caught her eye. He sat against a beam, his knees drawn up to his chest and his gaze glued to the floor at his feet. Gwen took a lantern off its peg and crouched down beside him. While he didn't appear too injured, she knew some of the worst wounds were sometimes hidden well.

"*Olá*," she began gently. "Are you hurt? *Ferido?*"

The man—boy, really—looked up at her, his brown eyes blank and empty. "*Não. É meu irmão*," he whispered, nodding over to something on Gwen's right.

"*Irmão*," she repeated. "Brother? Your brother?" Gwen glanced to where the boy gestured and saw a long bundle, wrapped tightly in cloth. Whoever was in there was clearly dead. She turned back to the boy and placed a hand on his trembling arm. "I'm sorry...*eu sinto muito*."

Gwen was about to move on to the next man, rolling up her sleeves as she went, but the sailor who bore her into the makeshift sickbay shook his head and pointed toward the back of the cabin. "*Não...capitão, sim?*"

She bit her lip, taking in the dead and dying. She was loath to leave them. "Have you a healer?" she asked. "*Curador*?"

He nodded and pointed to an older woman who was crouched in the corner over a pair of badly burned men. It was Sorcha, the woman from the village. She was a fine medicine woman and it eased her heart a bit to see these men in her capable hands. They shared weak smiles before the sailor touched Gwen lightly upon the arm.

"*Capitão.*" He led her through the lines of moaning sailors, back to a private cabin beside what served as the kitchen.

Gwen took a breath, although a shallow one, before opening the door. She prepared herself for the sight of Gaspar's body, and almost wondered what shape she would find him in. Would he be broken and bloody like some of his men? Would his skin be cold and gray—the appearance of one who had been too long in the waters? Or would he look as if he were merely sleeping? She prayed it was the third.

When the lantern hit the figure lying prone in the bed in the small chamber, Gwen's knees almost failed her. It wasn't Gaspar she saw, but the man she had first met on the morning of Flora's wedding—the one sailor, save Gaspar, who knew perfect English.

She knelt by his bed, seeing the slight movement of his chest. He opened his eyes as she drew near, but it took a moment for him to focus and he coughed a bit before he spoke.

"*Senhorita,* you should…you should no be here."

197

"Please…I am looking for your captain," she said in a low, but clear, voice.

"*Capitão…*" He grimaced. "His ship."

Gwen leaned in farther, careful to avoid the wrapped arm, which she was sure must be broken. "What of his ship?"

"He is there…his ship."

She sat back on her heels, unsure of what to think. He could be dead and it would only be his lifeless body. But he could be…she daren't even think it.

"Is Gaspar on *La Sereia*?"

"*Sim…La Sereia.*"

"Does he…" Gwen swallowed, holding on to the edge of the bed for support. "Does he live?"

"*Sim.*"

***

Minutes later, Gwen was back on the dock, waiting restlessly for one of the able bodied sailors to prepare the small rowboat that would take her to *La Sereia*. She could barely stand still. She shifted her weight from one foot to the other, refastened her cloak, ran her fingers through her hair to untangle the windswept knots, and paced the length of the dock before the sailor finally called for her.

She refused to look down at the pitch-black water as they glided over the small waves that rocked them. Instead, she focused her gaze upon their destination. She could see the strip of stained glass that she knew made up the windows in Gaspar's quarters. It was lit from the inside and she saw it as a lighthouse—the beacon of hope that would bear her over the unknown and into safety.

The sailor yelled something up to the ship as they stopped beside it and a rickety rope ladder was tossed unceremoniously over the side. The wooden slats that served as rungs clattered noisily against the hull as they came to rest just above the edge of the water.

Gwen glanced at the sailor, who pointed upward. When she didn't immediately climb, he mimed scaling a ladder, seriously saying something to her in Portuguese. It was then that she appreciated never being overly afraid of heights.

The wind made for an unstable ascent, despite the sailor holding tight to the foot, to try to keep it steady, his eyes tactfully turned to the side. Her skirts billowed up and around and Gwen wished she owned a pair of breeks, or at least wore a thinner or shorter skirt to make the climb a bit easier.

She heaved a sigh of relief as two men helped her over the side and onto the main deck. Gwen took a moment to acclimate herself to the slight movement beneath her slippers before brushing past the curious sailors and into the depths of *La Sereia*.

Her fingers shook as she turned the knob to the captain's quarters. Although the English speaking man had said Gaspar lived, she wouldn't allow herself to truly believe it until she looked upon him with her own eyes. Until that moment, he was still gone from her, and from this world.

The chamber within was just as she remembered it and she took a moment to take it all in. A fire crackled in the small, iron hearth, filling the room with healthy warmth. Maps were spread over the desk, along with several exotic odds and ends that made up a colorful array. The only thing that *wasn't* just as she recalled was the still figure on the four-poster bed.

Dropping her cloak to the floor as she walked, she made her was slowly—silently—to Gaspar's side. It felt as if her body wasn't her own and an unseen force propelled her forward. She was afraid of what she would see in the shadowed space beyond, but she knew she must gaze upon it…to face the truth.

It was as she feared. One side of his clammy face was black and blue, deepening the already dark-tinted stubble that touched his jaw. His breathing was shallow and ragged, as if each inhalation pained him. It made sense, as the bruising spread over the left side of his chest and down his flank, disappearing below the brocade covers. It was a heavy storm cloud that marred the striking landscape of his form.

"Gaspar?" she whispered as she gingerly leaned over the bed, trying carefully to hold back the flood of tears that threatened to fall.

Gaspar's lids fluttered and his gaze roamed aimlessly about the room before settling on Gwen. His cracked lips opened. "*Um anjo,*" he rasped. "*Um anjo…do céu.*"

He reached out a trembling hand and Gwen took it, pressing his rough palm to her cheek. "It's me. It's Gwen…Gwendolyn." She fell to her knees, still fighting to contain the sobs.

"Gwendolyn," he repeated wearily.

"Yes, it's Gwendolyn."

His eyes shut, but he muttered her name again as he drifted off into a fitful slumber.

It was then that she allowed herself to cry. But it wasn't tears of loss. She could hardly pinpoint the emotions that battled their way to the surface. Fear, anger, relief, despair all fought for supremacy in her heart.

She wished she knew of another sailor who spoke English, as she longed to know the extent of Gaspar's injuries. From what she could tell, his ribs were bruised at best, and broken at worst. He didn't cough up blood—a good sign that they weren't shattered, at least. The sheen of sweat upon his brow hinted at a fever, but his body shivered violently. She even dared a peek beneath the blankets and found a large swath of hip was bound. Gwen couldn't see what was beneath the dressing, but was content that the cloth was clean and there was no visible blood.

It almost didn't seem real. Gaspar was alive and in front of her, but she still didn't believe it. So she reached over and gently brushed his black hair away from his face, savoring the feeling of his realness beneath her fingers. And as she traced down his unmarred cheek, his lips rose in a small, sleepy smile.

But still, his body fought the small comfort, shaking harder in cold. Gwen looked over her shoulder at the fire, but it was burning well. And his brocade comforter was thick and warm. Still, he shivered.

Not knowing what else to do, Gwen took off her

slippers and slid fully dressed into the bed. Luckily, Gaspar's right side was largely unbruised, so she was able to carefully curve her body around his. Although she thought she might be enough to warm him, he still shook, his teeth beginning to chatter brutally.

Gwen paused, recalling the best way to warm a frozen man was with the help of a warm body. It was common knowledge in the Highlands, where men often got stranded on the hills together while fetching sheep or on long travels. So she quickly pulled her gown and shift over her head and placed her naked body beside him. As soon as she lay her head down next to him, the shaking stopped and his labored breathing calmed slightly.

In the back of her mind, she thought she should send word to the keep about where she was, but she dared not move from her place. She was finally back where she felt most at home in the world and Gaspar needed her and she needed him just as much.

As the firelight faded and the sun rose, she lay beside him, looking at each curve and angle of his face. She memorized the straight line of his nose and the arch of his brow. Her eyes traced the thick lashes and the swell of full lips and settled upon the strong, even pulse at the base of his neck. He didn't even stir when she pulled the crucifix and medallion over her head and moved to hang it upon his lamp as he had done the first time they lay together.

As each long moment passed, she watched him sleep and wondered how she would ever find the strength to say goodbye.

Chapter Sixteen

Gwen floated in the turbulent surf, nothing around her but clear blue skies and endless waves. She tried keeping above the water, but her heavy skirts weighed her down, the thick green velvet threatening to drag her under.

She sputtered as a swell broke beside her head, splashing her full in the face. She tasted the salt upon her lips and felt it sting her open eyes. The waves were getting stronger and she felt her strength begin to fade as she paddled.

But just as she began to slip into the sea, she heard the faint sound of men's voices. Gwen looked around, calling out, "Hello? Help! Help me!" until her throat was raw. And soon her prayers were answered; a sleek ship was gliding toward her, neatly cutting through the surf.

As it approached, she caught sight of the carved figurehead upon front of the boat. It was a beautiful mermaid; her sea foam green tail wrapped around the bow and her yellow hair streaming behind her like a banner of gold. But instead of the angelic face she always imagined the figure to have, it was that of a harpy. Red eyes flashed above a hook-like nose and a sharp-toothed grin leered down at her.

Gwen gasped. It was *La Sereia*.

She frantically waved her arms. "Gaspar! Gaspar, help me!"

But the ship continued on its path and soon it would be so close, she would be able to reach out and touch the dark wood of the hull. And as it finally came to be beside her, it set off a wake that sent her plunging under the sea and into the darkness. While she fought and clawed her way to reach the surface, Gaspar's voice called her name from above to where air, sky, sun, and life waited for her.

"Gwendolyn." It was a musical sound from his lips.

"Gwendolyn." It was closer then, as if he was under the water with her.

"*Gwendolyn.*"

Her eyes opened to see the brightly sunlit captain's quarters. It took a moment to control her rapidly racing pulse, but when she did, she heard her name again.

"Gwendolyn." It *was* Gaspar. He still lay beside her, his bruising even more vibrant in the daylight.

"Gaspar, you're awake." Her heart beat anew from joy rather than fear.

"No, *meu único ouro*," he croaked, looking at her through half opened eyes. "No, I...I must be...dead."

She leaned up on one shoulder and placed a hand upon his cheek. "Never, Gaspar. You're *alive*."

Gwen didn't know why, but tears were welling and she felt dizzy with emotion.

He shook his head and his lids fluttered closed. His lips were cracked with thirst, but still he spoke. "It cannot be."

"It's true."

"No, I saw *um anjo*...an angel last night...golden haired...a golden haired angel."

Gwen choked back a small sob, but a squeak still escaped.

He smiled softly. "An angel came. Now...must be heaven."

"No, you're alive, Gaspar, I promise you."

"I cannot...be so." His eye opened a sliver and he slowly reached up a shaking hand. Gwen thought he might be reaching to pull himself up, but instead he lifted up the blankets that covered her before glancing beneath. "*Sim*...I am surely in heaven."

"Oh, stop it, you," she giggled, tears flowing freely. Gwen felt lighter than she had in a week, for that fleeting moment. But then he tried to laugh as well and clutched at his chest, wincing. "Does it hurt much?"

He nodded, gritting his teeth.

Gwen slid from bed and quickly crossed the cold floor to the wardrobe, plucking the pink silk dressing robe from where it had been before. The fireplace was barren, but she didn't mind. The added smoke in the room may not have been a good thing. She glanced over her shoulder at Gaspar, who had his eyes closed, and went over to the window. The faint scent of blood and sweat permeated the cabin and she could no longer stand the stifling smell that was specific to injured and dying men.

The large stained glass windows behind the captain's desk were pretty to look at, but she wondered if they were functional as well. Upon closer inspection, she could see there were small, barred fastenings upon the center window, set in deep upon the sill.

Struggling a bit, she lifted the bar and pushed the window open, breaking through the salt that crusted upon the glass and wood outside. The fresh ocean air blew lightly in and she breathed great gulps, pondering her next move. But just as she was about to turn away to tend to Gaspar, she realized she wasn't looking out to the sea, as she would have had she been in her own bedchambers, but *toward* the cliffs and MacLeod keep.

She fell to her knees, her back to the wall beneath the window. Gwen had been too preoccupied with the fate of the Portuguese captain; she hadn't given much thought to being so far from land. It paralyzed her and she clutched her hand to her chest as her gaze darkened and she felt her stomach churn sickeningly.

But she had a sick man to care for, and that was all that mattered.

She hoisted herself up, carefully avoiding looking out the window.

His forehead was warm, but not overly fevered. Her light touch didn't stir him, so she thought he had fallen into another deep sleep. It would make her next job easier. The bandages that covered the wound upon his hip were still clean and she carefully removed them to see what hid beneath. To her great relief, the skin around the neatly sewn gash was free of the telltale signs of blood poisoning. And even the stitches were neat and straight. Gwen knew by the tiny sutures that Sorcha must have tended to him.

There had been a small box of medicines on the floor beside the bed when she came to see him, but she hadn't taken much notice at first. Now she placed it on her lap as she sat beside him.

She sifted through the small vials and packets of dried leaves and powders. There were a few she recognized as being remedies for aching heads and burns, but most of them were foreign to her. The majority of the labels were written in other languages—none of which she could rightfully identify. Even when she took delicate sniffs of some to try to recognize them by scent, she thought it would be too risky to take a chance. Her healing knowledge was good, but not good enough to risk Gaspar's heath.

While he was still sleeping, she dabbed at the cut with some vinegar-covered cloth to keep it free of infection. He moved a bit as she prodded gently, checking for pus and loose stiches as she went. But by the time she finished and was pressing a fresh bandage to his hip, she was satisfied that he had nothing more than some bruising around the ribs and some nasty-looking discoloration around his body.

Not wishing to disturb him by getting back into bed, nor wishing to leave him to return to the castle, she decided to send a message to Conner by way of a sailor, if there was one to be had. Finding a pen, ink, and fresh paper already on Gaspar's desk, she took a seat in his red leather chair and penned a short note.

Conner,

Do not fret, for I am well upon La Sereia. The good Captain Florencio has been gravely injured and I am tending to him aboard the ship.

–Gwen

It was a terribly short missive, but she didn't know what else to say. Surely she couldn't reveal to Conner why she cared so deeply about Gaspar's health, nor that she had spent the night in his bed. Saying she was well and taking part in the healing efforts was good enough for the time being.

Not bothering to seal the folded note, she quickly dressed and slipped from the room. The noise she had grown accustomed to upon the ship was still there as she recalled it, but it was muted, quieted with the lack of healthy men. Still, she hoped to find some unoccupied sailor to deliver her letter.

Her search didn't last long, as she soon found one sitting at the bow of the ship, idly sorting fishhooks and rolls of twine. After a bit of poor Portuguese and some elaborate hand gestures, he had nodded and taken the letter from her, tucking it into his shirt pocket. She watched as he collected another man to help with his task before disappearing over the side of the ship to the small rowboat below.

She knew Gaspar was in no immediate danger, so she stayed atop, taking in the fresh sea air and the bright sunlight that streamed down from a cloudless sky. It was hard for her to process that she was truly out at sea. Yes, land and her home were both clearly visible from her perch beside the captain's wheel, but she was still as far away from solid earth than she had ever been before.

Her father had loved the sea, and it had killed him before he had a chance to grow old, finish marrying off his children, or hold his first grandchild. He had never had a chance to finish rebuilding the clan to what it was before the failed rebellions decades ago. He had never had a chance to finish the life he was meant to have and they were all changed for it.

Gwen's mother had left the castle for good, choosing to stay with her daughters in other parts of Scotland and sometimes even with an aunt in Ireland. Conner had been thrust into leading the clan when he was merely on the cusp of manhood, and Gwen was left…well, not just fatherless, but fearful. She had filled her days with stable and unchanging numbers. Books had become her playmates as her siblings all grew up and began their own lives outside the castle. And healing had become her calling when she found she had little else to offer the world.

When it came to fixing people's bodies, she felt that she had found a true purpose, one of strength and necessity. While she couldn't save her father— not that she could have, as they hadn't found his body for days—she could use her head and hands to heal wounded men, injured children, and sick women. She could put her resilience in the face of death and dying to good use now. And what better use was there than saving Gaspar?

As she walked back toward the doors that led to the quarters below, Gwen noticed that the sailors paid her no mind. They went about their work with their usual serious demeanors, but a bit more subdued than before. Here and there, men had gashes upon the bared swatches of skin that showed on their tanned arms and faces. Or they stared ahead with blank expressions that Gwen knew only came from seeing a man die before you. But she was not upon the ship for those men—not that any were bad enough to need her attention. Her small talents were needed below deck, where Gaspar lay.

When she came back to his cabin, she saw he hadn't moved. His chest rose and fell beneath the brocade blankets easily. She had no reason to wake him, so she crossed the room to a glass-fronted cabinet that was set into the wall beside the desk. A number of books and maps lay stacked within, no real rhyme or reason to their positions. It almost made her cringe to see the leather bound books arranged so. But it wasn't her place to reorganize his belongings.

Once she had found a small book in English, she drew Gaspar's desk chair beside the bed and settled herself in to read. But even though it was something about Indian cultures she had never seen before, Gwen had trouble staying focused on the words. Reading them was one thing, but it was like her mind was incapable of processing what it said. The fact that her gaze kept shifting to Gaspar didn't help matters either.

After several tries at the volume, she gave up and stuffed it back into the cabinet with its fellows. She was about to find another when there was a sharp knock on the cabin door. It gave her pause. It wasn't as if she lived there—or whatever one referred to residing on a boat—but it also wasn't possible for Gaspar to leap into action and greet the guest.

"Hello?" Gwen called out as she reached the door.

"Open up, lass," ordered a voice from the other side.

She froze upon hearing the familiar Scottish lilt. And when she opened the door, she greeted her brother.

***

"Aye, he's a right mess." Conner shook his head. "He'll live, ye say?"

"Aye," Gwen replied wearily. "There's some bruising, but I think it looks worse than it is."

"Much better than some o' the lads. I've let them bring their dead inland to be buried under a priest."

She felt a pang in her heart. She knew Gaspar would regret not being able to lay his men to rest. "That was kind of you."

"It's no' kind, Gwen, it's just the decent thing to do. Now, I'll do the decent thing by the captain."

"What do you mean?"

"I know from your note that ye've been tendin'

to him, but I can hardly have ye out on this ship."

"You've come to bring me home?" she asked, trying to keep her voice even. But the thought of leaving Gaspar so weak and helpless in his cabin seemed unbearable. Even if Sorcha came to take her place, she still would find it impossible to stay away.

"Aye, I have. But do no' worry. We'll bring him up to the keep and have him set right. There are riders out collectin' more healers and such from the outer villages for the rest of the men."

"It'll be nice for Sorcha to have a rest," Gwen told him, feeling elated at being able to keep his vigil over Gaspar.

"I know." He ducked his head out of the cabin and said something to a small dark lad Gwen had often seen running about the ship before turning back to her. "I'll have his men bring him up when they can. I don't suppose he'll need much?"

"I'll pack him a few things, just in case." Gwen went to his wardrobe and pulled it up, sifting through the hanging garments until she found a worn leather bag lying empty at the bottom. She sat it on the floor and placed in several clean shirts, some pants, his boots, and a few other odds and ends before clasping it shut. And without thinking, she took his crucifix and looped it around her own neck. Then she felt a sharp chill, suddenly remembering that Conner was there, watching her pack up as if she knew where everything was—which was true, no matter how improper it looked.

"Will he mind ye takin' that?"

Gwen studied his face for a moment, but if

Conner suspected anything inappropriate, he gave nothing away. "I think that having such a token will soothe his soul in the coming days and I don't wish it to be lost in the sea during the trip back to the keep."

He nodded as if it made perfect sense and gestured for her to leave.

She glanced back at the bed. "But what about Gaspar?"

"They'll come along with him soon. Ye are to come back with me. I'm havin' a room made up for him now."

Feeling uneasy at the thought of leaving him behind, even for a few hours, she brushed the sensation away and led the Conner through the ship and out to the top deck. When she glanced over the side, she saw that a man stood waiting in a rowboat at the end of the rope ladder. Gwen grimaced. While climbing up wasn't particularly nerve-wracking, she imagined the descent would be another matter.

But as she climbed down the moving ropes that would take her to the little boat, her mind wasn't on the waves, or even Gaspar, but on the thought that she would never step foot on *La Sereia* again. There would be no point in it. Gaspar would come to the castle to heal then be off on his next adventures on the high seas. She would never again walk the deck, nod to the sailors who gave her respect. She would never lie beneath the brocade covers in Gaspar's cabin or sit at the desk below the stained glass windows drinking Italian wine from the bottle. Her time on the ocean was over and Gwen was more than sad to see it go.

Chapter Seventeen

She took a few moments to sort herself out while waiting for Gaspar to be brought in. She had hoped for some time alone to bathe and dress and possibly even eat something, but Flora was already waiting in her chambers when she opened the door.

"What's going on?" Flora began at once, her arms crossed over her chest.

She sighed, feeling a deep tiredness settle in her bones. "I assume you know well enough what's going on."

"No, I don't and I wish for you to tell me. Charlotte won't even speak of what's happened while I've been gone, save for some small talk. But I *have* heard that you've been in one of those boats."

"Yes, I have." Gwen brushed past her and went to the washroom. She filled up a basin with water and splashed her face several times.

Flora followed. "Why did you faint and run off when you found out what happened with the Portuguese?"

215

"I just wanted to help."

"That doesn't explain why you were so hysterical. You've seen much worse involving men you *did* know. Those sailors were little more than strangers to you."

"I was just surprised, that's all." She tried to leave the room, but Flora blocked the door.

"I *know* something's going on, Gwendolyn. You can't fool me. Now come clean."

Gwen didn't know what came over her. Perhaps it was the wave of tiredness that threatened to overwhelm her, or maybe the fear of finally saying goodbye to Gaspar, but she found the words spilling out of her. She told Flora of his advances, his promises to teach her Spanish and how close they became during their lessons. The only parts she omitted were the long afternoons in his bed. Those were sacred and belonged only to them.

"Do you love him?" Flora asked simply as they sat side by side on the edge of Gwen's bed.

"It's not that simple."

"Isn't it though? He asked you to go away with him."

"I'm engaged to the Spanish prince…well, almost engaged."

"So? Call it off! We'll send a messenger to Spain and you can go off to a life on the sea with a handsome captain. Wouldn't that be lovely?"

Gwen felt a lump grow in her throat. "It's not that simple."

"You keep saying that, but it *is* simple, Gwen. One letter is all it will take to end this whole farce of an engagement and allow you to be with…"

"Gaspar."

"Yes, Gaspar. I'll even talk to Conner for you, if you like. I'm a married woman now, so he can't be cross with me and hold back my pin money like he used to when we were young. I'll sort it all out for you," Flora said proudly, moving to rise to her feet.

Gwen grabbed her arm, pulling her back down. "No, Flora. Stop."

Flora pulled herself from her grasp. "What's *wrong*, Gwen? It's not like you love the prince."

"I'm afraid," she whispered, closing her eyes. It was shameful to speak such things aloud.

"Afraid of what?" Flora's voice was gentler. "Tell me, please."

"I can't be the person Gaspar needs me to be."

"That's what I thought when I met Andrew. I believed that someone like me could never be the wife of someone so pure and kind, but he adores me just as I am. I'm sure your Gaspar feels the same, not that you have anything to feel shameful about...unless there is more you haven't said?"

"It's not me, nor him...it's the ocean."

"What about it? You've been on the boat for almost two days now. Certainly you're overcoming it?"

She opened her eyes, the tears welling, threatening to spill. "Yes, but in view of *land* and in view of *safety*. I can't do it forever—I couldn't. And I couldn't ask him to give up the sea for me either."

"This is about Father." Flora's brows were heavily creased. "Gwen, what happened to him was a terrible tragedy. You can't give up your one great love because of fear of things that may never come to pass."

"Prince Eduardo could be my one great love," she countered lamely.

"Even you don't believe that."

"I must because I've made my choice." Gwen stood, wiping angrily at her damp cheeks. "What's done is done and there's no changing it. I'll help him regain his strength and then we both will go about our lives as we were always meant to."

Flora stayed silent for several moments. Gwen stripped off her mussed gown and dressed in a sturdy plum one. The sleeves went just to her elbows, making it perfect for the tasks she knew she would have to complete once Gaspar was in the castle. She glanced back at Flora and twisted her hair atop her head.

"Are you just going to sit there all afternoon and watch me?" Gwen asked, feeling annoyed at being thrust into such an emotional situation on so little sleep.

"I suppose not." She bit her lip and averted her eyes.

"What's that expression for?"

Flora paused a moment, her fingers idling toying with some lace on her skirt. "It's just…what if…"

She groaned. "What, Flora? Spit it out!"

"What if you're pregnant?" she hissed lowly. "You don't need to tell me that you and he had become quite…entangled. I can see it in your eyes."

"There are ways to prevent that," Gwen said, her cheeks hot.

"Good. I'm glad."

"Now you're finished with your interrogation?"

Flora nodded.

"Then we needn't speak of it again."

"But—"

Gwen rounded on her, her hands clasped in tight fists at her sides. "No. There came a time when you asked me to never speak of something that pained you and I didn't. I lay beside you and offered you my comfort and nothing more. Now it is my turn to ask the same of you."

Flora nodded, but her lips were pursed and she let out a deep breath through her nose.

"No more," she repeated sternly, stalking from the room to go to the guest wing.

She wasn't sure where exactly Gaspar would be, but it only took stepping into the corridor lined with guest doors to know. One opened and several Portuguese sailors filed out. They nodded to her in respect as they passed and she slipped inside before the door had a chance to shut.

The room was at the far end of the hall, one of the quieter chambers. It was dim, but not unpleasant, with one of the windows cracked open to allow a fresh spring breeze to drift in. Gwen was almost disappointed to see that this was one of the rooms that didn't face the sea, but the inner courtyard of the keep. Then she thought that it wasn't a shame, after all, to remind him what it was like to live on land. Besides, he would soon be back on his ship for good.

He lay upon the bed asleep, or unconscious, just as before. Even a light brush of her fingers against his cheek didn't stir him. It was in the faint afternoon light that she finally saw the faint sweeps of blood on his stomach and a dusting of black on his arms that might be gunpowder.

Since the initial danger was gone, she didn't see the harm in bathing him. She could have called up some manservants to take care of him, but couldn't bear the thought of someone else touching the skin she had so lovingly caressed. It was petty, but Gwen couldn't help it and tried to focus her energy on preparing a basin of warm water and some fresh soap.

As the daylight began to fade and a maid entered to light the fire and some lamps, Gwen slowly washed the remnants of battle and injury from his bruised body. She washed away the blood, changed the bandage on his hip, and brushed his tangled, black hair. Still, he did not wake until she had gently lifted his head to replace his cross and medallion necklace.

"*Meu único ouro.*" His voice was raspy and he spoke between shaking coughs.

Gwen hurriedly lifted a class of cool water to his lips. It pained her to see him this way, but she was glad to see him awake and speaking. "How do you feel?"

"Like...like I was stabbed. Like I...I was hit with the butt of a gun. And a cannonball was dropped...on my chest."

"Did those things happen?"

He looked as it he might laugh, but stopped short, grimacing in pain. "*Sim.*"

"A cannonball?"

"Maybe two."

"Do you need anything? Are you in any great discomfort? Shall I call for something for you to eat?"

His chapped lips lifted into a small smile. "This woman…I tell her I was…stabbed, beaten, and hit with a cannonball and she…she asks if I'm hungry."

"Well, *are* you?"

"No." He reached up a shaky hand and gingerly touched his swollen jaw. "Good thing I wasn't too invested in my looks."

"You look fine," Gwen lied, averting her eyes from the deep blacks and purples.

"And you…look beautiful."

"Do stop it and save your voice." She lifted the water to him again to drink.

"Do you have a fine singing voice, Gwendolyn?"

She was pleased to hear most of the coarseness of his speech was muted slightly. "Not at all! My mother used to say that I had a voice like a band of disgruntled barn cats."

"Soft and delicate like an angelic chorus?"

"You've never been around barn cats, have you?" she asked, sitting upon the stool beside the bed. "It's like the wailing of a thousand badly tuned fiddles."

"Sounds delightful. I am glad that it does not have…the same effect when you speak."

"Me, too."

His eyelids fluttered closed for a moment then sprang open as if he were trying to stay awake.

"You can rest if you like. I'll come back later this evening to see how you're doing."

"No, do not go. I do not wish to sleep yet."

"Why ever not? You've been terribly injured and need to rest."

His gray gaze shifted slowly to her. "I cannot."

"Too much pain? I'll go and fetch you—"

"No, no pain. I just do not wish to sleep."

"You really should."

His lips held the ghost of a grin. "You would leave a dying man?"

"Don't joke so," she admonished a bit more harshly than she meant. "You're not dying."

"Thanks to you."

"You weren't dying when I found you."

"But you came, all the same." Gaspar closed his eyes and held out his hand, as if searching for hers.

She took it, warming the cold fingers in her palms. He was always too hot-blooded, it was strange they should feel so. "Should I fetch you another blanket? Build up the fire a bit?"

"No, just…read to me?"

Gwen was surprised. He never really struck her as a pleasure reader; most of the books in his cabin were atlases and histories relevant to his travels. "What shall I read?"

"I do not care. I only wish to hear you speak, but I fear…I am too weary to talk."

"All right, I'll fetch something."

She rose, crossing the room to a set of tall bookcases that sat on either side of the fireplace. As it was a guestroom, she had no idea what was even kept on the carefully dusted shelves. She quickly skimmed the shelves, annoyed to see that Conner had placed plenty of nice looking—but rather boring—books in this particular room. German monarchs on the right, sheep breeding practices through the ages in the middle. Several of the volumes were even blank on the inside and merely for show.

Shaking her head, she plucked one at random from the right side and sat down beside the bed before looking at the title. "Well, it seems this little book covers the life of Henry IV, king of the Germans and the Holy Roman Empire."

"My favorite."

Gwen stifled a small laugh and began to read aloud. She told Gaspar of Henry's life and his experience in the Saxon wars before she noticed his breathing coming deeper and more even. She stopped reading and closed the book, then placed a hand on his forehead, gauging his temperature. Still no fever.

When she got to the door, she took one last look back at his prone figure. She wished she could climb abed with him and curl around his body as she had done so many times before. But she couldn't and she no longer had the excuse of warming a gravely wounded man to do it. Besides, they had true privacy aboard his ship and they might not have the same luxury in the MacLeod keep.

As dearly as she would miss it, she would be eternally grateful that he would live.

Chapter Eighteen

She rose just as sunlight began to creep between the curtains. It had been a restless night's sleep and Gwen was glad to be able to leave her bedroom. Every time she closed her eyes, she saw the dying men in the hold of the ship and Gaspar's battered body moaning her name in pain. And every time she began to doze, she envisioned them all fighting crashing waves and cannonballs as she watched from the safety of the MacLeod cliffs.

Even her reflection looked back at her exhaustedly. Dark circles sat below her eyes and her skin was paler than usual. She hoped a bath would rejuvenate her, and it did help. As soon as she submerged herself in the hot, fragrant water, she began to feel a little bit better.

When the bath grew cold, she dried and dressed and readied herself to go down to the kitchens. When she finished buttoning up her gown, her fingers brushed over Gaspar's crucifix, which still hung around her neck. Gwen made a mental note to return the gift for good, but tucked it into the neckline of her gown before going downstairs.

The kitchens had been alive for hours before she entered them. The scents of freshly baked bread and the tangy beginnings of cooking meat washed over her. She thought she should ask for help obtaining her items, but went on alone, not wishing to disrupt the breakfast preparations. They all worked together in perfect, unbroken harmony and she felt as if her requests at that hour would set things into unnecessary disarray.

But as soon as she found a serving tray to use, the plump cook was at her side, drying her hands on her apron. "Is there somethin' I can get for ye, Miss?"

"No, it's all right, I can manage…I think." In truth, Gwen wasn't much of a cook, not even a little bit. She could take inventory of the larder and prepare a meal list for the week, but if she were in charge of actually *preparing* the food, everyone in the castle would get poisoned.

"Just tell me what ye need, I'll do it," the cook said, a bit more firmly than before.

Gwen looked down at the empty tray, then around the room where the kitchen maids were busily chopping vegetables, kneading dough, and stacking clean plates. She knew enough to recognize when her "help would be more of a hindrance. "If it's not too much trouble, could you have some tea and good broth sent up to the guest room where the ship captain is staying?"

"Would he no' wish for somethin' with more substance?"

"No, too much rich food might make him ill.

He's not eaten for two days, at the least."

The cook nodded and shooed her out, promising to send a maid soon.

Gwen didn't wish to go to Gaspar empty-handed, so she went to the library to get some more interesting reading material on the chance he asked her to read for him again. But as soon as she opened the door, she felt her stomach drop. Upon the large desk where she usually did all of her work sat the portrait of Prince Eduardo.

Someone must have placed it there, thinking she would like to look upon her betrothed as she did her numbers. They were wrong. There was no one she would like to have seen less than the prince. And he looked so *angry*—as if he knew what she had been doing all the while their marriage contracts were being written up. She had never felt overly guilty about her doings with Gaspar, but the painted face drew up that very feeling within her.

His brown eyes seemed to glare at her from across the room and his mouth—while not the most pleasantly tilted to begin with—made him appear as if he was sneering in complete disapproval. Even his dark brow seemed furrowed coldly beneath his hair. The gaze followed her, daring her to make yet another wrong move.

It turned her stomach, but she found she was unable to tear her eyes away from it. She couldn't. He was to be her husband, and she, his bride. In a manner of weeks, she would be in Spain with a wedding ring upon her finger and him beside her in their marital bed. This complete stranger was to be her partner in this life and the next.

She flipped the painting face down and took a deep, stabilizing breath, willing it all to happen to someone else—anyone else. But it was happening to her and there was nothing she could do to stop it.

***

"You need to drink the tea, at least!" Gwen all but yelled at a very stubborn Gaspar.

He pursed his lips and shook his head.

She sighed in exasperation and frowned at his sunken, still-bruised cheeks. "You'll *never* get better if you don't at least *try* to comply with what I'm asking of you."

"I will be fine."

"Only if you eat." She picked up the cup of rapidly cooling broth again and thrust it under his nose. "You're no good to anyone if you starve to death."

He took it with a scowl and slowly sipped it.

Gwen smiled down at him. "There, isn't that better?"

"No. I need real food. No more broth."

She poured herself a cup of tea and began to drink it black, sitting beside the bed. "If you can keep this down, I'll get you something else this afternoon. It's good that you have an appetite, though. It means that there isn't anything too wrong, internally."

"It feels as though it is," he grumbled, setting the empty cup on the nightstand.

"Just a bit of bruising. Don't fret. You'll be right as rain before you know it and ready to return to the ships."

His gaze darkened. "*Sim*, the ships full of injured men."

Gwen set her teacup down and placed her hand on his arm. "They have been getting the best care. Sorcha, the healer from the village, has been there for days and Conner had more sent to tend to them."

"They were my responsibility and I failed them." He turned his face away from her.

"No, you didn't. You were attacked. It was just bad luck and there was nothing you could have done to prevent it." It was then that she remembered his necklace, tucked within her gown. Slightly embarrassed at having to remove it in his presence, she slipped it from around her neck and draped the chain carefully over his head.

Gaspar started and looked up at her, his fingers upon the cross. "You are giving it back?"

"Of course. If I haven't taken it, you wouldn't have…" Her voice caught in her throat. She had promised herself she wouldn't cry in front of him, but she felt so ashamed, the tears came before she could force them back down. "It's my fault."

With a slight groan, and a bit of effort, Gaspar sat up, taking both her hands in his. "You are the person who is the least amount to blame. You say it is not my fault, but it isn't yours either, *meu único ouro.*"

"It is. I had your tokens and after years of safety, you were almost killed! It isn't a coincidence."

"I have not had years of safety, Gwendolyn. The sea never offers safety."

"Men died," she whispered, her eyes trained on

her knees, her tears dropping onto the green fabric.

"As men always do upon the sea." He lifted up her chin, forcing her to look at him. "You have done nothing but helped me survive."

"You were never in any great danger. You would have lived no matter who helped you."

"It is not true." Gaspar caressed her cheek. "When the ship began to sink, I thought I would die and that it was my time to embrace death. But it was as if thinking of you gave me the strength to swim."

Her heart lurched. "I am glad of it."

"I could not die knowing that you still walked on land and breathed the air my lungs so desperately craved. So I fought to return to you. Seeing you again was the only thing that kept me alive."

"But you didn't know you would ever see me again."

"I did. I was returning to you when we came under attack."

She felt as if someone had poured freezing water over her head. "But why?"

He grinned, brightening his darkly bruised face. "Because I knew that if I kidnapped you, you would have no choice but to come with me. How could you run away if I take you to the middle of the ocean?"

"You're joking."

"I never joke about kidnapping," he told her seriously, still cupping her face. "I was coming back to take you with me."

She pulled back. "So it *is* my fault?"

"Stop taking the blame for things you have no control over."

Gwen averted her gaze and they sat in silence for several minutes. The thoughts whirled about in her head, more complex than even the array of emotions that fought for supremacy. She was sad for the dead men, guilty of putting the ships in harm's way, and made guiltier still by the disappointed expression on her betrothed's painted face. And she was also disappointed for the plan that never came to fruition. While a life at sea horrified her to no end, it would be as if the decision to leave with Gaspar would be out of her hands.

Then what would she think of it, when she had no way to fight the sea surrounding her? Would she have cursed him for taking her far from land? Welcomed him with open arms and packed a bag? She needed to know more, to imagine the feeling of her life going as she dared not wish.

"How would you have done it?" she asked before she could stop herself.

"Easily. I would send one of my ships in, flying the flag of the French, so you would not know it by sight. Then I would have sent a written message to the keep saying that someone was injured or ill within."

"Everyone can tell the Portuguese accent right away."

"*Sim*, which is why I would send a written message with one of the kitchen boys, and instruct him to be silent."

"And then what?"

"As soon as you were aboard, we would cast off…after sending a final note to your brother that you were well, of course."

"Of course. But you wouldn't be worried that he would seek you out?"

"I see no Scottish ships. Without a Navy, could he have done anything?"

Gwen smiled, despite herself. "That is true. And what if I wished to visit? Would you never face my brother again?"

"Once he saw how happy his dear, little sister was, I doubt he would have me killed. We would embrace like long lost brothers and have a family reunion."

"Very confident of you. But what if I fought you and didn't wish to go?"

"Would you have fought me, Gwendolyn? When you saw you were aboard one of my ships and I offered you a new life, would you have the ability to say no?"

She willed herself to look his way and his almost imploring expression pained her. His eyes were pleading and his mouth was set in a serious line. He was right, she wouldn't have fought him, not truly...well, until they were out of sight of land, then she might have died due to the distress and terror of being out in the open sea. But she still wouldn't have fought him.

"I-I have to go," she blurted out, rising from her seat.

"Please, Gwendolyn—"

"I have a...an appointment!" She daren't turn his way again and dashed from the room, waiting until she had slammed the door shut behind her before collapsing into the hallway in tears.

Chapter Nineteen

When Gwen finally mustered the courage to go back to see Gaspar, it was late in the afternoon. She hoped he wouldn't be cross with her, but she had run off so shamefully, she was rather vexed with herself in any case. She had behaved like a petulant child.

One knock, no answer. Another was also greeted with silence.

"Gaspar? It's Gwen," she called through the wood.

Nothing.

She slowly pushed the door open, so as to not wake him if he had dozed off, but the bed was strangely empty. The rumpled sheets were also cold to the touch, meaning no one had been there for some time. The washroom was also vacant, although the old, soiled wound dressings she had come to change lay discarded in the washbasin.

Gaspar was healing nicely, but she didn't think he was able to get around easily on his own. Surely that meant he was with a manservant, or maybe even someone from his ship. They could be in the library perusing the books, or maybe even out to the courtyard for stroll. The fresh air was sure to do him some good.

On her way down to the main hall, she came upon a maid carrying a bucket of firewood and asked, "Excuse me, do you know where the ship captain went?"

The girl frowned. "Aye, he came down the stairs and left through the front door."

"Did he say where he was going?"

"No, he just left."

"Was anyone with him?"

"He left alone."

Gwen thanked the girl and scurried to the main hall, not stopping for a cloak before going outside to find him. The air was light and warm and her head whipped around as she searched for him. The courtyard was still and quiet, apart from the stables, where a blacksmith was hammering horseshoes. There was no sign of him anywhere.

There was a distinct chance he had truly left her—gone back to his ship and called for the sailors to cast off at once. There were more than enough ports on the Scottish coast he could easily sail to if he so chose, to find new healers to help his crew. Or he could have left to go home, to the sea. They could have parted on such terrible terms and Gwen would never be able to take everything back and right all the wrongs.

Feeling her heart begin to race, she picked up her skirts and ran down the dirt trail that led to the docks. She didn't want him to leave without saying goodbye and thought that if she could just get to the docks, say her farewells, she could return home with a lighter heart. Without that small bit of closure, she feared she would never be able to enter into the next stage of her life. Without it, she would forever be frozen in time and her heart would slowly erode like the stone cliffs by the sea— smooth with waiting for a final goodbye.

By the time she reached the part of the path that rounded by the cliffs, there was a vicious stitch in her side and she fought to catch her breath. She slowed to a walk, her hand pressed over her pounding chest. But the sight of the ships still firmly anchored in the safe harbor greeted her warmly and she wrestled the urge to collapse in relief. She almost broke out in a new run when something caught her eye.

Gaspar sat on the edge of the cliffs, nestled within the outcropping of rocks. His back was to her and he looked out to the ocean. She knew it was him by the firm slope of his shoulders and his tousled black hair. He was so lost in his own thoughts that he didn't even turn when she approached.

"Hello," she said as she sat beside him, dropping her legs over the side next to his.

"*Olá*," he replied lowly, not turning to look at her.

"Are you all right?"

"*Sim.*"

Gwen bit her lip, waiting for him to say something else, but he merely continued his blank staring into the water. "How is your hip?"

"Well enough."

"I thought you left."

"I wanted to."

"Why didn't you?"

He took a deep breath. "I failed them for the first time and lost twenty-six men. There are sixteen lost at sea and the rest buried here, in strange lands, away from all they knew."

"I'm sorry that Conner couldn't wait to bury them, but they all had a Catholic service with a full mass. I believe one of your crew took note of where each was buried in our graveyard so we can place headstones for them when a man can be found to carry it out."

"I am not angry that they were laid to rest, I am angry with myself."

"I told you, it wasn't your fault. You are the captain they want and deserve."

"As they said," he conceded wearily, turning to her. "This is the first time a decision of mine resulted in so many deaths. I visited the injured once you left today, but I can hardly bring myself to return to my own ship."

"Why not?"

"It feels…blasphemous to take my seat as their captain."

"But that's what you are, Gaspar, you're the captain and they need to see you in command. That's the only way they'll feel secure in their place now. They need to see you as a confident leader."

He shrugged, toying with his medallion. "I do not feel very much like a leader."

"Come now, this isn't you. I know you've been

through something dreadful, but I also know you're stronger than this and if you don't confront those men and exude the traits I know you possess, then you truly *are* a coward."

"I am not a coward," he growled under his breath.

Gwen fought a smile as she found her little pep talk working. "Then go to your ship."

"Will you come with me?"

"Will you cast off as soon as I'm aboard with no regard to my personal wishes in a grand, dramatic kidnapping?"

He laughed. "No, not this time."

Gwen stood then helped him to stand. He was a little unsteady on his feet still, but if he was in pain, he did not show it. "Should you rest before going down? Perhaps take a meal?"

"Stop trying to feed me."

"You need to garner your strength. Now, will you take food and rest before you go down?"

"No, I cannot wait or I might lose my nerve."

They strode together in silence, their hands still tightly clasped together. If their walk and their future weren't so grim, Gwen might have thought it a lovely evening's stroll. The sun was just beginning to set and the fireflies that floated between the heather that had just begun to bloom promised a warm night.

The docked ship was quiet as they approached, but Gaspar called something sharply out and a teenage boy scampered down the gangway and began to untie the little rowboat at the ship's bow. The lad helped Gaspar into the tiny vessel and then

Gwen, followed by a lanky man who was to row for them. She held the boat on either side, her knuckles turning white with the effort it took to stop the shriek of alarm that threatened to burst free. She had to be strong for Gaspar, but without the pressing need to see if he lived like the last trip over the water, it was difficult to find the willpower to be brave.

His lips twitched in amusement as he carefully wrenched her fingers from the wood, encasing them in his palms. "Do not fear, *meu único ouro.* Just as before, I will tell you that no harm will come to you as long as you are with me."

"Oh? And do you think you have the strength to save us *both* from drowning?" she asked with a slight attempt at dark humor.

"With you by my side, I have the strength to do all things."

Gwen was glad that the deep sunset tinted everything pink, because she was sure her cheeks were just as red as the sky. His words were so sincere, it was hard to even listen to him speak. He had come to Scotland a terrible flirt and would be leaving her…a friend, at the very least.

"Ladies first," he motioned toward the rope ladder that dangled over the side of *La Sereia* as their rowboat hit the side of the hull. "I promise I will not look."

"Liar," Gwen grumbled, taking hold of the first rung.

Once onboard, she watched nervously as he climbed up behind her. But even gaunt from illness and injury, his powerful arms still held the sinewy muscle needed to propel his body upward. And once his feet hit the wood of the deck, it was clear he was in his element. He straightened his back and took a deep breath of the sea air, which seemed to revive him.

They got little more than the usual polite nods as they crossed to the door that led down into the galley. Gaspar led the way, his shoulders ramrod straight as he walked. He said something here and there to some of the men while she followed silently behind. Gwen almost felt like an interloper as they stared at her—or perhaps it was merely her guilt-ridden imagination that made her feel that way.

She was grateful when the cabin door shut behind them and let out an audible breath of air.

"Getting easier for you to be upon my ship?" Gaspar asked as he peeled his shirt off and dropped it on the floor beside his dresser, gingerly stretching from side to side.

"A bit. Are you sore?"

"A bit." He began to rifle through his shelves of clothes.

She peered at his lightly bruised face. The dark purple contusion over the sharp cheekbone was beginning to heal, slowly fading into the tanned skin of his face. "Should I leave you to rest?"

"No."

He pulled a clean shirt over his head and brushed his dark hair away from his eyes. She always wondered why he never tied it back, instead leaving it to hang in thick, black waves. When he stood before her, framed by the light coming in through the large windows, she thought she had never seen a better sight in all her life. He was alive and well, back where he belonged and she was content to look at him for as long as he stayed still.

"Might I ask something of you, Gwendolyn?"

"That depends. What is it?"

"Just for tonight, will you stay and pretend that…that none of this ever happened?"

"What do you mean?"

"I want you stay here…with me. I want to lie with you and hold you as if there were no rules and no limitations to what we could be."

On one hand, it didn't seem fair to play make believe in their quiet little cave of wood and art upon the sea. It wasn't fair to Gaspar, and it certainly wasn't fair to her own heart. But the idea was so tempting, so attractive…she couldn't bring herself to deny his request.

"Yes," she said, barely capable of forcing the word from her lips. "Just for tonight."

"Then may I give you something?"

"I suppose."

He walked past her, going to his hidden room behind the painting that held a small fortune of smuggled jewels. There was a bit of rustling from within before Gaspar emerged, something silver clasped in his hand. He stood before her then, staring down at the object as if waiting for it to speak to him.

Gwen was about to ask if he was well when he opened his mouth. "Just for tonight we will be as if there were no others on the horizon, so I must give you a token of that."

"Oh, you needn't give me anything, Gaspar."

"I must and you shall take it. We've already agreed that tonight there is only you and only me." He held out the piece of silver and she saw it was actually a small box in the shape of a closed clamshell with seed pearls inlaid around the edges.

"Goodness, it's lovely," she sighed, reaching out to stroke the pearls. "Thank you."

"I am pleased you like the box, Gwendolyn," he said with a slight smirk. "But there is something inside, which is the real gift."

There was a small click as the shells opened. Atop a tiny pillow of deep red velvet sat a beautiful sapphire ring. The flat, oval stone was of the richest blue she had ever seen. It was inlaid in gold, the gem surrounded by gilded webs where small diamonds were nestled like tiny birds' eggs.

"Gaspar." She could think of nothing else to say as he took her left hand and slipped the sapphire upon her ring finger.

"Now you have a token of our union," he said softly, pressing his lips to the stone. "It was made just for you, the only in the world. It is a sapphire from India, gold from France, and diamonds from Africa. Tokens from all the placed I wished to show you."

"I can't—"

"No. You can and you will. There is no one else, remember? There is just you and I here on this ship. You are my wife, at least for the night."

Gwen swallowed back tears she didn't know were lurking below the surface. She had done so much crying the last weeks, she could hardly believe there were more tears to be shed. But as she looked upon the ring, she thought of nothing more she wanted in the world than to keep it, and him, forever.

"It's beautiful."

"It is nothing compared to you."

As if drawn together by an unseen force, their lips crashed together and their hands tore through each other's clothes. His shirt, her dress, their shoes—all jumbled together on the hardwood floor. In their hurry to feel one another, their groping bodies almost didn't make it to the safety and comfort of the bed.

But as soon as Gwen's back hit the freshly changed sheets, she found shelter in his arms. She thought she'd never feel his skin against hers again, breathe him in, allow herself to give and take so freely, so selfishly. Their time together was almost over before it even began, but she was so blissfully happy to be back where she felt most herself in the world.

But she didn't. As he entered her, she could think of nothing else but him in that moment.

"*Meu único ouro,*" he groaned as he thrust into her again, his pace slowing to a deep and steady rhythm that made her breath catch in her throat.

Gwen ran her fingers over his back, careful to avoid the injured hip. She wanted to feel every slope and plane of sculpted body beneath her fingertips. And every so often, her hand would skim over his shoulder and she would catch a glimpse of the sapphire ring, the color flashing in the fading sunlight—like a lighthouse, a beacon in the dark.

***

Afterward, they lay together, their features only slightly illuminated by the light of the full moon that had risen at some point during their dalliance. Gwen's head was nestled against Gaspar's chest. He wound a curl lazily around his index finger, looking up at the embroidered canopy above. As for Gwen, her eyes were still trained on the ring, which much to her surprise, fit her perfectly.

He made a small sound like a hum.

She tore her eyes away from the ring and looked up at his freshly shaved face. "Did I hurt you?"

Gaspar kissed her on the forehead. "No, I am just happy."

"Me, too," she admitted.

"It's late."

"I know."

"Will they worry?"

She shrugged. "They'll be fine."

He lazily ran a hand down her arm, leaving a stream of goosebumps in its wake. "If it could only be this way forever."

Gwen said nothing about his comment, but closed her eyes, leaning into his touch. She did wish it could be that way forever—that they could stay in their little bubble together, away from the world. But a knock on the cabin door made it abundantly clear that they were not alone.

Gaspar groaned as he untangled himself from the bed and Gwen's arms. He pulled his pants on over his naked legs and fastened them low upon his hips before answering the knock. Ever the gentleman, he blocked the sliver of open door with his body, hiding Gwen from view. Still, she pulled the covers up to her chin.

Almost immediately, he brought something inside, closing and locking the door behind him. Grinning, he showed her a simple tray of meat, cheese, apples, and freshly baked bread. "Finally, some real food. No broth here."

Gwen pulled on her silk robe and sat up, eager for something to eat. He handed her the plate and knife then went to a small cabinet beside the desk, pulling out a bottle of red. It opened with a sharp *pop* and he offered it to her.

"My finest red from Portugal."

"Do you even own any glasses?"

He shrugged, taking a swallow and sitting across from her on the bed. "Why dirty two cups when we can drink from the bottle? Concerned you might catch the sailor's pox from sharing a dram?"

"Of course not. If you had the pox, I would have it by now, in any case," she replied, stifling a small smile at his look of surprise.

"Which I do not have, by the way."

"I am aware," she quipped, taking the bottle and sipping daintily before placing it on the floor beside the bed.

"You are a strange woman, Gwendolyn."

"Strange women are always the ones most worth knowing."

"This is true," he agreed, leaning over the tray between them to cup her cheek. "You have been so worth knowing, even though I admit that I could stay here with you for a thousand years and still never know enough. You always surprise me."

She turned her head and kissed his palm before taking his hand in hers. "And you, me. I was rather shocked when I found that it wasn't Spanish I had been learning, but Portuguese. You're a very sneaky man."

"Any wife of mine needed to be able to speak my native tongue…and I thought my wife would be *you*."

At the look of his downcast face, she regretted bringing up the lessons that initially sparked their romance. "For tonight I am."

"And the morning, *meu único ouro?* What comes then?"

"Please, let's not speak of it," she begged, squeezing his fingers.

"I cannot play pretend any longer." His voice was tired and his face appeared lined and weary in the moonlight. "I want nothing more right now than to cast off, taking you with me."

"You promised you would not."

He looked up at her hard, studying her face. "I know what I said, what I have not said, what you refuse to admit, even to yourself. There are so many words that are unsaid between us and it can go on no longer."

"What are you saying?" Gwen felt slightly alarmed. The playfulness they had enjoyed was gone, leaving darkness and moonlit tears in its wake.

"I'm saying that I was a coward and you pushed me to be strong for my men. But now it is *you* who are the coward."

244

"Me?"

"What do you feel for me, Gwendolyn?"

She pulled her hands away and pursed her lips, unsure of what to say. She was afraid if she dared to speak, she would betray the promise she made to herself to marry well, marry safely, and allow Gaspar to continue his life on the sea.

"*Meu único ouro*, just be honest with me for one night before I leave," he pleaded, running his hands through his hair. "I've nothing left to lose so I might as well lose my dignity by begging you to be open with me."

"Please, don't," she said weakly, leaving the bed and crossing to the open stained glass window. "Please."

He followed her and was behind her in an instant. He brushed the hair back from her shoulder, kissing the swatch of skin that showed where the robe had fallen a bit. "If you will not be honest, may I?"

"I cannot stop you."

"I love you, Gwendolyn," he whispered softly into her hair, his accent thick with emotion. "I love you more than my ship, the sea, the hundreds of diamonds I have no desire for anymore. I thought that a fleet and riches would keep me happy with my lot in life…but it cannot be so without someone to share it with."

"And you will find someone," she whispered bitterly, feeling the sharp pain of the eventual loss of him.

"*No*," he replied fiercely, moving his hands to her hips and digging his fingers into her flesh.

"There is no one else—will be no one else. You are mine and I am yours, if you wish to admit it or not."

"We can't."

"We can. I can care for you, Gwendolyn, more than I thought I ever could another person. I can give you everything your Spanish prince could and more…every gemstone, more silks than you could ever wear. You will have a home with me on my ship, another in Portugal—a grand one that overlooks the water with a garden you could read in and plant the heather that reminds you of home. And we could come here to see your family often, bringing them trade and news of your life with me. I could make you happy."

Gwen bit her lower lip, trying to quell the sobs that fought to escape. She couldn't let him see the cracks in her armor. She needed to stay strong so he would have the strength needed to return to his place at the head of his wounded fleet. The men needed him and he needed the ocean.

"My love for you has no borders, no limits, and I fear I will never escape you once I leave. Your eyes are the deepest blue of the sea, full of life and secret storms. The sea is my home, as are you when you look at me with those eyes and without your steady gaze to guide me, there is no shore for me. No safe harbor."

Still she said nothing, but her shoulders shook and her knees grew week under the weight of her broken heart.

"*Eu te amo*…I love you," he said again. "And I will do whatever it takes to prove it to you. You are not some woman I have at port to warm my bed, nor some passing fancy whom I will allow to marry some other man without confessing the extent of my feelings."

"You needn't prove anything to me," she managed, wiping at her damp cheeks with her arm.

He stepped around to face her, placing his hands on her arms to hold her still. "I must. You need to know that I would do anything for you, Gwendolyn. I would die for you, kill for you, *live* for you. If there is something I can do to keep you by my side, tell me and it will be done."

Her mind screamed, *tell him. Tell him to leave the sea behind and you will be his!* But she refused. She couldn't let him give up his life and livelihood for her. Besides, it was pointless. The Spanish messengers would arrive any day to finalize the match and she couldn't disappoint anyone. Things had already gone far enough.

"Do you even care for me?" Gaspar asked finally in a cool tone, releasing his hold on her arms.

"You know I do," she replied in a voice much harsher than she anticipated.

"Then tell me, Gwendolyn. Tell me what I can do if I mean *anything* to you!"

Tears slid down her cheeks. "You mean everything to me."

"Then come with me. Your family will understand and we—"

She silenced him with a kiss and he must have taken it to mean their heated exchange was over, replaced by the tender caresses and slow exploration that only lovers do. Soundlessly, quietly, he took her again. And afterward, neither spoke a word as they lay, spent, together in the dark. Their limbs interlocked, their hearts beating as one, they silently said their goodbyes as they watched the pale moonlight transform into the pale pinks of a new day.

Chapter Twenty

Gwen woke first that morning and stayed as still as possible so as not to awaken Gaspar. Instead, she listened to the sounds that made up his life—the calling of the sea birds, the low roar of the waves, the sound of ropes hitting the wooden hull as the men above went about their work. She didn't wish to leave the cabin, although she knew she would soon be missed at the keep, if they hadn't noticed her absence already.

But staying in the warm, safe cocoon of Gaspar's tan arms was far too tempting to even dream of leaving. They had stayed up until sunrise, locked in each other's embrace, not really speaking much, but just being together. Gwen knew she couldn't say the words she longed to admit and felt that Gaspar was silent due to her pushing away his romantic declarations. Still, she let her body speak where she was silent and she prayed it would be enough.

"Must you go?" Gaspar asked quietly, holding her tighter against his chest.

"How did you know I was awake?"

"I never slept."

"Oh, I see. Well…I do need to get back soon. It's well into the morning, if not the afternoon."

"I know. I did not wish to wake you."

"Nor I you."

He pressed his lips to her temples and asked, "Must you go?"

Not trusting herself to speak, she nodded, her fingers tracing a line down his arm.

"Will you not stay another day…and night?"

"I cannot."

"I know." He released her and she instantly felt his absence against her body.

Not wishing to delay the painful inevitable, she slid out of bed and pulled on her crumpled gown and tried to smooth her tangled hair. Then she watched as he dressed himself, slowly and deliberately, as if drawing out the moment. She almost wished he would say something to break the painful silence, but he didn't.

Instead, he took her by the hand and led her from the cabin, up to the top deck, through the crew and climbed over the railing. She swiftly followed and settled herself onto the wooden plank that served as a seat. She waited for one of the sailors to accompany them to row, but none did and Gaspar untied the small boat himself, pushing away from the hull before picking up the oars.

"You shouldn't do that, you'll hurt yourself," she told him, glancing nervously at his muscular arms as he rowed. It was true that he looked as if he had the strength, but he had been gravely wounded and had only just begun to heal. She thought it too soon for him to overexert himself so.

"If I did not take you to land by my own hand, I would forever blame whatever poor soul who did and that would be a heavy cross to bear."

The closer the rowboat came to shore, the sicker Gwen felt. But it wasn't seasickness that turned her stomach, it was her heart. With each stroke of the oars, she could feel the organ cracking in her chest, chipping off into painful pieces that were sharp to the touch.

When they reached the dock, he looped a rope around the piling and deftly leaped up. He looked down at her for a moment, the sun illuminating him from above. Then he held out a hand and pulled Gwen up beside him. He held her hard against him, his face buried in her hair and the breath was forced from her lungs. She clutched him just as tightly, not sure of what to do or say.

"*Por favor,*" he rasped as he drew back, his gray eyes portraying much more pain than those two words would have ever conveyed.

She said nothing, knowing she couldn't say what she wished, so ardently, that she could. If she could, she would tell him yes and brace the oceans to be tied to his side forever. But they were from too separate worlds of land and sea, she an ordinary woman whose feet belonged on solid ground and he a mysterious selkie, a mythical and beautiful creature of the deep. Just like in the old legends, the two lovers could never live in each other's worlds and were fated to forever be parted by circumstance. Gwen always hated those tales.

"Then this is where I must leave you," he said,

pulling back. His eyes were glassy with tears, pleading, begging, and imploring her to take action.

"Goodbye, Gaspar."

He covered her mouth with his, hungrily devouring her lips with a desperate need. She knew he was taking all that he could from their final moments together and she selfishly did the same. Before she knew it, she was sobbing into his chest, draining cries that echoed in the cliffs above. But she couldn't find it in her to care. She felt no shame, merely the excruciating burn of loss.

"Goodbye, *meu único ouro.*"

One final, fleeting kiss and he was gone, back into the boat, leaving her alone on the dock as he rowed away. Their eyes stayed connected, but soon the distance grew too great and there was nothing left for Gwen to hold on to. And when he was truly gone, she fell hard to her knees upon the wood and said her final goodbyes to the wind.

***

Gwen sat tucked between the stones on the cliff for hours afterward, her knees drawn up to her chest. She watched as the men below unfurled sails and went about their day, apparently unaware of their silent observer. They were too far away for her to be able to see which man might be Gaspar, if he were even upon the deck of the ship.

Part of her knew that staying there, watching the small fleet below, was doing her more harm than good, but she couldn't force away her gaze. After he had left her, she had tried to return to the keep, but only made it as far as the bluff before having to stop. The tears made her breath come short.

Horse drawn wagons were coming down from the closest village, heavy with barrels and crates. They towed their goods to the edge of the shore where swarthy sailors carried things up to Gaspar's ship, which had come to dock since she had left. She knew they had no great exports in their part of the Highlands, and assumed they were merely stocking up the boats with fresh water and food for the crew. Gwen knew they would be leaving—and soon.

Not wishing to watch their actual departure, she shakily pulled herself to stand, bracing a hand on the warm surface of the stone. She felt she had already said her goodbyes, in more ways than one, and couldn't stomach the idea of standing there any longer. Besides, she was tired, so dreadfully tired. It was the kind of exhaustion that one felt down to the marrow.

She shambled up the hill to the keep, brushing past maids and footmen, climbing each stair as if her shoes were made of lead. Luckily, no one of any merit was about to question where she had been. Gwen assumed that Conner would probably have a few choice things to ask of her, but that's what the heavy lock on her door was for.

The lock clicked thankfully into place and Gwen stripped off her gown as she went toward her dresser. Once she had kicked off her slippers and stockings and pulled a fresh nightgown over her head, she slid between the cool sheets of her bed. For a moment, she regretted not thinking to bathe beforehand, but that would mean washing away the faint prints Gaspar left behind.

She turned away from window, and as she did, something caught her eye. It was the oval sapphire. Started by its presence upon her finger, she shot up in bed. In the whirlwind of emotions that overwhelmed her at the parting on the dock, she hadn't noticed it was still upon her hand.

Questions flew through her mind. Did Gaspar know? Did he want it back? Did she want to return it? Could she even handle parting from her last piece of him?

Gwen pulled off the ring and studied it in the fading light. It was beautiful; he had amazing tastes for such an oddly crude man. It was delicate with its web of diamonds upon a lace of gold, but strong. And he had been right; the blue of the sapphire was so close to own eye color, it was almost alarming. He had an impeccable talent for jewels.

As she studied it, she noticed something amiss. Around the base of the stone, tucked into the gold and diamond web was the tiniest of hinges. It was so slight, she might have missed it if she hadn't been examining it so closely.

Intrigued, she pried the other side gently with a fingernail. The sapphire popped open and she peered inside, going quickly to the open window to see better in the dying light of the day. And as soon as the waning sun flashed upon the image within, she gasped. Etched upon a white base, hidden away, was a mermaid.

Gwen traced the tiny sea foam tail and the long golden waves of painted hair. The petite siren was almost a mirror image of the one upon *La Sereia* she knew had to have come from his own hand. She couldn't believe Gaspar had the figure placed within the sapphire ring without telling her. It was one final joke, one final, secret message from the man who taught her Portuguese instead of Spanish. One final hidden chamber for Gwen to discover.

One final goodbye.

Chapter Twenty-One

Gwen sat in the study the next morning, surrounded by the ledgers and notes she had all but ignored since her affair with Gaspar had begun. The numbers were comforting, unchanging and deliberate, not capable of changing their lot in life—much like her.

Groaning, she pushed away the papers and leaned back in her seat, a sharp headache breaking out behind her eyes. Staring at the tiny numbers did little to help matters, but she felt it was her responsibility to put things in complete order before she left. Conner was certainly more than capable of maintaining his own accounts, but she had changed things so much throughout her time managing the household and the lands, she worried he would find it difficult to decipher.

She was just about to ring for some tea when Charlotte entered with Flora at her heels.

"Darling Penelope's just sent word!" Charlotte exclaimed, holding out a letter.

Gwen's heart lurched as she was reminded of

Penelope and Drum's daughter, little Rose. "Good news, I hope?"

"Better news than I could have ever have hoped for. She'd like us to come for a visit as soon as we're able. Apparently, their house is finished now and there's plenty of room for all of us to stay on for a week!"

"Is she well enough for us to visit?"

"Perfectly. She really just misses having a bit of female companionship and apparently Drum is quite overbearing. Having Conner come to distract him would probably be of great help."

"Oh, I can't wait to see the baby." Flora sighed with a smile. "I bet she's a perfect little doll."

"She is," Charlotte agreed before turning back to Gwen. "So, would you like to go, Gwen? There may not be another chance before you leave and goodness knows it'll be difficult for us to go to you."

"Before I leave," Gwen repeated quietly. "Yes, I suppose this will be my last chance to see them for some time."

"When should we go?" Flora asked.

Charlotte thought a moment, tapping her chin with the tip of her finger. "As soon as can be arranged, I think. I haven't had the chance to tell Conner about it, but I'm sure he would take no issue with us taking a little visit. If we can, maybe we can go in two days' time…"

"I'll go speak with Andrew and ensure we can arrange to leave for London from Penelope's house," Flora said brightly before dashing from the room.

"Quite eager to leave." Charlotte laughed as the study door slammed shut, shaking a small portrait that hung beside the doorframe.

"It will be a lovely trip." Gwen had tried to sound just as lively as Flora had, but even she could tell the tone of her voice lacked the life it needed to sound sincere. She hoped Charlotte didn't notice, but by the look on her face, there would be no such luck.

"Stressful morning?" she asked with an air of seriousness.

"Yes, why?"

"You're rather pale and I noticed you hadn't much of an appetite at breakfast. Have you had lunch?"

She shook her head and straightened the papers upon the desk. "No, I was just about to take tea, though."

"Shall I do it? I'll fetch you a bite to eat as well."

"No, don't worry yourself over me. I have a bit more work to do now that I know we'll be leaving soon."

"You'll work yourself to death like this. Go on and get some fresh air."

Gwen thought to the ships in the harbor, their sails still visible over the edge of the rocks. She couldn't bear to see them. "No, I'm well."

"Just go for a bit. The sun and air will get you your appetite back."

She knew Charlotte wouldn't give in, so she rose, plastering a smile upon her face. "A ride certainly won't hurt things any."

"Good. I'll finish up things here. Lord knows I'll

need to learn more about the running of the lands. You know as well as I that Conner can be quite hopeless with numbers."

Gwen let Charlotte take her place at the desk and sullenly stalked out through the keep, almost tripping on one of little Ian's dogs on her way to the courtyard. She didn't feel much like riding, but she had neglected poor Faodail so terribly, she knew the poor creature would be ready for a good gallop. Besides, she was rather looking forward to getting some distance from her increasingly nosy family members.

But much to her surprise—and supreme annoyance—Conner was in the stable, looking over a tethered Faodail with an expert eye. She thought she might have be able to sneak away, back to the keep, without being questioned, but she brushed against an empty bucket as she snuck backward, knocking it over with a loud clatter.

Conner turned to her and grinned. "Gwen! I have no' seen ye for days."

"I was—"

She had been prepared to lie about how she was needed to tend to the recovering sailors, but as soon as she opened her mouth, Conner waved a hand and said, "Aye, I know ye were needed to heal upon the ships, ye kindhearted lass."

She chose to ignore his praise, as doing so would only heighten the sensation of guilt. "Is everything well with my horse?"

"Oh, aye. I was just seein' if the beast could fair well with sea travel."

"Take the horse upon the ship?"

"Would ye wish to leave her behind?"

"Of course not. I just hadn't thought about actually planning for her, I suppose."

"O' course you're a bit more preoccupied with your weddin' to think o' such trivial things. Gettin' excited, yet? Only last night I was tellin' Charlotte to begin helpin' ye with a gown."

"Lovely."

He placed a heavy hand upon her shoulder and his tanned features grew grave. "It's all right to be a bit nervous, lass. But there's naught to fear from marriage, nor the…marriage bed. If ye need to ask anythin' about the—"

"Goodness, no!" Her voice came out in a shrill shriek of alarm.

"I do no' mean *me*, ye daft lass!" he said between peals of laughter. "Do no' bring the roof down about us with your wailin', you're scarin' the horses. I was about to tell ye to seek out *Charlotte* if ye have any questions."

"May I go out riding now?" She was desperate to escape not only the confines of the keep, but the entire conversation.

"Aye, get on with ye, then. I've already cleared it with your betrothed—or his messenger at least— that ye'd bring your wee horse along if she could handle the time on the ship."

"I'm so pleased my betrothed gave his permission," she quipped sarcastically as a stable boy began saddling her mount.

Conner studied her beneath furrowed brow. "If there's somethin' amiss, or somethin' ye feel ye need to keep from me, do no' do so. I only wish ye well."

"I know."

He said no more, but kneeled down and cupped his hands, offering her a boost up to her saddle. With a final pat upon her thigh, he left her alone with her thoughts.

She left the stable in a hurry, more thanks to Faodail than to herself. She had been correct in assuming that the horse would be more than eager to flee the courtyard for the only land beyond the wall. They simply flew down the slope of the hill and weaved between the bramble bushes that dotted the landscape. Gwen was careful to steer Faodail to the right, away from the cliffs, but otherwise allowed the horse to set her own pace and their ultimate destination.

She felt free while riding, although arguably less than she felt on the ship. It still reminded her of old times before she grew from a girl to a woman, before the Spanish prince, before the Portuguese captain, before her life spiraled so far out of control she had no idea who she was anymore.

It was almost equally freeing to find that Faodail had taken her to the old stones. She hadn't been there since her first goodbye to Gaspar and she hoped to glean some comfort, but none immediately came. Still, they were a constant in good times and bad and she almost wept at the sheer sight of them.

She dismounted, leaving her horse to graze at her leisure, and climbed the gentle incline that led up to the stones. She sat down with her back against a particularly squat one on the far end of the almost perfect circle that made up what had probably been a hearth. The air was warmer than it had been in recent days, but the dark rolling clouds that loomed upon the horizon promised a storm, which she welcomed.

As she sat in the quiet, running her fingertips over the sprouting grass that brushed against her plum colored skirts, she tried to ignore the ring. But with each movement of her hand, the bright stone flashed in the sunlight, screaming to not be ignored. Taking it off was an option, one she had thought over that morning when she awoke, but she found it impossible to muster the strength to pull the gold band over a single knuckle.

Of course, it would have to go when a true wedding ring came to take its place. But then what? Would she put it in the back of a jewelry box, banish the gilded mermaid to a life of darkness? Leave it in Scotland or take it to Spain? Or be terribly dramatic and toss it into the ocean? She could give it back to Gaspar, but that would involve another painful goodbye and she could never dare manage it.

And there was another option, a dreadfully wild and almost unimaginable option. She could keep it on. She could throw caution to the wind and go on a life of passion and adventure. There could be exotic lands, foreign adventures, a world of unexpected joys, all with a man who loved her more than she could ever dream. Her life could be a rare voyage to rival any she ever thought possible...if only she were a braver woman.

"Why can't I do it?" she whispered to a white butterfly that landed just to the right of her knee.

"Why can't I just bloody do it?"

Gwen thumped a fist upon the ground in frustration, causing the small creature to hastily take flight. She thought it almost odd that the butterfly seemed braver than she. It knew not who she was, but came to sit beside her. It only left when frightened, but it grew near again, looking for a new place to land.

The ships would leave soon and Gwen would stay in Scotland to wait until she was beckoned to meet her husband at the altar. Logically, she knew it was silly to be so angry that the prince was stranger; after all, she was the one who'd pushed for the match and he could have been a perfectly nice man, but she found she suddenly hated him. What was once faint interest, then passive disinterest, had evolved into something akin to extreme revulsion.

She despised him so much, she couldn't even recall his name in that particular moment. However, she *could* remember that she loathed his mustache, the way a secretary wrote "his" note, how ridiculously bland his face was. There wasn't a single thing that endeared him to her. The prospect of being a princess was appealing on a childish level, but she had jewels, she had a position, she already lived in a castle. She couldn't pretend to love a man just so he would give her what she had since birth.

But Gaspar...Gaspar, she *did* love. For the first time she admitted it, even to herself. She loved him with every fiber of her being and ached for him so fervently, she could hardly stand the pain. It tore at her soul and mind, occupying her waking hours and even those she spent in slumber. A life without that deep love seemed almost meaningless—worse than drowning in the sea she feared.

"I-I need to go," she said aloud, scrambling to her feet. "Faodail!"

The horse trotted to her at once, looking equal parts eager and nervous for what was to come.

"I couldn't agree more." Gwen swung herself up to the saddle and kicked her heels into Faodail's sides. There was never a better time for the mare to display how fast she could go.

Chapter Twenty-Two

By the time the cliffs came into view, Gwen's eyes were stinging from the wind and Faodail was panting, unaccustomed to such frenzied flight. She nearly fell from her saddle when she saw the ships. Three were out in the open waters, their white sails opening fully to catch the wind, but she spied *La Sereia* still moored where it had been the day before. She didn't know much about boats, but she knew they were preparing to take full advantage of the blustering winds to carry them to their next port.

Feeling her heart hammer loudly against her breastbone, she urged her mount down the hill, cursing herself all the while. She needed to reach the shore before Gaspar's ship left as well. Once he was gone, there was no hope left for her—for them—and she refused to let this last chance slip through her fingers. But as *La Sereia* pulled up its ties and began to let down its sails, drifting away from the shore, she felt her heart being pulled away to sea.

Gwen leaped to the ground as soon as soon as

Faodial came a halt at the edge of the dock. But to her dismay, the ship had already begun to leave the dock behind, gone to join its fellows in the open ocean. She ran down the mooring, searching wildly on the deck of the ship for Gaspar. Although it was only perhaps less than twenty yards away, she couldn't see a single soul aboard.

"Gaspar!" she shrieked over the dull roar of the wave. "Stop! Gaspar, *stop!*"

There was no motion upon the ship. Gwen wasn't sure what she hoped would happen; perhaps that he would hear her and immediately turn the ship about to collect her on the dock? Gwen shook her head, trying to clear her muddled mind. With each wasted moment, the ship grew farther and farther away.

"Gaspar!" she screamed again, hearing her voice quaver and grow hoarse. Behind her thunder rumbled from the storm that crept ever closer, adding a ridiculous feeling of dread to the already stressful situation.

Not seeing another option, anything else to mend the sorry situation she had forced upon herself and Gaspar, Gwen jumped.

The day was warm, but the water was bone-chillingly frigid. It had been years since Gwen had swam in anything larger than her private bath, and her frozen limbs were too shocked to move her forward toward the ship as she had longed to do. It took all of her strength just to keep her head above the surf as her sodden skirts began pull her down.

"Gaspar! Gaspar!" Gwen cried, half choking when a wave brushed against her face. Her body was beginning to tire, but still she tried to swim toward the departing ship, screaming all the while.

With a sudden pang of dread, she remembered a dream she had when Gaspar was lying wounded that night she went to him. She had been drifting alone in the sea, begging for salvation as *La Sereia* came into sight. But instead of being plucked from the waters by Gaspar, the ship had passed her by, leaving her to her death. And as she struggled to allow air into her mouth instead of bitter salt water, she saw that nightmare becoming a reality.

Mustering the last of her strength, she called out for him once more. Perhaps it was her weakening resolve, or maybe it was what happened when one began to drown, but Gwen thought that there were no sounds in the air, save for Gaspar's name, which was lingering somewhere above. And perhaps it was just her imagination, but she thought she heard hers in return.

She squinted up at the departing ship just in time to see a figure dive from the top of the boat, cutting cleanly into the water like a seabird. Blinking several times, she hardly had time to process what she saw when a head popped up beside hers.

"Gwendolyn, what the *hell* are you doing?" Gaspar shouted as his arms clamped around her waist.

It was as if the silence was sucked out as quickly as it appeared, replaced with wind and waves and Gaspar speaking to her without being able to understand what was said. Gwen couldn't speak in return. Was she dead? If she was, she would be in purgatory at least, and not with Gaspar, if he were truly even there. Perhaps she was even hallucinating from drinking in too much seawater and on the edge of death.

"Gwendolyn, hold on to me!" he ordered as he began to swim with one arm toward the ship.

She complied, her teeth chattering painfully as her numb mind tried to understand what was happening. She tried to kick her feet, to help propel them forward, but all she managed to do was lose her shoes. But she had Gaspar—or at least she thought she did.

When they reached the side of the ship, the familiar rope ladder fell beside them from the deck with a loud clatter. He was saying something to her, but again she could hear little more than the ocean. Then, after apparently giving up on her being of any great help, he yelled up to his men. Before she knew it, her arms were looped over a ladder rung with Gaspar behind her, holding her in place. They were drawn slowly upward, finally being helped over the side of the ship by some of the sailors.

They collapsed together upon the hard deck, Gaspar atop her, searching her face with those gray eyes she had missed so much. She reached up a shaking hand to brush the dripping hair off his forehead, her fingers lingering upon his cheek. He was truly there and she was safe in his arms again.

"Are you...are you real?" Her throat was sore from screaming and swallowing the briny water.

"Of course, *meu único ouro.*"

He pressed his lips to hers and she tasted salt and didn't know if it came from the sea or her tears of relief and joy. But as quickly as his mouth had come, it left again. He stood and pulled her up.

"Are you hurt?" he asked fiercely, looking her over. "You could have died, had I not heard you. What in the world you thinking?

"I-I don't know."

"You don't know what?"

"I couldn't let you leave."

"But you told me to go."

"And I was a fool, a perfectly absurd little fool to do so," she managed to choke out through her emotion.

"How did you end up in the water?"

"I-I jumped."

His eyes widened. "You *jumped*? *Meu Deus*, can you even swim?"

Gwen nodded. He seemed angry with her. His tone was harsh. His fingers dug into her arms, and his gaze was almost wild. Even his crew hung back, silent and observant from afar. "What were you thinking? You could have drowned!"

"I couldn't let you leave. I made a mistake and I had to do something to stop you before I lost you forever."

He didn't respond at first, but loosened his grip, dropping his hands to her waist and drawing her close. He dipped his head down, touching their foreheads, his eyes closed. They stayed together like that for several moments and Gwen savored the feeling of being in his arms again. She would spend the rest of her life dripping wet and freezing if it only meant she could stay with him forever.

"What does this mean?"

"It means that I love you." She held up a hand to

show him the sapphire ring. "It means that I'm yours."

He pulled back to pore over her face, his brow furrowed and his eyes holding a pained expression. "And I love you, *meu único ouro*. But the sea…you cannot bear it."

"I learned that I can bear anything in this world except being apart from you. I cannot allow it to happen again. I need you, Gaspar, and I was a fool to not see it earlier and let you leave."

"And I will never leave you again. We will dock now and I will sell my ships, buy a home where your people live. And we—"

"No, you're not going to sell your ships or anything of the sort. When I chose you, I chose *all* of you. When I said that I was yours, I meant it. I will never be separated from you again and I want to be a part of your life in every way and your life is upon the sea."

"But you're so frightened."

"Once, you promised me that you would not let me fall, let me drown, let any harm come to me upon your ship. Do you mean to break that promise?"

"Never."

"Then I have nothing to fear."

Gaspar pulled her into a deep kiss, pouring all the unsaid emotion from his lips into hers, holding her so tightly against his chest, she could barely breathe. But she was happy, finally happy, so blissfully, *sinfully* happy. And now she was free.

"Now, *meu único ouro*, let us embark on the greatest adventure of all."

Epilogue

There had never been a wedding like it in all the years of the MacLeod clan. There was no church, no priest, no solemn wedding vows and no traditional masses. It was a ceremony of color and cultures unlike any the Highlands had ever witnessed.

Gwen wore a pale peach gown made of the lightest silk from Gaspar's stock. It was cut low, with slightly puffed sleeves hanging off her slim shoulders. Pearls trimmed the neckline and blooms of pure white, early summer rhododendrons were tucked in her loose curls. She thought they looked better than any wedding veil.

The ships only had to stay a week after Gaspar plucked Gwen from the sea. Just long enough for Gaspar to formally ask her to marry him, for both of them to press their case of marriage to Conner, and to send missives to Spain that the eligible heiress was no longer eligible. And it was just enough time to make a new gown for the occasion, at the behest of Gaspar. If it had been up to Gwen, she would have married him in the same wet, dirty dress she wore when she almost drowned.

"Are you ready?" Flora asked as she put the final flowers in Gwen's hair.

"I've been ready for weeks."

"You've only been engaged for six days."

"But I've been ready for much longer."

Flora smiled. "I know the feeling."

She dabbed a bit of the lavender perfume Gaspar loved so well behind her ears and replaced the vial upon her dressing table. The maids would collect everything she didn't pack to bring aboard the ship before they left in the morning. But she would miss her chambers dearly.

Before leaving, she took one final look around the bedroom she grew up in. It had served as her nursery upon her birth and now as her bridal chambers. One day, she might visit and sleep again in the familiar four-poster bed, or perhaps a child of Conner and Charlotte's would claim it as their own. No matter what the future held, it was no longer her room, her home. She lived in the sea now, joining the world of the selkies like in the tales and midnight stories of her youth.

Charlotte and Penelope were waiting in the hall when Gwen and Flora stepped out, their children safe with a hired nursemaid. They would serve as her wedding party and they giggled and made quiet jokes all the way down to the main hall, where Conner and Drum stood.

"Are ye ready, lass?" Conner asked, his eyes uncharacteristically misty.

"Everyone keeps asking me that and the answer

will always be the same."

"Ach, my wee sister," he said gruffly, taking her hand in his. "I hope ye'll be happy."

"I will," she promised in return as they stepped out into the sunlight.

The wedding was hastily planned and left no time for elaborate marital parades or for all their family and friends to join them. But that was all right by Gwen. She didn't need all attention on her, just a few words of promise between her and Gaspar.

Once a lone bagpiper had struck up a tune, the small party marched toward the cliffs overlooking the ocean. There was a large group of people gathered there, more than Gwen thought there would be. And as she grew closer she saw that most of the village had come, Angus and Grace, Sorcha with her family, the tavern owner with his barmaids, and every person Gwen had ever helped during their times of illness or injury. Mixed within the sea of plaid were the grinning, tanned faces of the Portuguese sailors, who would make up her new neighbors. But she had eyes for no one but Gaspar.

He looked quite unlike himself in a pair of black breeks and matching cutaway coat. His hair was brushed back off his face and he even wore a pale gray cravat that was the same shade of his eyes. He was freshly shaven and showed a set of brilliantly white teeth as he smiled at her.

She had no bouquet, making it easier to go to him at once, taking his hands in hers. They were steady and comforting, not that she was nervous in the least bit. This wedding was one born of love.

She could hardly wait for the ceremony to begin—and end—and looked around for the unofficial officiant.

The man pushed through the crowd and took his place with his back against the stones that jutted up off the edge of the cliffs. It was Gwen's special place on the MacLeod lands and she didn't think she ever saw a finer backdrop for her wedding, even though it would not be blessed by the church. The officiant was the lesser captain who sailed one of Gaspar's ships. Apparently captains were capable of officiating weddings and Gwen was not one to argue. She would have left with Gaspar even without a marriage certificate.

"Good day," the man began in heavily accented English. "We meet here today beneath a clear sky and beside calm waters to witness the marriage of Gaspar Christiano Alexio Florencio and Gwendolyn Isla MacLeod. May the seas that bear you never be a burden and may the breeze fill your sails with enough wind to always find one another. May your ship be your home and hearth, but may the anchor never cause you to sink. May the salt waters be the land beneath your feet, but your cups always filled with fresh drink. May you love, respect, and care for another and trust in our Lord as your compass. And may you find happiness together for all of your days on land and sea."

Gaspar squeezed her hands and cleared his throat before beginning to speak, his eyes always upon hers. "Gwendolyn, today before your family and friends and my own crew, I will make you several promises. I promise to always love you and protect you from harm. I promise that all I have, and all I will acquire, will be yours as well as mine. And I promise, above all, to never let you sink, for I shall always be by your side."

Gwen felt tears well in her eyes at his unexpected words. She didn't know there would be any personal exchange, but she had to say something. "Gaspar, I would like to make you some promises as well. I promise to always love you and to always love your crew as you do. I promise to explore the old world and the new with you, all upon your ship with you as my captain in all things. And I promise to always trust you, as I know you will never let me sink."

"As these people as my witness," the officiant began again in a booming voice, "I pronounce these two married."

Gaspar grinned and picked Gwen up and twirled her in his arms, crashing his lips to hers.

The spectators erupted in a roar of applause and cheers in several languages and Gwen laughed aloud in joy as Gaspar placed her back upon the earth. She was a married woman at last, and to a man she loved more than anything in the world. They would live aboard *La Sereia* and travel to distant lands together, taking in all the world had to offer. She would no longer experience things only through the pages of a book. She would be leaving the only home she had ever had for the unknown....

But she welcomed all the adventures yet to come.

***

275

Two Years Later

Charlotte sat perched upon the edge of the checkered picnic blanket, her hand on her swollen stomach. The child would be born soon and she was savoring the sweet, fresh air of early autumn. She knew she would soon be too pregnant and uncomfortable in her own skin to make the familiar walk down to the cliffs. She barely made it as it was, and relied heavily on Conner's strong support to guide her over the rocks.

She watched wee Ian take hold of Alec's hand as they ran away from Rose. The little girl was still a bit unsteady, but toddled after them all the same, her pink skirts lifted to her knees. The three children shrieked in laughter as one of Ian's faithful dogs bounded toward them, making them scatter like birds in a field. But they soon rejoined again, plucking sprigs of heather for some unspoken task that only children would understand.

Flora picked up her baby daughter, Fauna, when she whimpered in alarm, then ran her hand over the little girl's dark red hair. She murmured softly to her, quietly calming her back to sleep. Andrew was beside her, although his straight nose was buried in the newest of Drummond's unfinished manuscripts—a collection of pirate songs and histories. But he looked up when Flora began to speak to him, listening with the rapt attention he always gave his wife.

Nearby, Drum was conversing animatedly with Conner about something beyond the hills, his deep, vibrant voice echoing melodically around them.

Penelope watched him from her seat beside Charlotte, the corners of her lips upturned. She had been slow to smile since she learned she would never bear another child after Rose's difficult birth, but time—and Drummond's steady love—had eased that pain and the small family visited often, something Charlotte was grateful for.

She had just turned to call Conner to join her for lunch when Gwen and Gaspar strode up the incline from the docks. The youngest MacLeod lady was brown as a berry from her two years at sea and had first come home looking deliciously exotic with henna painted hands and wearing a gown of vibrant pink silk with gold embroidery. The pair shared a few words in animated Portuguese before coming to Charlotte, holding out the fresh bottle of imported champagne they had retrieved from *La Sereia*—a final gift from the worldly travelers before they departed again.

Noting the fine vintage, she happily popped the cork, calling all four couples together to share a toast. Soon they would all part: Flora and Andrew home to London, Penelope and Drum to their estate, and Gwen and Gaspar to their next adventure on the sea. Each had found their match and built a life outside the homes and families they had known. There was no telling when they would meet again in Scotland, or anywhere else for that matter, for they were naught but leaves, scattered to the four corners with no telling who would return—and who would not—come the next autumn.

It was only fitting they'd share one last glass—a parting drink.

When they were all joined, their children among them, silent for once, it was Drum who sang. His voice rang out across the green hills and rocky cliffs, sending the song through to the villages and out to sea. It was an old song, resurrected anew. It told of friendship, farewells, and the longings of love they had found, and those they had left behind. It was a promise for them to return when they could, to reconnect with the brothers, sisters, and friends who'd taken life's journey with them.

And then Drum was silent and each person raised a glass to their lips.

When each finished, Gaspar took Gwen by the hand and led her down the slopes to their ships, ready to cast off. Andrew and Flora collected their babe and got into the awaiting carriage that would bear them to the train back to England. Then Drummond and Penelope took Rose to their tethered horses, ready for the journey home.

All that was left upon the cliffs—just as it had been in the beginning before friends and marriages and children—was Charlotte and Conner. The MacLeod laird and the emerald queen, alone again at last.

Acknowledgments

Shout out to fellow author Sarah Fischer for loving this series as much as I do and putting in long hours "in the office" while I agonized over storylines and character development. A special thank you to my editor, Rosa Sophia, for making sure that my books were clean, organized, and always error-free. Love to my parents for always reading, sharing, and promoting my work—even when their copies ended up at the bottom of the ocean thanks to a hurricane. And some special sister snaps to Jacqulyn Paris King and all the lovely women who have joined the Σisters of the Σcottish Σtone.

About the Author

Kelsey McKnight is a university-educated historian from southern New Jersey. She has married her great loves of romance, history, and literature to create her first works that are set in Scotland. But she has recently begun to venture into the world of contemporary romance, drawing inspiration from true life. When she's not writing, Kelsey can be found reading, drinking too much coffee, blogging, spending time with her family, and working for two separate nonprofit organizations.

Facebook:
Facebook.com/Kissatmidnight

Twitter:
Twitter.com/KelseyMMcK

Website:
Kissatmidnight.wordpress.com

Instagram:
Instagram.com/akissatmidnight

Goodreads:
Goodreads.com/Kelsey_McKnight

www.ingramcontent.com/pod-product-compliance
Lightning Source LLC
Chambersburg PA
CBHW030113180626
46812CB00002B/395